WHAT WOULD SCOTLAND YARD DO WITHOUT DEAR MRS. JEFFRIES?

The Inspector and Mrs. Jeffries: When a doctor is found dead in his own office, Mrs. Jeffries must scour the premises to find the prescription for murder.

Mrs. Jeffries Dusts for Clues: One case is solved and another is opened when the inspector finds a missing brooch—pinned to a dead woman's gown.

The Ghost and Mrs. Jeffries: When the murder of Mrs. Hodges is foreseen at a spooky séance, Mrs. Jeffries must look into the past for clues.

Mrs. Jeffries Takes Stock: A businessman has been murdered—and the smart money's on Mrs. Jeffries to catch the killer.

Mrs. Jeffries on the Ball: A festive Jubilee celebration turns into a fatal affair—and Mrs. Jeffries must find the guilty party.

Mrs. Jeffries on the Trail: Mrs. Jeffries must sniff out a flower peddler's killer.

Mrs. Jeffries Plays the Cook: Mrs. Jeffries finds herself doing double duty: cooking for the inspector's household and trying to cook a killer's goose.

Mrs. Jeffries and the Missing Alibi: When Inspector Witherspoon is the main suspect in a murder, only Mrs. Jeffries can save him.

Mrs. Jeffries Stands Corrected: When a local publican is murdered and Inspector Witherspoon botches the investigation, trouble starts to brew for Mrs. Jeffries.

Mrs. Jeffries Takes the Stage: After a theater critic is murdered, Mrs. Jeffries uncovers the victim's secret shocking past.

Mrs. Jeffries Questions the Answer: To find the disagreeable Hannah Cameron's killer, Mrs. Jeffries must tread lightly—or it could be a matter of life and death.

Mrs. Jeffries Reveals Her Art: A missing model *and* a killer have Mrs. Jeffries working double time before someone else becomes the next subject.

Mrs. Jeffries Takes the Cake: A dead body, two dessert plates, and a gun. Mrs. Jeffries will have to do some serious snooping around to dish up more clues.

Mrs. Jeffries Rocks the Boat: A murdered woman had recently traveled by boat from Australia. Now Mrs. Jeffries must solve the case—and it's sink or swim.

Mrs. Jeffries Weeds the Plot: Three attempts have been made on Annabeth Gentry's life. Is it because her bloodhound dug up the body of a murdered thief?

Mrs. Jeffries Pinches the Post: Mrs. Jeffries and her staff must root through the sins of a ruthless man's past to catch his killer.

Mrs. Jeffries Pleads Her Case: The inspector is determined to prove a suicide was murder, and with Mrs. Jeffries on his side, he may well succeed.

Mrs. Jeffries Sweeps the Chimney: A vicar has been found murdered, and Inspector Witherspoon's only prayer is to seek the divinations of Mrs. Jeffries.

Mrs. Jeffries Stalks the Hunter: When love turns deadly, who better to get to the heart of the matter than Inspector Witherspoon's indomitable companion, Mrs. Jeffries?

Mrs. Jeffries and the Silent Knight: The yuletide murder of an elderly man is complicated by several suspects—none of whom were in the Christmas spirit.

Mrs. Jeffries Appeals the Verdict: Mrs. Jeffries and her belowstairs cohorts have their work cut out for them if they want to save an innocent man from the gallows.

Mrs. Jeffries and the Best Laid Plans: Everyone banker Lawrence Boyd met became his enemy. It will take Mrs. Jeffries' shrewd eye to find who killed him.

Mrs. Jeffries and the Feast of St. Stephen: 'Tis the season for sleuthing when a wealthy man is murdered and Mrs. Jeffries must solve the case in time for Christmas.

Mrs. Jeffries Holds the Trump: A medical magnate is found floating down the river. Now Mrs. Jeffries will have to dive into the mystery.

Mrs. Jeffries in the Nick of Time: Mrs. Jeffries lends her downstairs common sense to this upstairs murder mystery.

Mrs. Jeffries and the Yuletide Weddings: Wedding bells will make this season all the more jolly. Until one humbug sings a carol of murder.

Mrs. Jeffries Speaks Her Mind: Everyone doubts an eccentric old woman who suspects she's going to be murdered—until the prediction comes true.

Mrs. Jeffries Forges Ahead: A free-spirited bride is poisoned, and it's up to Mrs. Jeffries to discover who wanted to make the modern young woman into a postmortem.

Mrs. Jeffries and the Mistletoe Mix-Up: There's murder going on under the mistletoe as Mrs. Jeffries and Inspector Witherspoon hurry to solve the case.

Mrs. Jeffries Defends Her Own: When an unwelcome visitor from her past needs help, Mrs. Jeffries steps into the fray to stop a terrible miscarriage of justice.

Mrs. Jeffries Turns the Tide: When Mrs. Jeffries doubts a suspect's guilt, she must turn the tide of the investigation to save an innocent man.

Mrs. Jeffries and the Merry Gentlemen: When a successful stockbroker is murdered just days before Christmas, Mrs. Jeffries won't rest until justice is served for the holidays.

Mrs. Jeffries and the One Who Got Away: When a woman is found strangled clutching an old newspaper clipping, only Mrs. Jeffries can get to the bottom of the story.

Mrs. Jeffries Wins the Prize: Inspector Witherspoon and Mrs. Jeffries weed out a killer after a body is found in a gentlewoman's conservatory.

Mrs. Jeffries Rights a Wrong: Mrs. Jeffries and Inspector Witherspoon must determine who had the motive to put a duplicitous businessman in the red.

Mrs. Jeffries and the Three Wise Women: As Christmas approaches, Luty, Ruth, and Mrs. Goodge turn up the heat on a murderer to stop the crime from becoming a cold case.

Mrs. Jeffries Delivers the Goods: When poison fells an arrogant businessman at a ball, Mrs. Jeffries and Inspector Witherspoon must catch the culprit before the misanthrope murders again.

Mrs. Jeffries and the Alms of the Angel: When a wealthy widow is murdered right before Christmas, Mrs. Jeffries investigates what happens when money can't buy your life.

Mrs. Jeffries Demands Justice: Nigel Nivens may be a jealous, dishonest, spoiled man but when one of his associates is killed, Inspector Witherspoon and Mrs. Jeffries know he isn't capable of murder. Now they just have to prove it.

Mrs. Jeffries and the Midwinter Murders: When a powerful woman is strangled in her own home a week before Christmas, the Inspector and Mrs. Jeffries must deliver a stocking full of coal to a crafty killer.

Berkley Prime Crime Titles by Emily Brightwell

THE INSPECTOR AND MRS. JEFFRIES
MRS. JEFFRIES DUSTS FOR CLUES
THE GHOST AND MRS. JEFFRIES
MRS. JEFFRIES TAKES STOCK
MRS. JEFFRIES ON THE BALL
MRS. JEFFRIES ON THE TRAIL
MRS. JEFFRIES PLAYS THE COOK
MRS. JEFFRIES AND THE MISSING ALIBI
MRS. JEFFRIES STANDS CORRECTED
MRS. JEFFRIES TAKES THE STAGE
MRS. JEFFRIES QUESTIONS THE ANSWER
MRS. JEFFRIES REVEALS HER ART
MRS. JEFFRIES TAKES THE CAKE
MRS. JEFFRIES ROCKS THE BOAT
MRS. JEFFRIES WEEDS THE PLOT
MRS. JEFFRIES PINCHES THE POST
MRS. JEFFRIES PLEADS HER CASE
MRS. JEFFRIES SWEEPS THE CHIMNEY
MRS. JEFFRIES STALKS THE HUNTER
MRS. JEFFRIES AND THE SILENT KNIGHT
MRS. JEFFRIES APPEALS THE VERDICT
MRS. JEFFRIES AND THE BEST LAID PLANS
MRS. JEFFRIES AND THE FEAST OF ST. STEPHEN
MRS. JEFFRIES HOLDS THE TRUMP
MRS. JEFFRIES IN THE NICK OF TIME
MRS. JEFFRIES AND THE YULETIDE WEDDINGS
MRS. JEFFRIES SPEAKS HER MIND
MRS. JEFFRIES FORGES AHEAD
MRS. JEFFRIES AND THE MISTLETOE MIX-UP
MRS. JEFFRIES DEFENDS HER OWN
MRS. JEFFRIES TURNS THE TIDE
MRS. JEFFRIES AND THE MERRY GENTLEMEN
MRS. JEFFRIES AND THE ONE WHO GOT AWAY
MRS. JEFFRIES WINS THE PRIZE
MRS. JEFFRIES RIGHTS A WRONG
MRS. JEFFRIES AND THE THREE WISE WOMEN
MRS. JEFFRIES DELIVERS THE GOODS
MRS. JEFFRIES AND THE ALMS OF THE ANGEL
MRS. JEFFRIES DEMANDS JUSTICE
MRS. JEFFRIES AND THE MIDWINTER MURDERS
MRS. JEFFRIES AIMS TO WIN

Anthologies

MRS. JEFFRIES LEARNS THE TRADE
MRS. JEFFRIES TAKES A SECOND LOOK
MRS. JEFFRIES TAKES TEA AT THREE
MRS. JEFFRIES SALLIES FORTH
MRS. JEFFRIES PLEADS THE FIFTH
MRS. JEFFRIES SERVES AT SIX

MRS. JEFFRIES
AIMS TO WIN

Emily Brightwell

BERKLEY PRIME CRIME
NEW YORK

BERKLEY PRIME CRIME
Published by Berkley
An imprint of Penguin Random House LLC
penguinrandomhouse.com

Library of Congress Cataloging-in-Publication Data

Names: Brightwell, Emily, author.
Title: Mrs. Jeffries aims to win / Emily Brightwell.
Description: First Edition. | New York : Berkley Prime Crime, 2023. |
Series: A Victorian Mystery ; 41
Identifiers: LCCN 2023005363 (print) | LCCN 2023005364 (ebook) |
ISBN 9780593101117 (trade paperback) | ISBN 9780593101124 (ebook)
Subjects: LCGFT: Detective and mystery fiction. | Novels.
Classification: LCC PS3552.R46443 M6228 2023 (print) |
LCC PS3552.R46443 (ebook) | DDC 813/.54—dc23/eng/20230206
LC record available at https://lccn.loc.gov/2023005363
LC ebook record available at https://lccn.loc.gov/2023005364

First Edition: August 2023

Printed in the United States of America
1st Printing

*This book is dedicated to the best people in the world:
Richard, Matthew, and Amanda—with love and
thanks for their unwavering love and support.*

MRS. JEFFRIES
AIMS TO WIN

CHAPTER 1

"What's wrong now?" Luty Belle Crookshank put her champagne glass on the table and frowned at the tall, white-haired man sitting opposite her. "You've been starin' out that window for the last ten minutes. Glarin' at the storm ain't goin' to make it let up any quicker."

"That's easy for you to say, madam," Hatchet replied. "You're not the one who didn't get to compete. I've been practicing for weeks now and most of the Ladies' Division had finished. I was the first in my category to shoot, and if they'd let us stay out for five more minutes, I would have had my chance." He flicked a piece of lint off the sleeve of his jacket, picked up his tea, and took a sip.

Luty, a tiny, elderly American with snow-white hair, blue eyes, and a love of flashy clothes, shook her head. "If you'd stayed out for five more minutes, ya coulda been struck by lightning, and your outfit would have been ruined." She was dressed in a bright red cotton skirt with a wide blue cummerbund waist and a lacy white blouse with a high collar and puffy sleeves. Gold-and-pearl earrings dangled from her ears, and a gold broach in the shape of a frog playing a harmonica was pinned over her heart.

Hatchet glanced down at the blazer he wore over his starched white shirt. It was a deep green so dark that it almost looked black. His flat wide-brimmed matching cap was on the table next to Luty's gloves. "I'm not certain that would have been so bad."

He wasn't used to the garments they were required to wear for the competition. They were undignified, but when he'd mentioned the matter to Luty, she'd merely scoffed and said that wearing something other than his usual attire of black stovepipe trousers, white shirt, cravat, and old-fashioned black frockcoat was good for him. He'd decided it was pointless to argue with the woman, since her love of fashion made it impossible for her to understand that wearing different clothing made him uncomfortable.

The two of them were sitting by the window table in the common room of the West London Archery Club. Hatchet, who was supposedly Luty's butler, was drinking tea while Luty had opted for a glass of champagne. They'd come here so that Hatchet could compete in the annual archery contest, but owing to the sudden, vicious storm, everyone was now inside waiting and hoping for the bad weather to pass.

"I know you're disappointed and it don't seem fair that you had to miss your turn, but the contest ain't over." She glanced at the well-dressed men and women crowding around tables and milling about the huge room. She recognized a large number of people, most of whom were acquaintances rather than friends. "Archery ain't my cup of tea, but it's a better sport than horse racing. You can lose your shirt bettin' on the ponies."

"I'm not doing it just for the sport," Hatchet pointed out. "You know my doctor insisted I get more exercise, and archery is perfect. It provides the right amount of physical activity without making one desperately hot and miserable. You know how hard I've practiced, madam, and it isn't fair that my category was suddenly shoved to the end of the competition instead of at the beginning as is the normal custom." He jerked his chin toward the rain-streaked window. "If it had gone the way it was supposed to, I'd already be finished . . ."

"And you'd have first place," Luty teased.

"Possibly, madam, possibly," Hatchet replied.

The two of them had more than an employer-employee relationship. They had a strong bond, and it was because of this bond that Luty had used her considerable influence to get him accepted as a member. The archery club wasn't as class-ridden as most of London's athletic establishments, but they didn't encourage servants to join.

Luty knew every member of the Board and the Membership Committee, and as they wanted her to become a member, they agreed he could be one as well.

"Come on now, you know with the weather turnin' so fast that lettin' the young ladies shoot first was the right thing to do." Luty picked up her champagne flute and took a sip.

"Nonsense, madam, those young women all looked quite sturdy to me, as a matter of fact—"

"Look, look," she interrupted, "there he is." She nodded

toward a portly, balding man in gold-rimmed pince-nez eyeglasses as he stepped through the main door and into the crowded room.

"There who is?" Hatchet frowned irritably.

"Jeremy Marks, the fella I told ya about," Luty said softly. "The one everyone hates. I told ya what I overheard in the cloakroom."

"Refresh my memory, madam."

"There ain't nothin' wrong with your memory, Hatchet. Just admit it, you weren't listening to me," Luty accused. "But that's alright, I don't listen to you half the time, either. Like I told ya earlier, I was in the cloakroom gettin' my handkerchief and Mrs. McElhaney and another lady showed up. They stood just inside the door, which was open, and they didn't see me. They was too busy watchin' Jeremy Marks."

"How do you know they were watching the man?"

"At first I didn't, but then Alice McElhaney started talking to the other lady and she was madder than a wet hen. She kept sayin' that Marks wasn't supposed to be here, that he'd been banned from the club."

"Why was he banned?"

"She didn't say and I couldn't exactly ask, now, could I? But she went on and on about him. Kept tellin' the other lady what a no-good pole cat he was . . ."

"No-good pole cat?" Hatchet stared at her skeptically. "Mrs. McElhaney, an upper-class Englishwoman, used that expression?"

"Not those exact words, she used English insults, but the meanin' was the same," Luty shot back. "Anyways, her friend wasn't much help to her. She told Mrs. McElhaney that since Marks and Hannah Lonsdale had announced their engagement, she was bringing him here as a guest and they couldn't keep him out. Then Mrs. McElhaney said that she'd heard he was back but she hadn't wanted to believe it. But just in case it was true, she had a way to fix him. Once she had a chat with Hannah Lonsdale, he'd get what he deserved."

Hatchet crossed his arms over his chest. "Are you telling me that these two women had that kind of conversation with you standing there? That's not very discreet."

"I already told ya, they wasn't lookin' my way. They was starin' out at the corridor and watchin' Jeremy Marks."

"They didn't so much as glance into the cloakroom?"

"Well, they might not have realized I was standing there," she muttered as she watched Jeremy Marks. He weaved his way among the tables until he reached the door at the far end of the room. "I sort of moved back behind the rack of coats and jackets. I mean, I didn't want to embarrass the two ladies; I didn't want them knowin' their unkind words had been overheard."

"Nonsense, madam, you were out-and-out eavesdropping, weren't you? Come now, admit it."

"What if I was?" She glared at him. "You do it whenever it suits you, and you gotta admit, my being able to blend in with the woodwork has come in right handy on a number of other occasions."

She was referring to the fact that both she and Hatchet often helped out their friend, Inspector Gerald Witherspoon. He'd solved more homicides than anyone in the history of the Metropolitan Police Department. Naturally, he had no idea he was the recipient of such generous assistance and they, along with all the members of his household, were determined to keep it that way.

"Yes, but that's when we've been out and about on our investigations." He gestured around the room. "We don't have a murder now. This is a social activity."

"All the better to pick up a few useful bits and pieces." Luty grinned. "Besides, you never know when somethin' is goin' to happen."

A crash of thunder boomed overhead. It was so loud, half the room jumped. Hatchet leaned closer to the window. "Blast and drat, the storm is not going to end anytime soon and now it's as dark as midnight out there."

"Don't exaggerate." Luty took another sip. "You know what the weather here is like. It can be black as a coal miner's face, and ten minutes later, the sun's come out. Besides, the rain's been comin' and goin' since we came inside."

"Yes, but the lulls never last more than a few minutes," he complained.

A waiter pushing a tea trolley rolled up to their table. "More tea, sir?" he asked Hatchet.

"No thanks, this is sufficient."

"Would you care for more champagne, madam?" he asked Luty.

She shook her head and pointed to the door at the far end of the common room. "Where does that door lead?" On the previous two occasions she'd come to the club, she'd stayed out on the grass watching Hatchet.

"Outside, ma'am. There's a passageway to the practice room and from there out onto the range." He rolled the trolley over to the next table.

"There, there he is. I told you it was him. Good gracious, with all the money the fellow supposedly has, one has to wonder what makes him indulge in such nasty, cheap behavior." Chester Atwood nudged his companion in the ribs and then pointed to the target closest to the practice room.

They were standing on the small porch next to the stairs leading down to the kitchen waiting for a break in the rain. Despite the lulls between downpours, there was never enough time for them to get out to retrieve their arrows.

"Are you sure it's him?" Horace Miller's eyes narrowed behind his wire-rimmed spectacles. He jerked as another burst of thunder crashed overhead. "How can you see anything out there? It's too dark."

"Of course I'm sure. Just how bad is your eyesight, Horace?" Chester gave him an irritable look. "Honestly, you really ought to get your eyes examined again . . ." He broke off as he spotted Marks shining a lantern along the ground while he slowly made his way across the grass in front of the target. "What on earth is he doing?"

"Oh, I see him now, Good Lord, you're right, it's him, and you know good and well what he's doing out there. That's why we came dashing out here."

"This is all Matilda and Harriet's fault," he complained. "Between my daughter and your niece, we've half a dozen expensive arrows out there and that blackguard is going to get his hands on them if we don't take action. Good gracious, why on earth did they let him through the front door?"

"Good old Jeremy always finds his way back in," Chester muttered. "My wife told me at breakfast this morning that now that Marks is engaged to Miss Lonsdale, she can bring him as a guest. Once they're married, the Board will give him back his membership. They'll not want to offend the Lonsdale family."

"I think we should confront him," Horace declared.

"Don't be ridiculous. Unless he's got one of our arrows in his fat little fist, he'll simply claim he was looking for a cuff link or his purse or some such other nonsense. The man's a liar as well as a thief."

"I wish he'd go away for good. He's been here as long as I can remember, and no matter how dreadful his behavior, he always manages to keep his hand in." Horace shook his head in disgust. "What's he doing now?"

Marks had turned and, still keeping the lantern low, was going back the way he'd just come. When he reached the other side of the target, he turned again and moved slowly across the grass toward the main building. His pudgy frame was bent forward, holding the lantern as close to the ground as possible while he crept along.

"Why is he doing that?" Horace continued. "It's dark out there but he should be able to see without that lantern."

"Maybe he's going blind," Chester snapped. "But blind or not, if he picks up one of mine, I'm going out there and taking it back."

"God knows why he wants them," Horace complained. "He's such a bad archer, they'll be of no use to him."

"That won't stop him. He loves getting his paws on anything that's expensive. The broadheads alone cost a fortune."

"They should never have let him on the premises. If it wasn't pouring rain, I'd confront the bastard myself. How dare he?"

"It's not actually raining now." Chester looked up at the sky. "And the wind has died down. Should we go out there?"

Despite his bravado, he didn't relish the idea of confronting the man.

By this time, Marks had reached the place where the archers took their shooting positions. Then he turned quickly and walked slowly back the way he'd come again, this time bending so low with the lantern that the base brushed the top of the grass.

Chester cleared his throat. "Well, we can't really accuse him of stealing our arrows at this point. He's not picked any up, and besides, Matilda and Harriet were shooting at the two targets on this end of the range . . ." His voice trailed off as lightning flashed in the distance, momentarily illuminating the sky.

"True, and if Marks sees us out there watching him, perhaps he'll realize he'd better behave himself."

By this time, Marks was back where he'd started, in front of the target. Then he turned and began walking toward the one next to it, which was a good ten feet away.

"The lull in the storm is lasting," Horace said as another streak of lightning split across the whole sky, illuminating the area. Moments passed as flash after flash followed in succession then they waited for the inevitable booms of thunder. When he could be heard, he said, "Come on, let's get our arrows now. I don't care if Marks sees us. I'm disgusted with the fellow."

He broke off as he realized that Chester wasn't listening but instead was staring at a spot between the two targets, his expression one of horror. "Good Lord, man, what's gotten into you? What's wrong?"

Chester pointed at Jeremy Marks. But the man wasn't

moving about anymore. His lantern was on its side on the grass and he himself was lying next to it. But even in the dim light of the waning storm, it was obvious there was an arrow sticking out of Marks' neck.

"What's goin' on?" Luty muttered as two soaking wet men charged into the common room.

Hatchet stopped looking out the window as the men raced toward Rufus Farley, the club manager. He was standing by one of the tea tables, speaking to Mrs. Merchant, the housekeeper in charge of the common room. Farley turned as they rushed toward him. The men gesticulated wildly as they pointed toward the archery range.

"Whatever it is, it's serious," Hatchet muttered.

"Maybe we should go have a look." Luty got up, wincing as a sharp arthritic pain jabbed her left hip. "Come on, let's stick our noses outside and see what's goin' on."

"Really, madam, I don't think whatever is happening outside is any of our business." He frowned disapprovingly but rose to his feet. "Actually, you might be correct. If something untoward did happen, perhaps we should know about it."

"Something bad has happened. I can feel it. What time is it?"

He opened his blazer and pulled his watch out of his waistcoat pocket. "It's ten minutes past three."

Luty nodded and headed toward the door at the far end of the room.

Tucking his timepiece back inside his pocket, he followed her, weaving his way between the tables and noticing that most of the people were so engrossed in their own conversations, they hadn't seen the commotion at the front of the room.

Reaching the door, he glanced over his shoulder and saw that Farley, one of the field captains, and the two men were going back outside.

He and Luty stepped into the corridor leading to the practice barn. Even though they were in a narrow passageway, a cold gust of wind from the open-sided building blasted into them. Luty sniffed the air. "Dang, Hatchet, this place smells like a horse barn."

"That's because it used to be a stable," he told her as he led the way into the practice shed proper. The air smelled faintly of hay and damp as they hurried along the concrete floor of the old stable that now had one side completely open to the elements. A line of wide cupboards stood along the inside wall. At the far end were two bull's-eye targets, both of which were slightly smaller than the ones out on the range. Club longbows hung from hooks between the cupboards, and on the wall behind the targets there were assorted tools jumbled together, old leather quivers in various states of repair, arrow broadheads, and hand spools of heavy strings.

"They use this part for indoor practice," Hatchet explained as he and Luty reached the far end. From here, they had an unobstructed view of the row of targets. Luty gasped and started to race out into the storm. But Hatchet grabbed her arm and pulled her back into the darkened space.

"No, madam, let's see what is happening out there before we do anything," he warned as the two soaked men, the field captain, and Rufus Farley stood over what was definitely a body.

"I know what's goin' on." Luty pointed to the targets. "Someone's shot Jeremy Marks with an arrow."

"How do you know it's him?" Hatchet asked.

"'Cause he's the only one that came out here," she said. "Now we just have to find out if he's dead or not." She stuck her head back out. "And I'm pretty sure he is. He's got an arrow sticking out of his neck and it looks like another one in the middle of his chest."

Hatchet looked out over her head. "You're right, the fellow's not moving and these longbow arrows are lethal."

"That means they'll have to send for the police," Luty said. "We'd best get crackin', Hatchet. We've got us a case, and for once, we can get the jump on the others." She turned and headed back the way they'd just come. She'd gone ten yards before she realized that Hatchet wasn't following. "What are you waiting for? Inspector Witherspoon will be here soon, and before he gets here, we can find out who all here hated this feller." She turned and continued walking.

"How do you know our inspector will get the case?" Hatchet started after her.

"Because this place is in his district and he's on duty this afternoon. Now hurry up, time's a-wastin' and we have work to do."

Luty was perfectly aware that many would consider their actions outrageous, but as they'd both assisted Inspector Witherspoon on many previous occasions, albeit without his knowledge, her behavior was perfectly logical. Not just she and Hatchet, but his entire household as well as several of their friends assisted the great detective.

By the time they'd reached the door of the common room, it was apparent the news had spread as half a dozen people poured outside, brushed past Luty and Hatchet, and raced out onto the range. The two of them continued on inside. The room was buzzing, and the tables were deserted as groups of people clustered around the windows, talking excitedly and staring out at the range.

"Looks like everyone's heard the news," Luty muttered softly. "Come on, circulate."

"I'll start asking questions," Hatchet said. "I know many of these people, especially the men I compete against."

"So do I," Luty replied softly. "But I ain't sure about askin' questions."

"What do you mean?"

"I think it's best if we just eavesdrop. The killer might still be here and we don't want to arouse their suspicions."

"Madam, we don't even know that a murder has taken place," Hatchet warned. "It could have been a terrible accident."

"Nah, not with two arrows stickin' out of the feller." She started to move off into the crowded room, but turned suddenly. "And make sure you take note of who says what—that might end up bein' important."

"I'm quite aware of that, madam"—he sniffed disapprovingly—"and what's more, my eavesdropping skills are just as good as yours."

At the household of Inspector Gerald Witherspoon, Mrs. Jeffries, his housekeeper, frowned as she stared out the window over the kitchen sink. "Poor Phyllis is going to get caught in this downpour." She was a slightly plump woman of late middle age with streaks of gray in her auburn hair, freckles scattered across her nose, and a ready smile.

"She took an umbrella with her," Mrs. Goodge, the cook, replied as she pulled out a mixing bowl from beneath her worktable. "And this time of year, it isn't terribly cold out, just miserably wet." The cook shoved her wire-rimmed spectacles up on her nose. Her snow-white hair was neatly tucked up beneath her white cook's cap. She reached toward the flour canister but stopped as she heard the back door open and then footsteps running along the corridor.

Phyllis, the housemaid, raced into the room. She was a slender woman of twenty with sapphire blue eyes and porcelain skin. Tendrils of dark blonde hair had escaped from her hat and now framed her face. "I ran into Constable Griffiths outside and you'll never guess what's happened." She hurried to the coat tree, whipped off her bonnet, and hung it up. "We've got us a murder."

"Do we know where and who?" Mrs. Jeffries asked.

"Constable Griffiths was in a hurry and was actually grateful he'd run into me outside so he didn't have to come into the house and tell us the inspector might be late tonight."

"He didn't give you any details?" Mrs. Goodge asked plaintively.

"Not really, just that the inspector and Constable Barnes had been called to the West London Archery Club because a man had been killed." Phyllis hung up her light blue cotton jacket. "He was killed at the archery place but the constable didn't say how he died. Should I go upstairs and get Wiggins?"

"He's not here. I sent him over to Mrs. Palfrey's with that recipe she wanted to borrow," Mrs. Goodge said. "But he should be back soon."

Phyllis started to reach for the jacket she'd just hung up. "I'll nip over and get Betsy and Smythe," she offered. "They'll want to be here. We haven't had us a murder since Christmas."

"We had that one in February," Mrs. Jeffries reminded her.

"Humph," Mrs. Goodge sniffed. "We didn't do anything for that one. The killer practically left a note that he'd done it and our inspector had everything wrapped up in less than a day."

"That's true," Mrs. Jeffries agreed. "Good idea, Phyllis, go tell them and as soon as Wiggins returns, I'll send him across the garden to Lady Cannonberry's."

"What about Luty and Hatchet?"

"Wiggins can go there from Lady Cannonberry's," she decided.

"Shouldn't we send him to the West London Archery Club first?" the cook asked. "You know, to suss out what's what. We don't want to drag everyone here to have it end up like the last one."

Mrs. Jeffries thought for a moment. "You're right, that's the wisest course of action. At least that way we'll know if it's going to be a genuine investigation or merely an arrest."

Inspector Gerald Witherspoon and Constable Barnes stared at the front of the West London Archery Club. The inspector was a middle-aged man with thinning brown hair; a long, bony face; and just a hint of thickness about his waist. He wore a lightweight gray suit and a black bowler hat. Barnes was an older copper with a ruddy complexion, a ramrod-straight spine, and thick wavy steel gray hair under his policeman's helmet.

"I've been past this place dozens of times," Barnes said, "and didn't realize how big the property actually is."

The West London Archery Club was a three-story red-brick Georgian building set back from the busy road on an emerald green lawn. A walkway of polished black stone led up to a short flight of wide, white-painted steps flanked on each side by flowerbeds with red tulips, yellow daffodils, pink geraniums, and other colorful blooms. A trio of weeping willows, their long branches reaching the ground, stood on the right side of the turf while a low stone wall, crumbling in some spots, ran along the left edge of the property, and beyond that was a thick copse of oaks and elms.

Witherspoon headed up the walkway. "It is odd how we can see places frequently without really seeing them properly, isn't it? This place is less than a mile from the station, and like you, I've gone past it dozens of times without noticing very much about it."

They climbed the stairs, stepped inside the double front doors and into the foyer. The walls were painted a pale gray, the floor was black-and-white tiles in an intricate Wedgewood pattern, and overhead was a round brass light fixture topped with pale smoky white glass globes.

Just ahead of them, a red-carpeted corridor ran the length of the building with a staircase at the far end. Just inside the entrance was the reception counter. A chubby man with a towel around his neck and wet hair stood behind it, cleaning his spectacles with a white handkerchief.

Barnes cleared his throat and the man looked up.

"Thank goodness you're here." He raced out from behind the counter and they could see that his jacket was soaked. "What's taken you so long? We've had a terrible time trying to keep people back. I finally had two of the staff pull the targets together. I'm Rufus Farley, the club manager." He was a portly fellow with curly brown hair slicked down with rain, and a walrus mustache.

Witherspoon kept his smile firmly in place, but inside, he silently prayed that the manager or his staff hadn't trampled any clues in the crime scene. "I'm Inspector Gerald Witherspoon, and this is Constable Barnes. I assure you, sir, we got here as quickly as we could. More constables are expected any moment now and we'll send them out to safeguard the area. Can you tell me what happened?"

"It's dreadful, Inspector, absolutely dreadful. Someone has shot Jeremy Marks with an arrow . . . no, I tell a lie, not one arrow, with two of them. He's outside on the ground, and honestly, it's very upsetting. We've never had something like this happen here."

"Incidents like this are always difficult. Let's take a look. I've notified the police surgeon, so when he arrives, please have someone on your staff send him out to the body."

"Yes, yes, of course." He nodded distractedly, hurried to the double doors next to the counter, and stuck his head inside. "Mrs. Merchant, may I see you, please."

"Yes, sir," a woman's voice replied.

A few moments later, he returned. "Mrs. Merchant is in charge of the common room. She's sent one of the serving girls outside to wait for your constables. They'll bring them straight around to the back."

"Where is the body?"

"He's on the archery range." Rufus pointed toward the back of the building. "But the fastest way to get out there is through the storage pantry. It's this way." He turned to his right and strode down the corridor. They followed him past an open office door to the far end.

Farley stopped in front of a door, took out a set of keys, and unlocked it. "We keep dry goods and kitchen supplies in here," he explained as he waved them inside. They hastened through a room filled with shelves of flour, salt, coffee, tea, and sugar. Crockery, pots and pans, glassware, table linens, and serviettes filled the other shelves. A wicker laundry basket stood in one corner and extra chairs were stacked in rows along the only wall that didn't have shelves.

Farley crossed to a smaller door, opened it, and stood back so the two policemen could get past him. They went out to a covered porch that faced the archery range. "That leads down to the kitchen." Farley pointed to a narrow staircase off the left side of the porch. An expansive green lawn ran from the back of the building to the row of targets. Next to them was an attached structure with the side completely open. Witherspoon could see targets in there as well.

"That's the practice room," Farley explained. "It used to be a stable, but when the club bought the estate, they took all the doors off so the members could practice even if the weather was bad."

Just then, a young kitchen maid appeared from around the side of the practice room. Constable Griffiths and two other constables followed behind her.

Two of the targets had been pushed together and there were three men, two in jackets and hats and what looked like a kitchen lad, standing in front of the targets. Farley pointed at them. "I sent both of the club's field captains and our footman out to keep people away from Mr. Marks' body."

"Thank you, Mr. Farley, that was the right thing to do in the circumstances." Witherspoon stepped off the porch and started across the grass. Barnes was right behind him.

"Honestly, I don't understand how this could have happened." Farley hurried to catch up. "We'd stopped the competition when the storm got so dreadful. I've no idea why Mr. Marks went outside."

"You think it was an accident?" Witherspoon looked at him, as did Barnes.

"I don't know what to think, Inspector. As I said, nothing like this has ever happened here before." He shook his head in disbelief and continued walking.

"I'll take care of securing the area, sir," Barnes said as he shot ahead of them.

A few moments later, the field captains and the footman were gone, leaving just Barnes and the other three constables. "He's here, sir." Barnes pointed behind the bull's-eyes. "And the scene hasn't been too badly damaged."

"Thank you, Constable," Witherspoon said as he and Farley rounded the target and came to the dead man.

Seeing the body, Farley's eyes widened and he gasped. "Oh Lord, this is dreadful. Look at all that blood." He pointed to the corpse's chest, where blood oozed from the base of the arrow. "I didn't get this close before. Oh dear, oh dear, this is dreadful, absolutely dreadful."

The man was now so pale, the inspector was alarmed. "Mr. Farley, perhaps it would be best if you didn't look at the victim."

"Oh goodness, I've seen dead people before, but that was just my uncle George, who died of heart failure on New Year's Eve. I've never seen anything like this . . . so much blood." Farley immediately looked away and took a long, deep breath. "My apologies, Inspector, you must have questions. I'll answer whatever you like."

"First of all, if you feel faint or need to sit down, we can go inside." Witherspoon knew that the sight of violent death—and this was most certainly a violent death as the poor man had two arrows sticking out of him—was difficult for most people.

This time, Farley shook his head. "No, thank you, but I understand my duty. Ask your questions, Inspector."

"Can you confirm this man's identity?"

"His name is Jeremy Marks."

"Is he a member here?"

Farley swallowed and kept his gaze on the thick copse of trees on the other side of the wall. "Not now. He was, but he was asked to relinquish his membership last summer."

"Why was that?" Barnes, who'd just completed his own examination of the dead man, stood up.

"Mr. Marks was accused by several other members of cheating during a very important competition. The accusations were confirmed by the field captain and his assistant, so we asked Mr. Marks to give up his membership. He did so."

"If he wasn't a member, why was he here?" Witherspoon asked. He was trying to delay having to actually examine the corpse. Despite over forty homicide investigations, he was still squeamish around bodies.

"He came as a guest of Miss Lonsdale. They're engaged, or I mean they were engaged," he sighed. "Oh dear, there isn't going to be a wedding now, is there."

"No, sir, I'm afraid not. However, it is interesting that someone who was banned from the club ends up dead from two arrows," Barnes murmured. "Who were the members that accused Mr. Marks of cheating?"

Farley's eyes widened in surprise. "I can't tell you that. It's confidential."

"Mr. Farley, I don't think you quite understand," Witherspoon said. "This is an investigation into a very serious crime, murder. The matter can no longer be kept confidential. You really must answer the question."

"But that will cause all sorts of problems," Farley exclaimed. "I can vouch for the men who accused Marks. They're both fine fellows, excellent businessmen and stalwarts of the archery community. Neither of them would have done something like this."

"We're not accusing anyone of anything," Witherspoon explained. "We simply need their names so we can speak to them."

"Are they here today?" Barnes reached into his pocket and pulled out his little brown notebook and pencil.

"They are, but is it absolutely necessary to speak to them?"

"I'm afraid so," the inspector said. "What's more, we'll have to interview everyone who was here when this happened."

"Gracious, you're talking about a hundred or more people."

"Then we'd better get started." Barnes flipped open the notebook.

"Some of them might have left." Farley frowned. "We didn't know what had happened so there was no reason to ask anyone to stay, especially if they'd completed competing in their own category."

"Strange that people would leave once they knew a murder had been committed," Witherspoon mused. "Generally, people hang about for ages."

"But no one knew a crime had been committed," Farley protested. "What's more, I don't think you should call it murder. Perhaps it was an accident . . ."

"He was shot twice, sir," Barnes said dryly. "Shot once would be an accident, shot twice is usually deliberate. Now, may we have the names of the ones who reported him cheating?"

"Alright, if you insist. Marks was caught altering his target hits by Emmett Merriman and Warren Stanley."

"Target hits?" Barnes looked up from his notebook.

"I take it that refers to the system by which a winner is chosen? Is that correct?" Witherspoon wasn't just curious; past experience had taught him that the more he knew about any situation where a murder had been committed, the easier it was to investigate the case.

"That's right. We use the honor system and rely on our members to accurately report their hits, which leads to their final score," Farley explained.

"What kind of prizes are awarded for winning this sort of competition?" Witherspoon asked.

"There are some small monetary prizes awarded for the winner of each division, but mainly, the winner is allowed to compete at the regional and perhaps even national competitions."

"Did Mr. Marks cheat on the scoring for the money or to move on to the larger competitions?" Witherspoon asked.

Farley shook his head. "I don't know for certain, but if I was forced to guess, I'd say it was for the money prizes. To be honest, Marks was known to be a dodgy sort of fellow. There were all sorts of stories about him being less than honest in his business dealings. But we never had any official problem with him until last spring when Mr. Merriman and Mr. Stanley both saw him altering his score."

Witherspoon glanced at Griffiths, but before he could issue any instructions, Barnes pointed at two men standing at the edge of the practice room. "Are they the ones who found the body?"

"Yes, they raised the alarm. Do you wish to speak with them?"

"We'll do that as soon as we're finished here, sir," Witherspoon said quickly.

"When was the last time anyone saw Mr. Marks?" Barnes asked.

"He passed through the common room a few minutes before three o'clock and continued out through the back door."

"Was it still raining hard?" the inspector asked.

Farley frowned. "That's difficult to say. You see, the rain kept starting and stopping. It would be raining hard then there would be a lull, so I can't say for certain how bad it was when he went outside. I just assumed he was going out to the practice room to fetch something. We allow members and guests to avail themselves of our supplies. His fiancée, Miss Lonsdale, had already competed in her division and I thought he might be getting something for her."

"He wasn't competing?"

"No, only members are allowed to compete."

"Thank you, Mr. Farley. The more we know, the faster we can ascertain what has happened." Witherspoon looked at Griffiths. "Before you let anyone leave the premises, ask if they might have seen or heard anything. You and Constable Parker, follow Mr. Farley inside and begin taking names and addresses. Also, make certain you obtain the victim's address as well." He glanced at Rufus Farley. "Even though he's no longer a member, you do have Mr. Marks' address?"

"Of course, Inspector. It's in our files and I've not heard that he moved house."

"Thank you." He turned to Griffiths again. "Oh, but before you do anything, speak to the two men that reported seeing Mr. Marks cheating."

"Yes, sir, Mr. Merriman and Mr. Stanley."

"Mr. Farley will point them out to you. All you'll need to do is ask them for their movements and make certain they don't leave until Constable Barnes and I have spoken to them."

"Yes, sir," Griffiths said as he and Constable Parker headed back inside.

Witherspoon glanced toward the practice room. "Let's have a word with these two," he said to Barnes.

"What about the body, sir? Don't you want to have a look? Even though they pushed the two targets together, the crime scene didn't look too mucked about."

"Yes, of course." Witherspoon nodded at the one constable still standing watch over the corpse, steeled himself, and then focused his full attention on the dead man. One arrow was in the fellow's chest while the other had hit him in the throat.

"He brought a lantern with him." Barnes pointed to the lantern lying on the ground near the victim's leg. "He must have been looking for something."

"Let's hope we can find out what." Witherspoon stared at the spot where the lantern lay on its side. "But it was quite dark during the storm and the man does have weak eyes." He pointed at the spectacles that were still on the victim's face. He looked at the constable, a young lad with curly black hair and brown eyes. He appeared quite pale. "What's your name, Constable?"

"Constable Pritchett, sit. I'm new to the Ladbroke Station."

"I'm pleased to meet you, Constable Pritchett. Is this your first murder victim?"

Pritchett swallowed heavily and nodded. "Yes, sir, it is. I've seen dead bodies before, sir, but never one with arrows in it."

"You don't have to look at the victim if you'd rather not," he said softly. "Just stand guard until the police surgeon gets here. Constable Barnes and I are going to have a word with those two over there."

Pritchett smiled gratefully. "Thank you, sir."

The two policemen tramped over the sodden ground to the practice room. "Hello, I'm Inspector Witherspoon and this is my colleague, Constable Barnes," he said. "Mr. Farley said you gentlemen were the ones who found the body. Is that correct?"

"Yes, Inspector. I'm Chester Atwood," the taller of the two said, "and this is Horace Miller. It's been a terrible afternoon, sir. I can assure you of that."

"Tell me what happened here, how the two of you came to find the body."

Atwood cleared his throat. "Well, let me see, the competition was halted at two thirty. When the storm broke, everyone assumed it would just be a passing shower and that the competition would then resume. But as it turned out, it rained harder and harder, the sky got dark, and the winds were so strong, it would have been difficult to shoot."

Horace Miller interrupted. "It was impossible to do anything, Inspector, including picking up our arrows."

"I don't understand why you were outside then." Witherspoon's face mirrored his confusion. "Surely you didn't just go out there to stand in the rain?"

"No, no, no, Inspector." Atwood shook his head. "We weren't in the rain." He pointed to the covered porch Witherspoon and the others had come out of themselves. "We were under there. The rain was coming and going, and I was hoping for a long-enough break so I could retrieve my arrows."

"So you had already competed?" Witherspoon asked.

"No, Inspector. My daughter and Horace's niece are in the ladies' group and we'd lent them our arrows. They'd already competed, but the storm broke so quickly, they dashed inside without picking them up. I was very cross."

"As was I," Horace added. "Those arrows are made especially for us in France and they cost the earth."

"They left your expensive arrows out on the wet grass?" Barnes pressed. "And you came out to get them during a storm? Why didn't you just wait till the rain stopped?"

"We couldn't risk it, Constable," he explained. "We saw Marks crossing the common room to the back door."

"Why did seeing Mr. Marks go outside make you go outside yourselves?" Witherspoon asked.

"Because we were afraid he was going to steal our arrows," Chester said. "We both know what kind of cad Jeremy Marks is, and the minute we saw him hurrying through the common room, we decided to make sure he didn't get them."

"Are you saying that the victim, Jeremy Marks, deliberately went outside during a thunderstorm to steal arrows?" Witherspoon looked skeptical.

Neither of them answered. Instead, Chester Atwood sighed and Horace Miller simply shook his head. Finally, Miller said, "I know it's unbelievable, but yes, that's precisely what we're saying. Aside from being a cad and a thief, he was a very strange person."

Witherspoon decided to examine the dead man's character at a later time; there were other, more pressing questions that needed to be answered now. "While you were outside on the porch, did you see anyone?"

"Other than Marks, no," Atwood replied as Horace gave a negative shake of his head.

Barnes stopped writing and glanced up. "How much time had elapsed from your first sighting of him until you saw him lying on the ground between the targets?"

"I didn't see him." Horace jerked his thumb toward Atwood. "Chester spotted him first. He's got better eyesight than I do."

"We watched him for a few minutes." Chester told the two policemen about Marks walking slowly back and forth in front of the target closest to the practice room and then moving between the bull's-eye and the archer's starting position before moving toward the next target. "And even though the rain had stopped, there were was so much thunder and lightning that we were distracted. When the next bolt of lightning flashed, we saw him lying on the ground. But I don't know precisely how long it was, maybe a minute."

"It was less than that," Horace said. "My guess is it was about thirty seconds."

"And in that thirty-second period of time, someone managed to fire two arrows into Mr. Marks' body?" Witherspoon murmured.

Chester shrugged. "As I said, Inspector. I really couldn't say how much time had passed between seeing him alive and dead.

Horace is probably right. It could have been as little as thirty or perhaps forty seconds."

"Marks was moving between the bull's-eye targets when he was shot," Barnes confirmed.

Both men nodded in the affirmative.

"How good an archer would one need to be in order to shoot and hit someone moving?" the inspector asked.

Chester looked at Horace and then at the two policemen. "That depends on where the person who fired the lethal arrows was standing. It wasn't pitch-black out here, but it was quite dark. If anyone fired from over there"—he pointed toward the copse of trees and the crumbled wall dividing the club from the adjacent property—"we'd not have seen them because we weren't looking at anyone other than Marks. But considering how strong the wind was, I'm fairly sure that whoever did this wasn't merely a competent archer; in my opinion he would have to be an expert."

CHAPTER 2

After they'd completed the interviews with the two men, Inspector Witherspoon and Constable Barnes spent ten minutes looking around the grounds before heading back inside. When they stepped into the foyer, Constable Griffiths was at the reception counter writing in his notebook.

He put down his pencil and straightened to attention. "As you instructed, sir, I've spoken with the two gentlemen," he reported, "and they claim they were in the common room from the time the competition was stopped until they heard Marks was dead. They've both agreed not to leave the premises until you've interviewed them. Constable Parker is in the common room taking statements and addresses."

"Good work." Witherspoon saw Rufus Farley step out of his office and head toward them. "Constable Barnes and I have done a cursory search of the immediate area, but we need a far more thorough one. I want the grounds next door searched as well. The place looks abandoned, so there shouldn't be any problem with having a good look around. The police surgeon has arrived so I sent Constable Pritchett to the station to get more men. When he gets back, you'll need to break off taking statements and take charge of the search."

Griffiths flicked his notebook shut, picked up his pencil, and dropped them into his pocket. "Yes, sir," he said before heading to the common room.

Farley joined them but waited till the double doors closed behind Griffiths before he spoke. "Is the body still here, Inspector?"

"Only for a few more minutes," Witherspoon assured him. "The police surgeon will do an examination and then Mr. Marks will be moved to the hospital mortuary for a postmortem."

Farley frowned. "Why can't they take him straightaway? Surely there's nothing a doctor can see that you and Constable Barnes haven't already noted. Honestly, Inspector, I've already had messages from two of the club's directors and they weren't pleased. Jeremy Marks' death is already wreaking havoc with our reputation. Now there's even press out front. God knows how they managed to learn about this so quickly, but that will make things worse. We want this matter over and done with, and frankly, getting the late Jeremy Marks off the premises might help."

"Murder rarely pleases anyone but the perpetrator, Mr. Farley," Witherspoon said patiently. "But it's important not to rush things. Everyone, including the police surgeon, must be thorough. But I do understand your concerns and I assure you we're working as quickly as we can. Now, if you could show us where we can conduct our interviews, that would be most helpful."

Farley opened his mouth as if to argue, closed it, and shrugged. He pointed to an open door farther down the corridor. "You can use my office."

"Thank you, Mr. Farley."

"I'll send Emmett Merriman in. He was the first person to make the accusation against Jeremy Marks."

"The constables have begun interviewing everyone else who is here—as Inspector Witherspoon said, they'll mainly just ask if they'd seen or heard anything or if they might know anyone who had a reason to want to harm the victim. We'd appreciate it if you would stay in the common room and keep an eye on things for us," Barnes said.

His brows drew together. "Why do I need to do that? I've told you everything I know."

Barnes doubted that was true, but he was a smart-enough copper to let the statement stand. "The constables may need you to verify a statement or perhaps even explain the different aspects of the club's policies," he pointed out. "People say odd things when they're talking to the police, and it helps to have someone such as yourself available to clarify matters."

Farley thought for a moment. "I can understand that. Of course I'll stay. As I said, right now our priority is to get this matter resolved quickly. God knows what the rest of the directors will think of this whole wretched mess."

"Thank you, Mr. Farley," Witherspoon interjected. "We appreciate your cooperation."

"I don't have much choice now, do I," he muttered as he disappeared.

"Wait till we catch the killer and it goes to trial," Barnes murmured as soon as the door closed behind Farley, "and the club's name is on the front page of every newspaper in the country. That's when the poor man will really have something to complain about."

Inside the common room, there was a steady buzz as everyone expounded on their opinion of the dead man. Luty, feigning a slight limp, crept around a particularly gossipy table, moving slowly so she could catch every word. A tall, buxom blonde woman wearing a jaunty boat-shaped blue hat was holding forth: *"Hannah Lonsdale must be devastated."*

"She can't be. You'll notice that she isn't here, so how would she know he's dead?" a plump brown-haired matron in a green day dress said. *"I'll wager she and Marks had a row. Right after she competed, she stormed off. I saw him running after her and she looked very angry. When he grabbed her arm, she shook him off and jumped in her carriage."*

"That doesn't mean they rowed," buxom blonde woman charged. *"She might just have been in a hurry."*

Green day dress snorted. *"Don't be absurd. You know how competitive Hannah is. She never leaves before seeing who wins her division. She must have been furious."*

Luty stopped as Hatchet stepped in front of her. "Madam, let's move over here," he said softly. He took her arm and gently tugged her to a more isolated spot beyond earshot of the tables.

"Why'd ya interrupt me? I was gittin' an earful," Luty complained.

"As was I, madam." He glanced over his shoulder at the room. "As you surmised, the deceased was not well liked. Furthermore, as you've noticed, gossiping ladies can tell us quite a bit. But we've a more pressing problem."

"What problem?"

Hatchet pointed to the front of the common room. "That problem. Constable Griffiths is here, and oh blast, he's heading our way. What do we say?"

"Tell 'em the truth—we're here because you're competin'." Luty dropped her voice to a whisper.

"What about everything we've overheard?"

"Let's keep it to ourselves for now. We don't know that everything we heard is true; maybe we ought to do a bit of investigatin' on our own before we say too much. We can pass 'em along to Constable Barnes later."

Barnes had figured out years ago that the inspector was getting help and it hadn't taken him long to realize precisely where the assistance came from.

Hatchet chuckled. "Excellent, madam."

In Rufus Farley's office, Constable Barnes opened his notebook as Inspector Witherspoon took off his bowler hat and laid it on the side of the desk before sitting down in Farley's chair. There was a sharp knock on the front door, and a moment later, a tall, blue-eyed man with thinning dark blond hair stepped into the room. "I'm Emmett Merriman. Your constable said you wished to speak to me."

"We do, Mr. Merriman. I'm Inspector Gerald Witherspoon, and this is my colleague, Constable Barnes."

Merriman, his back ramrod straight, nodded politely.

Witherspoon gestured at the empty chair next to Barnes.

"Please take a seat, sir." He paused while the man settled himself and then said, "Mr. Merriman, I take it you're aware that Jeremy Marks has been killed."

"Everyone here is aware of it," he replied. "I'm not surprised. Marks had plenty of enemies. It was only a matter of time before someone he ruined decided to do something about it."

"I understand you and another gentleman accused him of cheating during an archery competition, and because of that, he was dismissed from the club."

Merriman smiled broadly. "That's right. We caught the blackguard altering his score sheet. He wasn't even trying to be subtle about it. Stupid fool did it in the cloakroom. Luckily, I wasn't the only one who saw him. Warren Stanley saw him do it, too."

"Was he angry with you when he was dismissed from the club?" Witherspoon asked.

Merriman shrugged. "Of course, but there was nothing he could do about it."

"Why didn't you like him?" Barnes asked.

Merriman turned and looked at the constable. "You mean aside from the fact that he was a disgusting excuse for a man?"

"Can you be a bit more specific, sir?" The constable stopped writing and looked up from his notebook.

"He cheated people. He did it all the time. My family owns Merriman Cabinets and Cupboards, we've three shops in London, and we do good work. Ten years ago, Marks hired us to refurbish all the cabinets and cupboards in a house he was renovating. We did the work and sent him the bill, but he wouldn't pay. He kept stalling us, and when I began to insist upon payment, he started denigrating our firm all over town. I finally threatened to sue the bastard."

"He paid what he owed?" Witherspoon asked.

Merriman shook his head. "Only part of it. He claimed he wasn't going to give me the full amount because the work wasn't up to the standards we'd agreed upon. By that time, I was so sick of the fellow, I took what he offered just so I wouldn't need to deal with him again." He broke off, his expression disgusted. "But when my wife and I joined this club, I found out he was already a member."

"This isn't the only archery club in London." The inspector leaned forward. "If you disliked him so much, why did you stay a member?"

"Because of my wife, Inspector. Her uncle is one of the directors, and most of her friends are members here. I will admit that I tried warning both her uncle and the other directors about Marks' character, but they wouldn't listen. They only cared about collecting the membership fees. But I was proved right in the end."

Witherspoon said, "How so, sir?"

Merriman's eyes narrowed. "Within three months, Marks was suspected of stealing Frank Burkhead's crossbow."

"I've no idea how valuable a crossbow might be," Witherspoon said curiously.

"This one cost upwards of fifty pounds. It was made by a master craftsman in Scotland."

"Was Marks arrested?" Barnes asked.

Again, Merriman shook his head. "Burkhead refused to press charges. There wasn't enough evidence for an arrest. But Jeremy Marks was the only person who was seen going into the practice room during the period when the bow was stolen. The members often hung their bows in there when they came inside for tea. After that incident, many of our members took care to avoid leaving anything valuable where Marks might get his grubby paws on it."

"Did the club take any action against him?" Barnes asked.

"No, they claimed they could do nothing. As I said, Burk-head didn't press charges, and without evidence of wrong-doing, the directors were hamstrung as well. Mind you, as you already know, last year Warren Stanley and I caught him cheating, and with two witnesses, the directors finally had a reason to get rid of the man. He was forced to resign his membership."

Witherspoon nodded. "Did you see Mr. Marks today?"

"Yes, I saw him going through the common room and out the back door." His brows drew together. "It must have been just a few moments before he was killed, because no more than ten minutes later, I could tell that something had happened when Chester Atwood and Horace Miller rushed in and raced over to Rufus Farley. A few seconds later, the three of them went outside."

Barnes shifted to a more comfortable position. "Were you alone when this happened?"

"No, I was sitting at a table with four other people." Merriman frowned slightly. "I assure you, Constable, I might have loathed the man, but I didn't kill him."

"May we have the names of the people you were with?" Barnes flipped to a blank page.

"Mr. and Mrs. Belton were there, as was Henrietta Storch and Miss Linwood, her companion, no, I tell a lie, Mrs.

Storch had sent Miss Linwood to the kitchen for something. It was just the three of us, not four."

"Thank you, Mr. Merriman," Witherspoon said. If the man was being truthful, he couldn't have murdered Jeremy Marks. "Did you notice if anyone else was missing during this time period?" He made a mental note to do a timeline. Dozens of people must have seen Marks in the common room and a few moments later the fellow had been struck with two arrows. A good timeline of who was where during the fateful moments could be very useful indeed.

Merriman shook his head. "Not that I can recall, Inspector, but then again, the only thing I was interested in at that moment was a hot cup of tea." He rose to his feet. "Is there anything else?"

"Not for now, sir," Witherspoon replied. "Would you ask Mr. Farley to send Warren Stanley in?"

While they waited for the next interview, Barnes went over his notes and the inspector stared off into space, thinking about the case. Witherspoon mentally debated various methods to devise a workable timeline. The trouble was there were so many people involved, it might be impossible to determine who was where at the precise moment Marks was killed. But surely, there must be a way to do it. Surely. His reverie was interrupted by a soft knock on the door. "Come in."

"Hello, I'm Warren Stanley. I understand you wish to speak with me." He was a short, thin fellow with a friendly manner and a Liverpool accent.

The inspector introduced himself and the constable as Stanley took the spot vacated by Emmett Merriman. The interview wasn't very long as he confirmed everything Merriman had told them. "We caught Marks cheating right and proper. Fellow wasn't even embarrassed about it."

"Were you well acquainted with Mr. Marks?" Witherspoon asked.

Stanley laughed. "Not likely, Marks looked down his nose at men like myself. I got a bit lucky and did well in business. I'm retired now, but I'm not ashamed to say I'm a working-class man."

"Did you ever do business with Jeremy Marks?"

"No."

Barnes looked at him, his expression curious. "Do you feel welcome here?"

"I do." Stanley grinned. "Archery clubs aren't like those fancy London men's clubs. All you need to be admitted here is an interest in archery, a recommendation from a member, and the means to pay the annual membership dues."

"Did Mr. Marks' attitude toward you cause you any problems here?" the inspector pressed.

"There's a few like Marks, but most people are polite and decent."

"Did you see Jeremy Marks when he went through the common room and out the back door during the storm?"

"I did. I was sitting with George Ellingson and his wife. We were having tea and champagne when Jeremy Marks came inside and then went right back out the back door to the practice room. It wasn't long after that we heard he was dead."

"Thank you for your cooperation, Mr. Stanley." Witherspoon rose to his feet. "We've got your address if we've any more questions."

Stanley stood up as well. "I didn't like Marks much, but no one deserves to die like that."

As soon as the door shut behind Warren Stanley, Barnes closed his notebook and said, "What do you think, sir?"

"The victim was obviously a controversial figure here." The inspector's spectacles had slipped down his nose, so he reached up and shoved them back into place. "But I didn't get the impression that Warren Stanley had any real personal animosity towards him."

"Probably because Stanley never did business with the fellow." Barnes tucked his notebook into his pocket. "We can't say the same about Mr. Merriman; he clearly hated Marks."

"True, but if the timeline of Marks moving through the common room minutes before he was spotted lying dead is correct, Merriman has an alibi. He was sitting with other people and probably in the full view of everyone else." Witherspoon stared off into space as an idea popped into his mind and then popped out just as quickly. "Gracious, Constable, for a moment, I had an interesting thought, but honestly, it suddenly flew out of my head."

"Goodness, Mrs. Crookshank, it's you." Constable Griffiths stared at the woman standing in front of him.

"It's surely me, Constable Griffiths. I'll bet you're real surprised I'm here."

Surprise didn't even begin to describe it, Griffiths thought. Over the years, he'd seen Mrs. Crookshank several times at Inspector Witherspoon's home. Originally, she'd been a witness in one of the inspector's early cases and that had resulted in a friendship between them. "Are you participating in the contest?"

Luty laughed. "Not me, Constable. Hatchet's the archer."

Hatchet, who was right behind Luty, gave a quick wave. "I'm in the Men's Novice Division. My doctor recommended it as a way to get more exercise, and I must say, except for today's incident, it's been very rewarding."

"Yes, I'm sure it has. Except, of course, for the, uh . . . uh . . . incident. You know, Mr. Marks getting killed," Griffiths blurted out. He didn't normally babble but finding personal friends of Inspector Witherspoon's here at the scene of the crime was a bit unsettling. He took a quick breath and got ahold of himself. "Er, did either of you know the deceased?"

"Jeremy Marks." Luty shook her head. "Nope, but I've heard an earful of gossip about the feller."

"I didn't know the man, either," Hatchet volunteered.

"I don't think anyone in this room liked him much," Luty continued. "But I imagine you're not interested in listenin' to gossip. Policemen want facts," she declared as she sat down in the chair he'd placed on the other side of the table. "Now, go ahead and ask your questions."

For a moment, Griffiths wasn't sure what to say. In truth, he'd heard both the inspector and Constable Barnes make comments that listening to gossip was important, but he wasn't sure if he should admit that to a civilian. "Uh, of course. Did you see anything today that struck you as odd?"

"Not really."

"Did you see Mr. Marks earlier in the day, before the storm?"

"Not before the storm," Luty said. "But we both saw him walkin' through the common room."

"I saw him earlier," Hatchet volunteered.

Griffiths leaned forward eagerly. "What did you see?"

"I was watching the Ladies' Division when I suddenly realized that I'd left my hand guard in the carriage. I went out to get it and I saw a lady, a lady I'd just seen competing, leaving the club. Then I saw Jeremy Marks. Of course, I didn't know his name at the time, I found out who he was later. He was racing after her and he grabbed her arm, but she shook him off and hurried on to her carriage."

"What happened then?"

"The lady shouted something at her driver, I couldn't hear precisely what it was, but he got down and helped her into the carriage."

"What did Marks do?"

Hatchet shrugged. "I've no idea. Once I saw that the lady was safe, I went about my business. It was only later that I heard the man was Jeremy Marks and the lady in question was his fiancée, Miss Hannah Lonsdale."

"And how did you come by this information?"

"I overheard another lady recounting the same incident I had seen," Hatchet said. "She happened to be outside when it happened and had seen what I'd witnessed."

"I see." Griffiths broke off as he spotted Constable Pritchett coming toward him. "Is there anything else either of you can tell me?"

"Neither of us knew the man," Luty explained. "So other than repeatin' some of the gossip, there ain't much we can tell ya."

Hatchet nodded agreement.

Griffiths almost told them hearing gossip might prove useful but then decided that might not be wise. But he did make a mental note to mention it to the inspector.

Pritchett was out of breath by the time he reached Griffiths. He glanced politely at Luty and then turned his attention to Griffiths. "Sorry it took so long to get back here with more constables, but there was a bit of a dust-up at the station. One-legged Billy got into it with Harry Wartle when the two of them were bein' led off to their cells. They was goin' at it hard and fast—it took seven of our lads to pull them apart. But we're 'ere now and we've brought along a few hand lanterns so we can keep searchin' even if it darkens up."

"Right then, let's go." Griffiths nodded politely at Luty and Hatchet, then he and Pritchett left.

"Do you think I said too much?" Hatchet whispered.

"Nah, you told him the truth, and as you said, you weren't the only one seein' Marks' fiancée stormin' off in a huff."

"Oh goodness, madam." Hatchet put his hand on Luty's shoulder. "There's the inspector and Constable Barnes."

The two policemen spotted Luty and Hatchet at the same moment. Witherspoon gaped at them but Barnes, after a brief look of surprise, got his expression under control.

"Gracious, Luty, what on earth are you doing here?" Witherspoon said as he reached the duo. "Are you a member?"

"Yes indeedy, but it's Hatchet who likes shootin' arrows. Where I come from, Inspector, a bow and arrow ain't considered sport, it's a weapon."

It took a moment for the inspector to understand what she meant. "Of course, Luty. It must seem very odd, considering that you're from the American West. I've read about the conflicts between the Indians and the settlers."

"Madam has been very kind about my archery efforts."

Hatchet patted Luty's shoulder. In truth, he knew good and well that Luty had never witnessed an engagement, battle, or even a mild skirmish in her life.

"His doctor said he needed more exercise and Hatchet's always wanted to try his luck at archery." Luty waved her hand dismissively. "But I'm bettin' you're not interested in why we're here, but what we might have seen or heard."

Witherspoon smiled. "That's true, Luty."

"We did hear the victim wasn't well liked, but we already told that bit to Constable Griffiths before he went off with that other feller to search the grounds."

Barnes said, "How did you hear that Marks was disliked?"

"It wasn't hard. Soon as the word came up that someone had sent a couple of arrows into the man, everyone in the place started talkin' about him and most of 'em didn't keep their voices down," Luty replied.

Witherspoon glanced around the room. Rufus Farley stood by the door, his arms crossed and his expression glum, people stood in haphazard lines in front of the remaining constables taking statements, and the serving staff was tidying up. Except for a few groups of people still clustered together talking, the room had emptied out substantially. Suddenly, an older, well-dressed woman broke away from a trio by the window and hurried toward Rufus Farley. The inspector watched as the woman spoke to Farley. A moment later, he nodded his head and came toward the two policemen.

"Inspector, Mrs. Robinson has mentioned something very important," he began. "She said that Miss Lonsdale,

Mr. Marks' fiancée, will read about his death in the evening papers if you don't go and see her straightaway. Really, Inspector, that would be cruel. She lives quite close by so it shouldn't take you long."

"I understand your point, Mr. Farley, and the Metropolitan Police certainly don't want Miss Lonsdale to read about her fiancé's death in the evening papers, but we need to search the premises and the grounds thoroughly," Witherspoon told him.

"But there are constables outside searching now, so I don't see why you can't take a few moments to speak to Miss Lonsdale. Her godfather is one of the club's directors and her uncle is an advisor to Her Majesty."

Barnes realized that his superior, though one of the best men he'd ever known, placed far more significance on serving justice than keeping the rich and powerful happy. He generally admired this characteristic of the inspector, but Mr. Farley had a valid point. Not letting the lady know what had happened would be seen as cruel, and deliberately upsetting an advisor to Her Majesty when one didn't need to was foolish. "Exactly how far away does Miss Lonsdale live?" he asked quickly.

"Less than a mile from here," Farley exclaimed. "You can get there, give her the sad news, and be back by the time your men have finished their searching."

Barnes looked at Witherspoon. "What he says makes a lot of sense, sir. Griffiths is an experienced officer and he knows what he's doing. By the time he and the men finish searching the property here, the one next door, and these premises, we'll be back."

Witherspoon nodded in agreement. "True, we should

also send a constable to Mr. Marks' home so his household doesn't read about it in the papers, either."

"I'll send Constable Parker, sir." Barnes looked at Farley. "We'll need Mr. Marks' address, sir."

Witherspoon climbed out of the hansom cab and stared at the six-story redbrick town house that belonged to Hannah Lonsdale.

"From the looks of this place, she isn't poor," Barnes muttered as he joined the inspector on the pavement. The white front door and all the window frames appeared freshly painted, the brass lamps were brightly polished, and two exotic orange trees in huge green ceramic pots stood sentinel on each side of the wide stairs.

"I do hope she isn't alone. We're about to give the poor woman some dreadful news." Witherspoon was grateful that Constable Barnes was with him. Barnes, having been married to his good wife for many years, would probably be very helpful should Miss Lonsdale get upset or, God forbid, hysterical when she learned her fiancé had been murdered.

"She'll at least have a housekeeper and other servants around her," the constable said as he and Witherspoon started up the short walkway to the staircase.

Barnes banged the iron knocker against the wood. A moment later, the door opened and a tall, balding man in a butler's uniform appeared. "May I help you?"

"I'm Inspector Gerald Witherspoon, and this is my colleague, Constable Barnes. We're here to see Miss Hannah Lonsdale."

"Miss Lonsdale isn't receiving." The butler started to close the door.

Barnes stuck his foot in the opening. "Whether she's receiving or not, she'll want to hear what we have to say. Now, you can either go and tell your mistress that we're here or you can let her read that her fiancé has been murdered in the evening papers."

The butler's mouth gaped open and he quickly stepped back. "Oh dear, oh dear, this is not good. Please come inside. I'll tell Miss Lonsdale you're here."

They stepped inside.

"Thank you," Barnes said as the butler disappeared down the wide, Oriental-carpeted hallway and through a set of double doors. The constable turned slowly, studying the foyer. The oak floor was polished to a high gloss and covered with a red-and-black Oriental rug. The walls were painted a very light brown inset with white paneling that set off the curving staircase and oak banister. A huge vase of pink roses sat on the side console table opposite which was an emerald-and-white ceramic umbrella stand. "It's a very nice place, sir."

"Indeed, it's a lovely home," Witherspoon murmured.

The butler stepped back into the hall and waved them forward. "Miss Lonsdale will see you now."

They headed to the drawing room, but Witherspoon stopped before stepping inside and said to the butler, "Does Miss Lonsdale have any relatives here, or perhaps a good friend or someone like that?"

"No, Miss Lonsdale lives alone," he whispered. "But I think it might be wise to get Mrs. Leary. She's the housekeeper. We'll both stay just outside here in case Miss Lonsdale gets upset."

"Meadows, what are you whispering about?" a female voice said from inside the room. "You said the police are here. Send them in. I've not got all day."

"Yes, ma'am." He took a deep breath and waved them through the door.

The room was huge, with pale-blue-painted walls, a deeper-blue-and-gold-patterned carpet on the floor, and a black marble fireplace. Gold candelabras with white candles stood on each end of the mantle and above that was an old-fashioned portrait of a young girl.

"Meadows said you wished to speak to me." A woman of late middle age stepped out from where she'd stood by the window. She was of medium height and build. Her face was long, her complexion splotchy, and her dark hair liberally threaded with gray.

"I'm Inspector Witherspoon, and this is Constable Barnes. You're Hannah Lonsdale?"

"I am. What do you want? I've an appointment soon. I'm expecting my solicitor."

"Miss Lonsdale, I'm afraid we've some very bad news," the inspector began. "Perhaps you should sit down. It concerns Jeremy Marks, who we were told is your fiancé."

She made no move to sit down; she merely crossed her arms and stared at them. "He was, but that is no longer the case. Hence, the reason I'm waiting for my solicitor."

"You're no longer engaged?" Barnes blurted out.

"I ended the engagement earlier today." She uncrossed her arms and moved to the chair and sat down. "Now, what's this all about? I hardly see that my personal affairs are any business of the police."

"I'm afraid you'd be mistaken about that," Witherspoon replied. "You see, Mr. Marks was murdered this afternoon."

"Murdered?" Her mouth dropped open for a brief moment before she caught herself. "But that's absurd. People like us don't get murdered."

"I'm afraid Mr. Marks did," Witherspoon said.

"But I saw him only a few hours ago. What happened?"

Witherspoon was relieved she was taking the news so well. He thought it odd and perhaps a tad cold, but nonetheless, she hadn't become hysterical, and for that, he was decidedly grateful.

"He was shot with two arrows at the West London Archery Club."

She drew in a deep breath and closed her eyes for a split second. "That's not what I expected to hear."

"What did you expect to hear, ma'am?" Barnes regarded her curiously. She wasn't crying, and except for the quick drawn breath, she seemed in control of her emotions.

"I'm not sure, but it certainly wasn't that. Jeremy is a survivor . . . oh dear, I mean he was. I suppose everything suddenly caught up with him. Do you know who killed him?"

"No, ma'am." Witherspoon saw Barnes taking his notebook out of his pocket. "May we sit down? We've a number of questions for you."

"Yes, please do." She looked embarrassed. "I'm sorry, I'm a bit shocked . . . no, that's not the right word. I'm nowhere near as shocked as I ought to be. That's terrible, isn't it—you come tell me that the man I almost married has been murdered and I'm not genuinely surprised."

Witherspoon and Barnes both took a seat on the sofa

opposite the wing chair where Hannah Lonsdale had just sat down.

The inspector said, "When did you last see Mr. Marks?"

She exhaled softly before she spoke. "Just before the storm started this afternoon. I'd finished competing and I saw him right as I left. I'd told him earlier today that I was ending our engagement."

"When exactly did you tell him?"

"Just before I competed."

"Was there a specific reason you ended your engagement today?" The inspector wondered if the engagement ending and Marks' murder were somehow linked.

Her eyes narrowed. "I don't see how my personal life is any business of the police."

"Unfortunately, in this case, it is very much our business," the inspector replied. "I know this must be awkward for you, Miss Lonsdale, but Jeremy Marks was murdered only hours after you ended your engagement."

"I certainly didn't kill him," she snapped. "He was alive and well after I left. My coachman can attest to that."

"We also have a witness who saw you leaving the archery club," the inspector said quickly. "But you do understand, we must pursue every avenue of inquiry. Did you return to the club after leaving?"

"Why would I? I'd already competed and I had no wish to see Jeremy again."

"You've been here all afternoon," he pressed.

She leaned back and stared at him. "No, Inspector. Before I came home, I went to Jeremy's home. I left the engagement ring he'd given me with his housekeeper. Then I

came home. You can speak to my servants if you don't believe me."

"No disrespect is intended, Miss Lonsdale, but I must ask
these questions. Mr. Marks was murdered by a weapon that
few people are adept at using. From what I understand, you're
an excellent archer." He had no idea if that was true or not,
but he wanted to see her reaction. Yet her expression didn't
change; she simply stared at him for a few long moments.

"As are many others at the club," she finally said.

"May I ask why you ended your engagement?" Barnes
asked.

"Is it pertinent?"

"It might be."

"I ended it because I found out that Jeremy was only marrying me for my money." She stared at him coldly.

"How did you find out such a thing?" Witherspoon
asked. Asking such questions was awkward, but he knew it
might be important.

"It was easy, Inspector." She smiled cynically. "His previous, shall I say 'paramour,' waylaid me. She had in her
possession a letter written by Jeremy to her on the very day
he proposed to me. In it he ended his engagement to her. As
she is far more beautiful and quite a bit younger than myself,
it was clear that his interest in me was motivated solely by
money, not by love."

"Was he upset that you ended your engagement?" Witherspoon shoved his glasses back up on his nose.

"He didn't make a scene or anything like that," she said.
"But I could tell he was upset. He pretended to be devastated
and hurt, but the real truth was, Jeremy was furious."

Barnes looked up. "What's the name of the lady who showed you Mr. Marks' letter?"

She hesitated. "Alice McElhaney. She confronted me in the practice room a few moments before I competed." She broke off with a harsh laugh. "Actually, once I saw the letter, I was so outraged, I hit the target more than I've ever done before."

Wiggins ducked behind a tree as he spotted Constable Griffiths and half a dozen other constables moving steadily toward the low, crumbling wall that separated the archery club from the abandoned property he'd decided was a safe place to hide.

Cor blimey, he thought, this is gettin' blooming hard. He'd spent the last hour dodging from carriage to tree trunk then just plain keeping his head down and hoping the constables that knew him would be too busy to notice him. But they were everywhere, and to avoid them, he'd taken refuge here. On top of that, the one serving girl he'd managed to speak to had told him if he didn't leave her alone, she'd call one of the constables. But he had discovered one thing: Luty Belle and Hatchet were here and surely they would have kept their ears open.

Blast it, could this day get any worse? Short of making a run toward the carriage house, he didn't know what to do.

He stuck his head out to have another look and then realized the ruddy tree trunk wasn't wide enough to conceal him. Frantically, he turned and surveyed the area, desperately trying to find something to dodge behind. But this copse of trees was young and all of them had skinny, useless trunks. He began backing away, keeping his gaze glued on the advancing line of constables.

Suddenly, the wind picked up and Wiggins felt raindrops slapping against his neck and face. He knew he didn't have much time. Don't panic, he told himself, use your head, there's got to be a way out of here. He took a quick look around: The grass was overgrown and unkempt, but not long enough to hide him even if he flattened himself to the ground, the ruddy trees were useless, and from the angle of the derelict gravel drive that led to the main road, he'd be spotted the second he headed that way.

But they were getting close, so he began backing up, trying to make himself as small as possible while still staying out of the constables' line of sight as he retreated and they advanced. They were close enough now that he could hear them.

"Keep your eyes peeled, lads," Constable Griffiths' familiar voice said. "You know what Inspector Witherspoon needs us to do. Call out if you see anything that looks out of place, anything that the killer might have dropped."

"I thought we was lookin' for the murder weapon," another constable said.

"We are, but a good copper keeps a lookout for everything."

Wiggins stumbled as he tripped over a protruding tree root. He sucked in a deep, ragged breath as he righted himself, glanced toward the line of approaching constables, and thanked his lucky stars it had started raining so hard, no one had heard him staggering about like a stupid git. He knew there was only one thing to do—he had to get to that carriage house. It was probably locked tighter than a bank vault, but if he could get out of sight and behind it, he could get away. Cor blimey, he'd had a right miserable afternoon, and if he didn't get out of here, it was going to get worse.

The rain was coming down even harder now and the wind had picked up as well. Wiggins turned, and moving as quickly as he could, he went toward his destination. He kept his body hunched over and as low as possible.

The carriage house was a two-story brown brick structure with huge double-wide doors that could accommodate even the grandest carriage. There was a covered porch to the left of the carriage entrance that probably led to the driver's quarters upstairs. The roof of the entryway sagged precariously, but that didn't stop him—he dived into the dimly lighted space. His heart raced and his breath came in short, ugly bursts. Keeping his gaze focused on the line of constables who had now reached the wall, he moved backward.

"Constable Griffiths, are we going over?" a constable from the far end of the line shouted.

"We are. Inspector Witherspoon wants those grounds searched as well." Griffiths pointed toward the run-down property. "But have a good look along the wall on this side before going over. We don't want to miss anything."

Wiggins backed up more just as a huge gust slammed into him, pushing him harder against the door. It flew open, clattering against the inside wall. He fell through the doorway, landing hard on his backside. Frantic, he scrambled to his feet, hoping the storm was loud enough to mask all the noise.

Some of the constables were now climbing over the low crumbling wall. His heart beat so loudly, it sounded like thunder; he had to get out of here. Too many of the constables knew him. This place might be close to the inspector's house on Upper Edmonton Gardens, but there was no excuse he could give if he were caught here. It was too late to try and get around the ruddy place; he had no choice but to go inside. Sucking in a long, deep breath, he entered the building.

There was no foyer, merely a long, narrow, old-fashioned kitchen. A sink with half the water pump gone was at the far end, and next to that was a window with no glass left in it. A small table and two chairs, both with missing spindles, were in the corner and halfway down the right-hand wall was a door next to which was a narrow staircase. A cooker with the lopsided warming door stood on the left-hand wall, right by a bed of what looked like moth-eaten wool blankets. Wiggins looked at the scarred and scuffed brown linoleum floor that was littered with old newspapers, dead leaves, tin cans, and even a set of big muddy bootprints.

From outside, he heard shouting. The constables had found something! Maybe there was a chance he could see what it was. He whirled around and raced for the entryway. But as he neared the door, he heard voices again, this time closer than ever.

"Get the inspector and Constable Barnes," someone shouted.

Then Wiggins heard someone else yell, "They just arrived."

He skidded to a halt and hesitated, torn between his desire to know what was going on outside and his real need to stay out of sight.

Another constable said, "Over here, Inspector, we've found . . ."

Wiggins frowned because he couldn't catch the rest of what was said.

"What about the carriage house, sir?" he heard another constable ask.

Wiggins glanced at the empty window. Whoever had broken in here seeking shelter had done him a favor. This was his way out. He ran to it, double-checked there was no glass on the inside or the outside of the frame before grabbing the sill and swinging his right leg over it. He stuck his head out, checking both ways, before hoisting his left leg over and leaping out. He stopped for a second, took a deep breath, and then ran as if the devil were on his heels.

CHAPTER 3

Wiggins raced down the back hall and into the kitchen. Phyllis, Mrs. Goodge, and Mrs. Jeffries were at the kitchen table, waiting for him.

He skidded to a halt, bent down and gave Fred a quick pat, and then straightened. "Where's Smythe and Betsy?"

"They weren't home." Phyllis reached for the teapot and poured him a cup.

"I remember Betsy mentioned that they were going to take our little one for an outing to the seaside," Mrs. Goodge said.

"That's right." Mrs. Jeffries nodded. "Smythe said they wanted to do a few special things with her before the new baby comes."

"Luty and Hatchet weren't home, either." Phyllis slid the tea across the table to Wiggins, who had just sat down. "But I left a message for them to come here tomorrow morning."

"I think we'll see 'em before tomorrow." Wiggins grinned. "You'll not believe it, but they're at the West London Archery Club, and knowin' the two of them, I'd bet a hot dinner they've been keepin' their eyes and ears wide open."

"Gracious," Mrs. Jeffries exclaimed. "That's certainly useful. Did you speak to them? Did you tell them to come here, that we were having a meeting?"

"I didn't get the chance to say anything. To tell the truth, I had a right miserable time," he explained. "There were constables everywhere and most of them know me by sight." He went on to tell them the details about his afternoon. "Thank goodness I was able to get into that carriage house; otherwise, I'd have been caught for sure. But the day wasn't a complete waste of time. I found out who was killed and where 'e lives."

"Who?" Phyllis demanded.

"'Old yer horses." Wiggins took a quick sip of tea. "I'm gettin' to it. His name was Jeremy Marks and he lives on Wakeman Crescent and that's right close by, so we should be able to make contact with someone from his household."

"Where on Wakeman Crescent?" Mrs. Goodge asked.

"I didn't get the 'ouse number," he admitted. "Truth to tell, I was hidin' behind a carriage when I overheard the constables talking about the dead fellow."

"Did you find out anything else about him?" Mrs. Jeffries reached for the teapot and poured herself another cup.

"Not much, only that Marks was a widower and that they needed to find out who the next of kin might be."

"So it's likely that he lived alone." Phyllis frowned. "I hope Jeremy Marks had servants. They're so useful to us."

"Let's not make any assumptions," Mrs. Jeffries warned.

"We've walked that road before and it never does any good." She looked at the footman. "You said there were footprints on the carriage house floor—"

"More like bootprints," he interrupted, "and whoever made 'em had big feet."

"But there was a bed in the corner," Mrs. Goodge said. "Could that have been where the killer slept?"

He looked doubtful. "The window was broken, Mrs. Goodge. That's 'ow I got out. But I think someone must 'ave broken in this past winter, you know, because it was so cold out. There's not many empty 'ouses where someone can get out of the wet in this part of London."

"Why do you say that?" Mrs. Jeffries regarded him curiously.

"Because when I climbed out, there wasn't any glass lyin' about the floor or the sill."

"And the murder happened only today," the housekeeper murmured, "so if the killer had broken in with the express purpose of lying in wait to murder Jeremy Marks, he or she would have to have cleaned the glass up and then disposed of it somewhere."

"I didn't see glass anywhere and I didn't see anything like a broom or a dustbin, either," Wiggins said. "I think that window's been broken for a long time. All sorts of rubbish was lyin' about on the floor, like it had been blown in."

"I hope Miss Lonsdale wasn't dreadfully upset." Rufus Farley stared anxiously at the two policemen. The three of them were standing by the reception counter. "But on behalf of the club, I'm grateful you saved her from reading about Mr. Marks' death in the evening papers."

"Miss Lonsdale certainly wasn't happy, but she didn't become hysterical," Witherspoon assured him. "Apparently, Miss Lonsdale and Mr. Marks had decided to end their engagement earlier today."

Farley's eyes widened in surprise. "Really? That's certainly news to me. They seemed quite taken with one another when they arrived here today."

"I assure you, it's true. Miss Lonsdale told us herself," Witherspoon replied.

Farley frowned thoughtfully. "Perhaps that's a good turn of events. It may keep the press at bay a bit longer. The Lonsdales are an important family, and if the papers don't catch wind that Miss Lonsdale was previously engaged to Marks, perhaps it will keep them out of the newspapers."

"That won't stay a secret for long," Barnes warned him. "But it might be a day or so before an enterprising reporter susses it out. I'm not sure the murder happened early enough in the afternoon to make the evening papers."

"It most certainly did," Farley replied. "The press are already here and snooping about asking questions. That's why I was so grateful you gave Miss Lonsdale the news this afternoon." He broke off as the front door opened and a tall, burly woman wearing a short lightweight blue mantle and straw boater stepped inside. She looked to be in her mid-fifties with graying brown hair pulled back in a bun at the nape of her neck.

"Hello, Miss Linwood." Farley stared at her. "I thought you and Mrs. Storch had already left."

Miss Linwood smiled. "We did, Mr. Farley, but Mrs. Storch forgot her spectacles and I've come back to retrieve them. I believe she left them at our table. If you don't mind,

I'll just nip in and see if I can find them." She kept her gaze on the two policemen as she spoke.

"Are you the Miss Linwood who was sitting with Mr. Merriman this afternoon?" Witherspoon asked quickly.

"I am." Her smile broadened. "May I ask if you're Inspector Witherspoon, the one who solved the Andover murder?"

"I am." Witherspoon was flustered but pleased. She'd obviously read the newspaper accounts of his last murder investigation.

"It's so wonderful to meet you, sir." She charged toward him with her hand outstretched. "I'm a huge admirer of yours. I've been following your cases ever since I returned to England."

Embarrassed, he could feel his cheeks turning red as they shook hands. "That's very flattering, Miss Linwood, but Constable Barnes here and the other members of the Metropolitan Police do just as much as I do in apprehending criminals."

"You're just being modest, sir." She laughed as she turned to Constable Barnes. "I'm delighted to meet you as well, Constable. Is there something you'd like to ask me about today? I was at the table with Mr. Merriman and several others. It was such a pity that Mrs. Merriman couldn't join us."

"Was Mr. Merriman at the table with you the whole time this afternoon?" Barnes asked.

She thought for a moment before answering. "Actually, I wasn't there the entire time. Mrs. Storch sent me on an errand."

"What time was that?" Witherspoon interrupted.

"Three o'clock or thereabouts," she replied. "She asked me to supervise taking her picnic hamper out to her carriage. Well, there was no point in opening it; it was too wet to eat outside so she asked me to go to the kitchen and make certain it was put properly in the carriage. I was gone a few minutes and frankly"— she frowned—"I think he was there when I returned, but I'm not sure. I stopped a moment to speak to Mrs. Perry and then . . . well, you know what happened then. We found out Mr. Marks had been killed and everyone began moving about."

Witherspoon nodded. "Thank you, Miss Linwood."

"Of course, Inspector. I'm pleased to have met you, sir, but I'd best see about finding Mrs. Storch's spectacles."

"At least we found the murder weapon," Barnes muttered as he took the seat opposite the inspector. They were in a hansom cab and driving to the Marks home. "Not that it did us any good. According to what Mr. Farley said, it was one of the archery club's bows."

"Now, don't be so miserable, Constable. We did learn something."

"What? Mr. Farley said they keep the things hanging on the wall of the practice room; anyone could have grabbed it and done the murder. If it's the murder weapon, and I'm not sure we can know for certain it is."

"Why not?"

"Because it could have been dropped out there by some lazy person who couldn't be bothered to take it back inside, especially as it didn't belong to them."

"That's possible, but considering where the constables found the bow, I think it's more likely it was the murder weapon. It wasn't just lying on the other side of that wall in the grass. Constable Barlow said it looked as if it had been deliberately shoved up against the stone and covered with wet leaves."

"As if the killer wanted to hide it," Barnes mused. "But why? A club bow doesn't tell us anything."

Witherspoon shrugged. "We can only speculate. Perhaps the killer wanted to muddy the waters a bit, have us waste time trying to answer a question that has no bearing on the murder."

"Do you think the killer planned it out or that he just grabbed an opportunity to kill Marks?"

The inspector hesitated. "To be perfectly honest, I don't know, but I think it's a distinct possibility that the murder might have been a spur-of-the-moment decision. After all, the reason the murderer wasn't seen was because the storm had hit. The killer couldn't possibly have predicted that the competition would be halted and everyone would be in the common room."

"Which means it could be anyone at the archery club," Barnes murmured.

"Unfortunately, yes, in which case we have to keep our eyes on everyone. It's too bad that Miss Linwood couldn't confirm Merriman's alibi." Witherspoon glanced out the window. "That would have been quite helpful."

"It would have eliminated the one person we know hated him."

"True. Goodness, it is getting late, Constable. Your wife must be getting worried."

Barnes shook his head. "No, sir, Constable Griffiths sent messages to both our households that we had a murder. My wife will keep my dinner warm for me." He glanced out the window as well. "Constable Parker has already told them what happened to Marks, so hopefully, his household has had time to get over the shock."

"Perhaps this shouldn't take too long," Witherspoon said as the hansom slowed and pulled over to the pavement.

Jeremy Marks' home was at the end of a row of elegant town houses. "It's a big place, sir," Barnes said as he joined the inspector on the walkway. "Especially just for one person. According to Mr. Farley, except for his servants, Marks lived alone."

They started up the walkway. "Let's hope his housekeeper knows who his next of kin might be," Witherspoon said.

When they reached the door, Barnes banged the knocker, and a moment later, a short, thin middle-aged woman with wire-rimmed spectacles stared out at them. "Good gracious, it's more police. Don't tell me you've caught the killer this quickly."

"Unfortunately, we have not. I'm Inspector Witherspoon, and this is Constable Barnes. May we speak with you?"

"Why?" She burped gently. "That constable told me what happened to him. Must say, I wasn't surprised."

"That's precisely why we need to ask you a few questions." Witherspoon wasn't sure, but he thought he smelled whisky. "As a member of Mr. Marks' household, you might be able to help us understand who might have wanted to harm him."

She snorted faintly but then held the door wider and waved them inside. The woman moved so fast that neither man had time to get much more than a cursory glance of the foyer and the hallway before she led them into the drawing room.

The room was filled with heavy, dark, old-fashioned furniture, the walls painted a pale green and adorned with portraits of men and women dressed in old-fashioned clothing. Potted ferns, tables covered with fringed gold runners, and knickknacks stood beside settees and chairs. The floor was covered with a brown-and-gray carpet and there were beige-and-gold-striped curtains at the two windows. She gestured to the nearest sofa as she took a seat on the chair next to it. "Make yourself comfortable. I'm Ivy Lewis, the housekeeper."

Witherspoon sat down in the corner of the sofa and angled his body so he faced her. "I take it Constable Parker told you what happened to Mr. Marks?"

"He did. But he wasn't the first person here with bad news today, Inspector. Mr. Marks' fiancée, Miss Lonsdale, arrived this afternoon. She insisted on leaving the engagement ring Mr. Marks had given her and told me that she never wanted to see 'that wretched man' again. Her words, sir, not mine."

"What time was this?" Barnes glanced at Witherspoon. Hannah Lonsdale had been telling the truth when she'd claimed she'd gone to the Marks home.

"Early this afternoon. I didn't notice the exact time. I could tell Miss Lonsdale was upset. When I invited her inside, she said she'd never set foot in here again. Now, what was it you wanted to ask me?" Her hand flew to her mouth as another burp escaped. "Excuse me."

Witherspoon glanced around the room and spotted a serving trolly on top of which was a cut-glass whisky decanter ringed by a circle of matching glasses, one of which was half full of dark amber liquid.

Ivy Lewis followed his gaze and giggled. "I've had a bit to drink. Not like he can do anything about it now he's dead. You said you had to ask me questions; can you get on with it?"

"As you know, Mr. Marks was killed this afternoon," Witherspoon blurted out. "He was shot with arrows at the West London Archery Club. It appears Mr. Marks was targeted by someone who wanted him dead. Do you have any idea who might have wanted to harm him?"

She said nothing for a moment; she simply looked down at her lap and gave a shake of her head. "Not really. It could be anyone. He had a lot of enemies. I wish I could say I was shocked, but I'm not. The way he lived, the way he treated people, it's no wonder it's come to this."

"How long have you worked for Mr. Marks?" Witherspoon asked.

"I've been here fifteen years, Inspector. But I've only worked for him for the last two years." She waved her hand around the room. "This house belonged to Mr. Marks' late wife. I worked for Miss Fairfax and her family before she married him. When she died two years ago, Mr. Marks asked me to stay on."

Barnes stopped writing. "How did Mrs. Marks die?"

"Pneumonia, sir. It was sad watching my poor mistress struggle to breathe." She sighed heavily.

Witherspoon drew back as a blast of whisky breath hit him. "I'm sure it must have been dreadful, Mrs. Lewis."

"Mrs. Marks was a good mistress, sir." She blinked hard but her eyes teared up anyway. "Not like some, sir. She was good to all of us."

"Did you like working for Mr. Marks?" Barnes asked.

She stared at the constable as if he were a half-wit. "Does it sound like I liked working for him? He's not a nice person and he's a real skinflint, but he paid my wages on time and let me run the household as long as I didn't spend too much money on food or heating the place."

"How many servants are there here?" the constable asked.

"A cook and two maids. There were a lot more when Mrs. Marks was alive, but he got rid of her personal maid, the tweeny, and the footman when she passed away."

"Do you know the name of Mr. Marks' solicitor?" Witherspoon asked.

"I do. He's here quite often." She gave him a lopsided smile. "The one thing Mr. Marks didn't mind paying for was good legal advice. But you're not interested in my opinion about the matter. He's represented by Miles Wiley of Wiley and Upton. They have offices on the Brompton Road."

Witherspoon nodded encouragingly. "Thank you, that's very helpful. Do you know who might be Mr. Marks' next of kin?"

"That would be Frederick Marks. He's in Wolverhampton."

"May we have his address, ma'am?" Barnes said quickly. "We'll need to send a telegram to the local constabulary so they can let him know about his brother's death."

"That might take a few moments. I know it's somewhere in his study." She started to get up.

"We'll get the address before we leave, Mrs. Lewis," Witherspoon said. "Right now, we need to continue."

She slumped back into her seat. "Of course, go ahead.

Oh, wait a moment, I might as well tell you now that Mr. Marks and his brother haven't spoken in over twenty years. Mr. Frederick Marks didn't even come to his brother's wedding."

Witherspoon relaxed slightly. She wasn't having any problems answering his questions. Perhaps she'd not had as much to drink as he feared. "Do you know why they're estranged?"

"Mr. Marks wasn't one to air his family's dirty linen in front of a servant." She laughed. "But I overheard a spat between him and Mrs. Marks, and during that argument, she said he was such a miserable human being that his own brother couldn't stand the sight of him. That's all I know about it."

"Was it an unhappy marriage?" Barnes shifted on his seat.

"Not at first. In the beginning he was kind, loving, and attending to her every need, but it wasn't long before he showed his true colors." She took a deep breath and belched.

The whisky breath was in full sway now, and the inspector leaned as far away from her as possible.

"I'm not one for speaking ill of the dead, but he was a terrible man," she continued. "He lied, cheated, stole, and made her life a misery. That's one of the reasons she spent most of her time at her family's country house in Surrey. Her family didn't like him. Mr. Marks was a bit scared of them, I think."

"I see. But do you know of anyone specifically who would wish to harm Mr. Marks?" Witherspoon winced inwardly. It was the silliest of questions, even from the small amount they'd learned about the victim; the inspector had a feeling the dead man had a long list of enemies.

"I'm not sure how to answer that question, Inspector. As I've already said, he was quite an awful person, and the truth is there are a lot of people who hated him. But just because they loathed the man doesn't mean any of them committed murder." She burped again. "I'd not like to talk out of turn and get anyone in trouble."

"Please don't worry about that, Mrs. Lewis," the inspector assured her. "We only make an arrest when all the evidence points to the guilty party."

She didn't look convinced, but finally, she shrugged. "I suppose it's alright then. I'll tell you what I know. But it's from a long time ago. The first time anything untoward happened, by that I mean the first time I ever heard the name of someone Mr. Marks had cheated, was a few months after Mr. and Mrs. Marks had married."

"What happened?" Barnes interjected.

"Mr. Marks was in business with a man named Stephen Mueller."

"What kind of business?" Witherspoon asked.

"Something to do with property. I'm not certain but I think he was buying up houses and converting them to flats. What I do know is that Mr. Marks pulled out of the deal and Mr. Mueller showed up here and accused him of all sorts of terrible things."

"What kind of things?" Barnes asked quickly.

"I'm a housekeeper"—she laughed—"and the master of the house certainly didn't call me into his study to tell me all the details."

"Do you remember anything else about the incident?" the inspector interjected. "Anything at all?"

"All I remember is Mr. Mueller shouting that Mr. Marks pulling his money out would cost Mr. Mueller everything, that'd he'd end up bankrupt."

"How did Mr. Marks react?"

"It was a long time ago, Inspector. Frankly, I don't recall how Mr. Marks responded. What I do remember is when the shouting started, Mrs. Marks rushed into Mr. Marks' study. A few minutes later, Stephen Mueller left and the master and mistress had a dreadful row that ended with him storming out of the house."

"Do you happen to know if this Stephen Mueller is a member of the West London Archery Club?" Witherspoon asked.

"I've no idea, sir." She yawned and glanced at the half-filled glass of whisky. "But it's getting late and I've more to tell you. Mr. Mueller was just the first. Mr. Marks wasn't an honest man. I don't like to repeat gossip, sir, but our old cook told me that Mr. Marks had done some really nasty things to his other business partners."

"Your old cook?" Witherspoon repeated. "I take it that means she no longer works here. Where is she now?"

"She's dead. She passed away a few years ago." She broke off as another burp escaped. "But she claimed she'd worked for a family years ago and that Mr. Marks had ruined them doing the same thing he'd done to Mr. Mueller."

"How long ago?" Witherspoon asked.

She shook her head. "I don't know. She didn't bother sharing the details. All she said was that it was ages ago and that the entire family was gone because of Marks pulling out of a business deal."

"Do you happen to recall the family's name?"

Her eyes narrowed thoughtfully. "I'm not sure . . . I think it was Tower or Howard or something like that. I'm sorry, I can't remember the name. It was a long time ago."

"That's fine, Mrs. Lewis. I'm sure the family's name will crop up in the course of our investigation if it is relevant."

Barnes flipped over a new page in his notebook. "I take it Mrs. Marks' family had money?"

"Yes, sir, the Fairfax family is very wealthy," she replied. "Miss Fairfax was past the age when most women marry when she met Mr. Marks. The truth is, she'd been engaged years ago but her young man died. She'd more or less resigned herself to being a spinster, but when she met Mr. Marks, she was swept off her feet. It's surprising, really. Mr. Marks wasn't a handsome man but he could be very charming, and before you knew it, the two of them were engaged."

They heard the clock chime the hour. Witherspoon nodded at Barnes and the two policemen got up. "You've been very helpful, Mrs. Lewis."

"Is that all, sir?" She stumbled slightly as she stood.

"Do you have more to tell us?" Witherspoon asked.

"Not really, just more gossip, but I expect you'll hear plenty of that on your own, sir."

"I imagine so, Mrs. Lewis. If you do think of something pertinent or remember names of other business associates Mr. Marks may have wronged, please contact the Ladbroke Road Police Station. If we could just trouble you for the address of Mr. Marks' brother, we'll be on our way."

*   *   *

"I tell ya, that man had more enemies than an old man has chin whiskers," Luty declared.

Mrs. Jeffries nodded. Luty and Hatchet had arrived a few minutes ago, but it was already getting late and she was concerned the inspector would be here soon. "Do tell us, Luty. What did you find out?"

"To begin with, I got me an earful when I was in the cloakroom. I accidentally overheard someone talkin' about Jeremy Marks."

Hatchet snorted. "Don't be fooled. She was blatantly eavesdropping."

"You eavesdropped, too." Luty glared at her butler.

"Only after we found out Marks had been murdered," he argued, "and then I was doing it because we had a case."

"Come on now, time's a-wastin' and the inspector might be here any minute. Tell us what you found out," Mrs. Goodge ordered.

"No he won't," Luty said. "He and Constable Barnes were gettin' into a hansom as Hatchet and I were leavin' and I heard the constable tellin' the driver to take 'em to Wakeman Crescent, that's where Jeremy Marks lives, so we've got some time."

"How do you know where Jeremy Marks lives?" Hatchet demanded.

"I asked Mrs. Merchant, you know, the lady in charge of the common room. But as I was sayin' before I was rudely interrupted . . ." Luty shot Hatchet a triumphant grin and then told them what she'd overhead in the cloakroom as well as what she'd picked up in the common room.

"This lady's name is Alice McElhaney?" Phyllis asked.

"Yup, and she was talkin' to another woman and she was furious. I found out later that Alice McElhaney was engaged to Jeremy Marks but he broke it off when he met Hannah Lonsdale."

"I heard the same thing," Hatchet added. "Apparently, Marks was quite brutal when he broke off the initial engagement, and supposedly, he broke it off with Mrs. McElhaney because he'd met someone with more money."

"Mrs. McElhaney?" Mrs. Goodge frowned. "She's married?"

"Widowed," Hatchet said. "Her husband left her well off, according to the gossip I heard, but not nearly as wealthy as Miss Lonsdale."

"Is Hannah Lonsdale a member of the archery club?" Wiggins asked.

"She is and she was there today." Luty nodded. "And after what I overheard in the cloakroom, I just know that Mrs. McElhaney said somethin' to Hannah Lonsdale."

"You're only saying that because of what I saw," Hatchet challenged. He'd told them about seeing Marks chasing after his fiancée and how she'd shaken him off.

"That ain't the *only* reason I said it. That Mrs. McElhaney sounded madder than a wet hen." She broke off and frowned. "I gotta tell ya, I saw the feller before he was killed and he weren't much to look at."

"Sometimes charm is more important than appearance," Mrs. Jeffries mused.

From outside, they heard a hansom pull up in front of the house. Phyllis jumped up and ran to the window over the sink. "It's the inspector."

"Nells bells." Luty stamped her foot as she got up. "How'd he get here so fast? We ain't finished yet."

"The Marks house is close. Wakeman Crescent is less than half a mile from here," Wiggins pointed out.

"Come on, Hatchet," Luty said, but he was already getting up. "We gotta skedaddle."

"Yes, madam, I do believe it's time to exit the stage."

The records room of the Metropolitan Police was located on the lower ground floor of Scotland Yard. Shelves lined the walls, three quarters of which were filled with paperboard boxes, folders held together with twine, and old-fashioned box files. There was a single desk in one corner of the room. Inspector Nigel Nivens sat behind it.

Nivens smiled to himself as he reached for the top file on the stack in front of him. He'd been waiting for this moment. He'd known it would come, that the dreadful man who'd almost cost him everything would eventually get a new case. He'd had to wait until Chief Superintendent Barrows and even the rank and file had taken their eyes off him before he could make his move. But now that Witherspoon had a case, if anyone noticed he'd taken the files off their shelf, he had a perfect excuse; he was holding them on his desk so when the "brilliant Witherspoon" solved this newest homicide, they could be moved to another shelf that had more room.

They'd done their best to keep him off the police force, but political power was more important than administrative decisions, and thanks to dear Mama, he'd been back on the force for several months now. Barrows and his lackeys had overplayed their hand and he'd carefully manipulated them. They'd put him in charge of the records room as a punishment, a way of keeping him caged, but that's exactly what he'd wanted. They were fools, but he wasn't.

At first, it had been difficult; he'd had to kowtow to everyone, including Chief Superintendent Barrows. But the worst was, he actually had to do the work of keeping the records in order and making sure that when a file was needed, it was available to whoever wanted it.

But those days were over now. Thanks to his own clever machinations and a loan to a chief inspector who had foolishly let his love of gambling get the better of him, Nivens managed to get a constable assigned to assist him.

The door opened and Constable Paul Quigley, Nivens' assistant, stepped inside. He was a tall, thin, brown-haired lad. He carried a stack of files. "These have just come in, sir."

Nivens pointed to an empty spot on one of the bottom shelves behind his desk. "Put them there. I'll get to them later."

Quigley hurried across the room and dumped the files. "Anything else, sir?" He edged toward the door.

"Bring me a cup of tea," Nivens ordered as he opened the file in front of him.

"Yes, sir," Quigley replied as he rushed out.

Nivens knew his assistant didn't like him; in fact, one of his "informants" on the force had told him that the young constable had put in for a transfer. But Nivens wasn't in the least bothered by the fact that he was one of the most unpopular men in the force; he was used to that.

But Quigley wasn't going anywhere. The lad had sealed his own fate by being too efficient. He was excellent at sorting the folders, writing the few reports that were required, and best of all, he could lay his hands on a file if any of the upstairs brass needed it. All tasks that Nivens didn't have time to do himself now. He had other fish to fry, as they say.

He picked up the first page of the open file and began to read. It was Witherspoon's final report on the murder of Dr. Bartholomew Slocum.

Witherspoon handed Mrs. Jeffries his bowler hat and unbuttoned his jacket. "I'm so sorry to be late, Mrs. Jeffries, but there's been a murder."

"Yes, sir, we know. Constable Griffiths was able to get a message to us this afternoon."

"That's good." He smiled wearily. "I'd hate for one of Mrs. Goodge's fine dinners to be ruined because you didn't know I'd be late."

Mrs. Jeffries hung up his hat and reached for his coat, putting them both on the coat tree. "There's no problem with dinner, sir, if you'd like to have a sherry. Mrs. Goodge made a lovely lamb stew and it's in the warming oven."

"That would be wonderful." He let out a deep breath. "It's been such an odd day. I do believe a drink and chat is very much in order." He headed down the corridor to his study.

Mrs. Jeffries hurried after him. The two of them had long had the custom of discussing his cases over a pre-dinner drink. When she reached the inspector's study, she went directly across to the mahogany cabinet while he settled into his old overstuffed leather chair. The room had recently been refurbished with a new maroon-and-cream Oriental rug, red-and-ivory-striped curtains at the two windows, and a new office chair behind the inspector's desk. Despite Mrs. Jeffries' pleas, he'd refused to part with his beloved leather chair and sofa, both of which were worn and, in her opinion, on their last legs. Yet she understood his feelings—he was sentimental about them—as they were both from the home he'd shared years ago with his beloved mother.

She poured two glasses of Harveys Bristol Cream sherry, handed him his drink, and took her own seat on the sofa across from him. "Now, sir, do tell. You know how much I love hearing about your cases. Who was murdered?" This was always the part where she needed to take care. It wouldn't do for him to realize she already had a substantial amount of information.

"A man named Jeremy Marks." He took a quick sip. "And I must say, the manner of his death was most unpleasant. The poor man was shot with arrows. Two of them."

"Arrows? Gracious, that's certainly an odd way of killing someone."

"Indeed, and from what we learned today, whoever shot the arrows must have been an expert archer."

"That should make it much easier for you to track down the killer, sir," she said.

He sighed. "If only that were true. But it won't be as easy as it should be because the man was shot at one of the competitions at the West London Archery Club."

"Oh dear, sir, I imagine that means there are quite a few expert archers at such a place."

"I'm afraid so." He took a quick drink.

"Were there any witnesses, sir?"

"Unfortunately, no. The competition was halted because of that dreadful storm we had this afternoon. Marks was outside on his own when he was killed so it's not as if we have anyone who saw the deed itself."

"Why was he outside in a downpour?" Mrs. Jeffries sipped her sherry.

Witherspoon gave a shake of his head. "That's the strange part, Mrs. Jeffries. Honestly, I don't know what to make of the whole situation. The two men who raised the alarm seem to think Jeremy Marks was outside stealing arrows."

"What?"

"I know it sounds insane, especially as Marks wasn't a poor man. He lived in a huge house on Wakeman Crescent and had been married to a very wealthy woman. He was a widower." He told her everything he'd learned from Chester Atwood and Horace Miller.

She listened carefully as she realized this was very important information. When he'd finished, she put her glass on the side table and said, "So you know precisely what time it was when he was shot?"

"Not precisely, but very close. It was between five and ten past three this afternoon. The alarm was raised almost immediately and that helped give us the time frame."

"I should think so, sir. If these gentlemen, Mr. Atwood and Mr. Miller, were 'on the scene' in a sense, that means you'll be able to narrow down who had the opportunity to do it."

"One *would* think so," he said glumly. "Except for Atwood and Miller, everyone else claimed they were in the common room of the club having tea and sandwiches or champagne. But you know how those situations are—everyone gads about going from table to table chatting and greeting friends. It will be difficult to pin down precisely where everyone was at the moment Mr. Marks was murdered."

"It will be difficult but not impossible, sir," she assured

him. She could tell by his expression he was having one of his moments of self-doubt. They were few and far between these days; after all, the man had solved more murders than anyone in the history of the Metropolitan Police Force. But he still had times when he lost confidence in his abilities. She was having none of that. "You're very good at such things; you've always had a wonderful head for details and timelines. What's more, your 'inner voice,' as I like to call it, has never let you down."

"That's very nice to hear, Mrs. Jeffries." He smiled self-consciously. "You're right, I mustn't get discouraged at this point in the investigation. Oh, I didn't tell you the most remarkable thing about today. Luty Belle Crookshank and Hatchet were there. Hatchet has taken up archery and was going to compete today."

"Really, sir? That must be useful. Did they see anything?" She knew they had, of course.

"Oh yes, Constable Griffiths took their statements because Constable Barnes and I had so many others to interview. We are hoping to be able to speak to Luty and Hatchet tomorrow if possible. Luty did make it a point to tell me that the victim was not well liked. It will be interesting to hear what she and Hatchet have to say. Luty is very good at picking up information."

A frisson of alarm raced up Mrs. Jeffries' spine. It wouldn't do to have the inspector realizing any of them were out and about sticking their noses into his case. She thought they'd all been more discreet but, apparently, not discreet enough. "She does have an ear for gossip and she certainly isn't shy," she murmured. "What did you do next, sir?"

He took another quick sip of his sherry. "We had a word

with the director of the club, Rufus Farley, and he confirmed that the victim wasn't a member of the club, but was there as a guest. However, he'd previously been a member and had been asked to leave because he was caught cheating." He told her about his interviews with Emmett Merriman and Warren Stanley.

"Goodness, sir, it sounds as if Mr. Merriman genuinely loathed the victim."

"He did." Witherspoon drained his glass. "But he appears to have an alibi. He claimed to be sitting with several other people when Marks was murdered. We did try to verify his statement and we spoke to a lady who'd been at his table, but Miss Linwood couldn't confirm Mr. Merriman had been there during the time period Marks was killed. But it should be easy enough to determine if he is telling the truth, since there were others at the table who were there the whole time. After that, we went to speak with Marks' fiancée. She lives very close to the archery club and luckily she was home."

"That must have been dreadful, sir. I know how much you hate informing people they've lost a loved one." She finished her sherry and got to her feet. "Another one, sir?"

"Oh yes." He gave her his glass. "That is the worst part of my job, Mrs. Jeffries, and truthfully, I was dreading the task. But Miss Lonsdale wasn't in the least brokenhearted. As a matter of fact, she told us she'd just broken off her engagement to Mr. Marks that very afternoon." He told her the details of the interview. He took his time and repeated everything Hannah Lonsdale had said almost word for word.

When he'd finished, Mrs. Jeffries asked, "Did she tell you how she found out he was only marrying her for her money?"

"Indeed she did." Witherspoon winced. "Frankly, Mrs. Jeffries, it was a bit embarrassing, at least for me. Yet she didn't seem concerned at all. She told us that just before she'd competed, another member of the club, a woman named Alice McElhaney, had pulled her aside and insisted she read a letter. Now, you must understand, Mrs. McElhaney is a widow who was once engaged to Jeremy Marks. The letter was from Marks to Mrs. McElhaney and in it he broke off his engagement to her."

"How did that prove he was only marrying Miss Lonsdale for her money?"

"The letter was dated the day Marks asked Miss Lonsdale to marry him."

"In other words, he proposed to one woman while still engaged to another." Mrs. Jeffries nodded.

"Precisely. Furthermore, Miss Lonsdale said that Mrs. McElhaney is much younger and, well, one hates to say it, but it was her words, not mine, she said that Mrs. McElhaney is much prettier than she is. Honestly, Mrs. Jeffries, I didn't know what to say when she said such a thing, but luckily, I didn't have to say anything."

"Why not?"

"Because she also said the letter had made her so angry that she hit the target more than she'd ever done. Then the butler came in and said her solicitor was there to see her so we terminated the interview. I will speak to her again."

"Did she say why her solicitor was there?"

"Oh yes, she was quite happy to tell us. Just as we were leaving, she said she was taking Marks out of her will. Apparently, she'd already made him her heir."

"Before they were married?" Mrs. Jeffries frowned.

"That's very odd. Most marriage settlements become effective after the wedding."

"I know, Mrs. Jeffries, and that's one of the things I'm going to ask her about. After that, we went back to the archery club. We happened to arrive just after the constables had found a bow that I believe is the murder weapon. It was actually on the property next to the club; the place is uninhabited so I instructed the constables to search those grounds as well as the club property. But that's neither here nor there. What is important is the bow was shoved up against the stone wall separating the two properties and Constable Griffiths said it appeared to have been deliberately covered up with leaves."

"Goodness, sir, were you able to find out who it belonged to?"

"No, it was one of the club bows that hang in their practice room. Anyone could have taken it."

"Oh dear, that's unfortunate," she murmured.

"Very, but it was getting late, so I sent the constables back to the station, and Constable Barnes and I went to the Marks home. We had quite an enlightening chat with his housekeeper. Mind you, she was a bit in her cups, but not so much so that she couldn't understand or answer my questions."

"She'd been drinking?"

"Yes, we'd sent a constable to the Marks home earlier to inform his household, and apparently, once Mrs. Lewis realized her employer was dead, she helped herself to his whisky. It was obvious from the way she spoke of her late employer that she didn't like him very much." He put his glass down on the table and told her about the interview with the Marks housekeeper.

When he'd finished, she said, "Gracious, sir, Jeremy Marks really wasn't well regarded, was he."

"Thus far, we've not spoken to anyone who had a good word to say about the fellow. Nonetheless, we'll do our best to find his killer."

"Of course you will, sir. I think the hardest thing for me to believe is that he was outside in the storm collecting arrows. There was so much lightning. It must have been very dangerous."

"Yes, I agree, *if* that is what he was doing out there. Marks was far from poor. His late wife left him well off and it seems he's made quite a bit of money from his own business ventures. Despite what Mr. Atwood and Mr. Miller told us, there's something about that arrow-stealing business that doesn't ring true. Why would such a wealthy man risk his life?"

"Do you think they were lying?" She wanted his opinion. Witherspoon was one of nature's gentlemen, and tended to see the best in everyone. But he wasn't easily fooled anymore. He really did have an "inner voice" and she trusted it.

"I'm not sure; it is possible. At times, human beings do very odd things," Witherspoon mused. "Everyone we spoke to confirmed the man was very cheap and very much the sort of person who would steal other people's valuables, and apparently, those arrows are quite expensive."

"Marks does sound peculiar, sir. What will you be doing tomorrow?" She wanted to find out where he'd be so she could let the others know.

"We'll be going back to the archery club." He took another drink. "Mr. Farley said the competition still needs to be finished. It works out quite well, as we'll have another chance to question the club members who were there today. Then, I'm going to interview Alice McElhaney, and after that, if we've time and nothing else urgent comes up, I'll have another word with Miss Lonsdale."

"But didn't she leave the club before he was murdered?" Mrs. Jeffries asked.

"That's what she said," Witherspoon replied. "And despite her apparent calmness at finding out Marks was only marrying her for her money, I've learned that where matters of the heart are concerned, it's always best to be sure there isn't a hidden layer of rage and hurt."

"Do you think she went back to the club and killed him?"

Witherspoon looked thoughtful. "I've no proof she did, but her home is very close to the club. She could have easily gone back, taken the bow and arrows from the practice room, and shot him. When I do speak to her, I'm going to have Constable Barnes have a word with her coachman. The weather was so inclement, I doubt she'd have walked. Don't misunderstand me, Mrs. Jeffries, there's no evidence the lady killed him, but there's a reason that the first person to be examined closely in a homicide is the spouse, or in this case, the fiancée of the victim."

CHAPTER 4

Betsy and Smythe were the first to arrive for their morning meeting. Usually, Betsy was a lovely, blonde-haired matron with a bulging baby tummy and bright blue eyes, but today there were faint circles under her eyes, wisps of hair escaping from her topknot, and an exhausted look on her face. Smythe, her husband, stood behind her with his hand on her shoulder. He was a good fifteen years her senior with a hard, sharp face, dark brown hair with gray at the temples, and kind brown eyes.

Mrs. Goodge started to ask where her goddaughter, Amanda, was but clamped her mouth closed when she saw Smythe give a negative shake of his head.

"I know you wanted us to bring Amanda this morning," Betsy said. "But she's with our neighbor. We had such a big day out in Brighton yesterday that she's tired and fussy. Frankly, I just didn't have the energy to cope with her today."

"And so both my girls were up 'alf the night." Smythe pulled out a chair for his wife just as Luty, Hatchet, and Lady Cannonberry arrived.

Luty quickly surveyed the kitchen and then snorted when she saw the two of them. "You left my baby at home again?"

"We did." Smythe helped Betsy into her chair. "She's been a right little madam this mornin', but if she behaves, we'll bring her this afternoon, I promise."

Lady Cannonberry, or Ruth, as she insisted they call her when the inspector wasn't present, took her seat as well. She was a middle-aged widow of a lord of the realm. She had delicate features, blue eyes, and blonde hair, which darkened to brown in the winter. She also had a ready smile and a fearless disposition. She was the inspector's "special friend" and loved helping with his cases. But like the others, she was very discreet and made certain that her dear Gerald never knew of her involvement in his work.

The daughter of a country vicar who took seriously Christ's admonition to "Love thy neighbor as thyself," she cared for the poor, fed the hungry, and fought tooth and nail for justice. Believing that all human beings were equal in the sight of God, Ruth was a tireless worker for women's rights.

"I'm so glad everyone is here on time," Mrs. Jeffries said as they settled down. She looked at Luty and Hatchet. "Before I tell everyone what I heard from the inspector, you two tell us the rest of what you heard and saw yesterday. We'll bring everyone who wasn't here yesterday up to speed a bit later."

Luty went first, telling them every morsel of gossip she'd picked up before turning to Hatchet. "Your turn."

He took up the story and gave them the information he'd overhead and then glanced at Mrs. Jeffries. "As we mentioned yesterday, the man was not well liked."

"Not well liked?" Luty laughed. "We overhead a dozen people talkin' about the feller and none of 'em had one good thing to say about him."

"That's what the inspector heard as well," Mrs. Jeffries said. "But I wanted everyone to hear what you two had to say in your own words before I reported what the inspector said."

"Before you tell us," Phyllis interjected, "did you have time to speak to Constable Barnes this morning?"

"No, he was late getting here so he had to go straight up." When they had a case, Constable Barnes always stopped by the kitchen before going up to the inspector. He and Witherspoon used the walk to the station to discuss the case undisturbed and to plan the day's activities. "But he said he'd be here early tomorrow morning so we can pass along anything we learn today."

"And we can 'ear what he's got to say," Wiggins added.

"Alright then, let's get on with it." Mrs. Jeffries then gave them a quick and concise update on what she'd heard from the inspector. It took a good twenty minutes, and when she'd finished, she glanced at the faces around the table. "I'm afraid I agree with the inspector. This one might be very difficult."

"Why do you say that?" Phyllis asked. "We know exactly when the victim was murdered. Shouldn't that make it easier to catch the killer?"

"In theory, yes, but as the inspector said, there was so

much moving about in the common room that accurately placing anyone will be difficult. But we'll not let that stop us. Now, who would like to do what?"

"I'll take the local merchants," Phyllis offered. "I can ask about Jeremy Marks and Hannah Lonsdale and I'll mention the West London Archery Club as well, just to see what I might be able to learn."

"Excellent." Mrs. Jeffries nodded.

"I'll have a go at the hansom drivers," Smythe said.

"You should be able to hear somethin' useful; there was a whole line of carriages there yesterday," Luty said.

"I know a few of those drivers as well." He looked at his wife. "When you get 'ome, you need to rest before you get the little one."

"That sounds heavenly. I'm really tired today." Betsy gave him a grateful smile and then looked at the others. "I'll get out and about tomorrow. I'll do my share."

"Don't be daft," Mrs. Goodge ordered. "You've always done your fair share. You need to rest and take care of your-self right now."

"That's right," Luty agreed. "Yer health is important."

"I'll 'ave a go at the staff from the archery club again"— Wiggins made a face—"and 'ope I 'ave better luck than I did yesterday. If I don't find out anythin', I'll 'ave a go at the servants at the Lonsdale and Marks homes."

"Don't forget Alice McElhaney," Luty said. "As I told ya, she had a real burr up her nose over Marks, and she was the one who got Hannah Lonsdale all stirred up."

"And Emmett Merriman loathed him as well," Mrs. Goodge pointed out. "We mustn't forget him, either. Do we have his address?"

"Not yet. I'll get it from Constable Barnes tomorrow morning," Mrs. Jeffries said. "Will you be contacting your usual sources?"

Mrs. Goodge nodded. "I've the butcher's boy coming today and the laundry is being picked up as well. But just in case I don't get anything out of those two, I'll send off some notes to two of my old colleagues and invite them for tea."

The cook did her investigating without ever leaving the kitchen. Every delivery boy or tradesman who stepped into her domain was plied with tea and treats until she'd squeezed every crumb of gossip out of them. Surprisingly enough, she often found out a wealth of information about the victim and suspects. She also had a number of old coworkers who had spent most of their lives in "service," and they'd contributed useful bits and pieces as well.

"I can ask my sources about both Miss Lonsdale and Alice McElhaney," Ruth offered. "I'll also drop Emmett Merriman's name and see if anyone knows anything."

"I'll have a snoop in everyone's finances," Luty said. She glanced at Hatchet. "What're you goin' to do?"

Hatchet smiled. "What I do best, madam. I'll find out every single thing I can about everyone!"

"I've had an idea," Witherspoon said to Barnes as they stepped into the Ladbroke Road Police Station. He greeted the constable behind the reception counter with a smile and a wave as they headed past him and down the short hall to the duty inspector's office. "Something that might help us solve the problem of who was where at the specific moment the murder was committed."

He whipped off his bowler as he stepped inside the room.

"It came to me as I was falling asleep. Actually, it's been poking at me since yesterday but it didn't focus in my mind until last night. We're going to need a few supplies."

"What kind of supplies, sir?" Barnes took off his helmet and put it on the empty chair by the door.

"Paper. We'll need at least four to five large sheets." He hung his hat on the coat tree in the corner and then sat down behind the desk. "Do you know if any of the lads who were at the club yesterday are good at drawing?"

"Not that I'm aware of, sir, but I'll ask them."

He thought for a moment. "How many tables do you think are in the archery club common room?"

"Ten. I counted them yesterday. There are three rows with three tables each and then the one table closest to the door. What are you thinking, sir?" The constable took a seat opposite the inspector.

Witherspoon grinned. "Well, as I said, just as I was falling asleep last night, I realized that one way to determine where everyone was when Marks was murdered could be with a variation on my timeline system."

Barnes thought about it. "That would be useful, sir. They've worked in the past. Are you thinking of doing a separate timeline for every single person who was there yesterday?"

"That would be ideal, of course." Witherspoon glanced around the room, his gaze stopping on a rather bedraggled-looking hyacinth in a green ceramic pot on the windowsill. "But it would take far too long. No, I've come up with another method." He broke off, went to the window, and grabbed the plant. Sitting it in front of him, he yanked open the top drawer and drew out a blank piece of paper. He took the pot, set it on the paper, grabbed a pencil, and then traced around the base.

"Works perfectly. It appears we won't need any artistic constables after all." He lifted the pot from the paper to reveal a five-inch round circle. "What I'm thinking is that we draw all ten tables on several sheets of paper. Then we add the names of those that sat at each table. Everyone who is working this case will have a copy, you, me, all the constables from yesterday. Many of those we interviewed yesterday will be at the archery club today to finish the competition, so we'll start there."

Wiggins reached the corner of the building a few feet away from what would be considered the "servants" entrance of the West London Archery Club. He stopped to have a good look around. He wanted to get his bearings, but more important, he wanted to be sure there weren't any constables lurking about.

However, he saw no one except a groundskeeper raking leaves. He considered having a go at the fellow to see if he knew anything, but before he could move, the servants' door opened and a young kitchen maid carrying a wicker shopping basket stepped out.

He moved farther back so she wouldn't notice him and then stuck his head around the side so he could get a better look at her. He didn't want to risk running into the girl he'd spoken to yesterday. That had been a right disaster. But he didn't recognize this one. She was a slender young lady with brown hair tucked under her maid's cap and even, rather pretty features. He stepped out onto the walkway as she headed in his direction.

Surprised, she stumbled slightly. "Who are you?"

He gave her his best smile. "I'm so sorry, miss. I didn't mean to startle you. My name is Arthur Harley-Jones and I work for the *Evening Echo*."

Her eyes narrowed. "You're from a newspaper?"

"Yes, miss, I'm a reporter. I'm here about the murder of Jeremy Marks," he replied. "If you have a few minutes, I'd like to speak to you. It'll not take long and I'd be ever so grateful."

"Mr. Farley said we weren't to speak of what happened yesterday." She cast a quick glance over her shoulder at the closed door.

"Come on, if I don't go back with something, I'll be in trouble with my editor. It'll only take a little time and I'll not let anyone know you spoke to me. Look, you'll probably not believe me, but I can't afford to get sacked."

"Neither can I," the girl shot back, "and there's no reason I should risk my position so you can keep yours." She started off toward the front of the club and the street.

Wiggins hurried after her. "You're right, I'm sorry, miss. I had no business asking for your help. But if you wouldn't mind tellin' me, is there anyone else on the staff that wouldn't say 'no' to a shilling or two for their time?"

By now, they'd reached the front of the building. She glanced over her shoulder again and then looked at Wiggins. "A shilling or two? Are you serious?"

He knew he had her then, but strangely, he took no satisfaction in it. Mrs. Jeffries always kept a handful of coins in the top drawer of the pine sideboard so that both he and Phyllis could help themselves when they were "on the hunt." A number of their previous cases had shown that a couple of shillings went a long way to loosening tongues. But he also understood what it felt like to need that extra bit of coin, to be so desperate you'd risk your job. It made him feel uneasy, because he knew that, despite his assurances, if any of them were caught or even suspected of talking to a newspaper reporter, they *would* be sacked. The fact that he wasn't a real reporter made no difference whatsoever. Still, he was going to learn everything he could from this young lady. "Exactly what I said, miss. I know that the staff talking to a reporter like me might be 'ard for some people and my guv at the paper always gives me a shilling or two to 'elp 'em out a bit." He didn't bother to change his normal way of speaking as he usually did when he was pretending to be a reporter. This girl seemed the type to be more willing to help someone more like herself than a toff.

They had reached the corner and were well out of sight of the archery club.

"I see." She stepped off the pavement and onto the road, looking both ways to see that nothing was coming. Wiggins kept pace with her but stayed quiet.

"You're sayin' you'd give me two shillings if I talk to you?"

"Well." He didn't want to seem too eager. "I'll give you one shilling, and then if you tell me anything useful, I'll give you the other one."

Her brows drew together. "But what if I don't know anything your paper could use? I'll not risk my position for a shilling."

He tried not to smile. This one drove a hard bargain. "Tell ya what, do you have time for quick cup of tea? If ya do, you answer my questions and I'll give you both shillings."

She thought for a moment before nodding. "They'll not notice how long I take, so I have a few minutes for tea. Everyone in the kitchen is all het up because the members are coming back to continue the competition and no one is paying attention to anything. The police are back again and even Mrs. Leigh, she's the head cook, keeps running up to the common room to see what's what. By the way, my name is Janet Marshall."

"Pleased to meet you, Miss Marshall"—he nodded politely—"and I'll never tell anyone that you spoke with me."

"There's a decent little café next to the greengrocer's." She pointed toward the High Street. "We can get a cup there."

Five minutes later, he ushered her to a seat at the back of the small café and went to the counter. "Two cups of tea and two currant buns."

The counterman poured the tea first and Wiggins took both mugs to the table, came back, and paid. He picked up the small plates with the pastries and went back to where she sat. "Here you go." He put a currant bun in front of her. "I'm always hungry and I thought you might be, too."

"Ta." She smiled widely. "They feed us tea and a lunch meal at the club and the food is better than most places I've worked, but the portions aren't generous."

He returned her smile. "I know what ya mean." He said nothing for a few moments, and the two of them ate in silence. When she'd swallowed the last of her food, he said, "Did you happen to see anything yesterday? I mean, about the time of the murder."

She shook her head. "We were too busy in the kitchen to do anything but run up and down them stairs carrying tea, champagne, and sandwiches. That ruddy storm comin' in so hard mucked up everything. The tea wasn't supposed to be served until much later, when the competition was finished, but with everyone comin' inside, Mr. Farley insisted we start servin' immediately. We didn't even have time to finish our own meal and it was Mrs. Leigh's Lancashire hotpot, which everyone loves. We left our plates half finished, and by the time we got back to them, the potatoes were stone cold and the lamb was congealed."

"Ugh, that sounds awful." He smiled sympathetically and it was genuine. He remembered what life had been like for him before he began working for the inspector's late aunt, Euphemia Witherspoon. He'd eaten some right miserable food. "I 'ate missin' a good meal."

She shrugged. "Mr. Farley's decent, not like the other manager we had before, so he had Mrs. Leigh and Helen, she's the scullery maid, make up ham sandwiches for everyone when he saw what had happened to our meal. But you're not 'ere for that. If you've more questions, ask 'em now."

"When you was runnin' up and down them stairs, did you overhear or see anything odd?" Wiggins sipped his tea.

"Let me think for a minute." Her eyes narrowed slightly. "The only thing that sounded strange was Mrs. Woolsey. She's one of the older members. Mrs. Leigh says she's been a member since the club was established forty years ago. But that's not important and you probably want to know what was so odd about Mrs. Woolsey."

Wiggins nodded.

"It was before we found out that Mr. Marks had been killed. Half of our members wanted champagne, not tea, so we were gettin' through it fast. Mrs. Leigh told me to take another bottle upstairs because one of the members had come down complainin' it was takin' too long to refill the glasses. So the minute Mrs. Leigh popped the cork on the thing, I raced up the stairs, and when I got to the top, Miss Vetterly, she's Mrs. Woolsey's good friend and even older than Mrs. Woolsey, stood up and waved me over to her table. Both them women like their drink. The two of them were havin' a right brouhaha about whether or not some older gentleman across the room was a member from years earlier."

"How much earlier, did they say?"

"I heard Mrs. Woolsey say that it had been years and years since either of them had set eyes on the man, that after all this time it was impossible to know for sure, and that Miss Vetterly should get new spectacles."

"Did they mention the gentleman's name?" Wiggins asked.

"Oh yes, when Mrs. Woolsey told Miss Vetterly to get new eyeglasses, Miss Vetterly said no matter how many years had passed, she'd know the face of Stewart Miller . . ." She broke off, frowning, "But it wasn't Miller, it was something else. But I can't remember exactly what it was."

Wiggins was disappointed but did his best not to let it show. Two old dears having a quarrel about someone from days long gone probably had nothing to do with the Marks murder. But he'd report it properly at their meeting this afternoon. "Did you notice anything else? I know you were busy, but there's windows in the kitchen and you've got that little porch. Did you see anything, anything at all?"

She picked up her teacup and took a drink. "Not really. The only other thing I noticed was two members showing up on the porch just as I was goin' upstairs to fetch the brine pot. Mrs. Leigh needed it as she was out of vinegar. But I had to wait a bit until they moved . . ." She frowned. "I guess that must have been when they came inside and got Mr. Farley. But Mrs. Leigh was still annoyed with me takin' so long, but what could I do? They were standing there like a couple of statues and I didn't want to get in trouble by tellin' two of our members to move aside so I could get at the brine pot."

"What time was this?"

"It was five minutes or so past three."

"You're sure of the time?"

"The kitchen clock chimes the hour and it had struck a few minutes before, so yes, I'm sure."

"Did you notice Mr. Marks when he went through the common room and out on the archery range?" Wiggins asked.

"No, no one in the kitchen saw him." She picked up her cup and drained it. "If it's all the same to you, I need to go now. I've got to go to the greengrocer's and the butcher shop. We need more food now that the members are back today."

Wiggins rose to his feet and reached into his pocket. He pulled out the coins. It wasn't Janet Marshall's fault that she hadn't seen or heard anything useful. He handed her the money. "Thank you for talking with me."

She took it, smiled awkwardly, and then quickly looked away. "I'm sorry I didn't have more to tell ya. But I'll not lie just to make an extra shilling or two."

"You told me enough. I've got something to take back to my guv and that's all that matters."

Relieved, she smiled. "I'm glad. You seem nice and I'd not

like you to get into trouble." She looked down at the two shillings in her hand. "This will put Mick's nose out of joint. He's my cousin. He's supposed to be a footman, you know, helpin' ladies with their bows and bits, but he's more a general dogsbody around the place than a footman."

"He'd resent you gettin' a bit of coin?"

"Not really, but he does like to be better than everyone else." She laughed. "Yesterday, he was struttin' around like a peacock because he'd carried a picnic hamper out to some lady's carriage and she give him a shilling." She giggled. "But I've got two of 'em."

"I doubt there will be many at his funeral." Octavia Wells smiled over the rim of her teacup, took a quick sip, and then put the delicate pink-and-white porcelain cup on the saucer. "By all accounts, he was an absolutely dreadful person who vacillated between being cheap and ruthless."

Ruth Cannonberry smiled at her friend and fellow suffragette. Octavia was the treasurer of the Women's Suffrage Alliance. She was a tall, well-rounded woman with flaming red hair, a lovely complexion, and a smile that could charm even the most churlish misanthrope. Today she was wearing a teal-and-black-striped skirt with a teal cummerbund waist, a white blouse with mutton chop sleeves, and a gold broach in the shape of an apple on her lapel.

Octavia gave the impression she was nothing more than an upper-class matron obsessed with clothes, parties, and balls. The reality was she had a mind like a steel trap and she used her considerable intelligence to ensure that not only did their local group have money for their cause, but she also worked for the National Union of Women's Suffrage Societies, the organization for *all* the groups in England, Scotland, and Wales.

On the London social scene, she knew who was likely to join and be active, who wouldn't join but would sympathize and donate, and who wasn't worth her time.

"That's a very sad commentary on a human life," Ruth remarked.

They were sitting in Octavia's morning room. Ruth knew she could trust her friend to be discreet. Octavia had assisted her on several of the inspector's previous cases. The woman was a godsend, because she knew more than just gossip—she understood the politics of upper-class relationships, and her memory was astounding.

"Of course it is." Octavia put her cup on the side table. "The low attendance at Marks' funeral means his life was an utter waste. But that's to be expected. When you spend your entire existence chasing rich women and cheating your business associates, that's what happens. The man has been embroiled in one dreadful scandal or another for years."

"What kind of scandals?" Ruth asked.

Octavia's eyes narrowed in thought. "Much of what I've heard about him involved his business dealings. Apparently, he doesn't pay his bills promptly, and on at least two, possibly three, occasions, his actions have ruined those that went into business with him."

"What does that mean?" Ruth wanted to be sure she understood.

"It means he wasn't to be trusted. He'd pull investors and partners into various enterprises, and if something went wrong, he made certain that none of his money was ever lost."

"In other words, he pulled out of the deals without warning his partners," Ruth murmured.

She nodded. "That's right. The first time it happened was about twenty-five or so years ago," she explained. "I don't recall every little detail, but I do remember that Marks and another man named Henry Howell had bought property in Leicester for a factory that was supposedly being built by Cosgrave's. They'd also purchased an adjacent piece of land for an additional commercial interest."

"Cosgrave's the shoe and bootmakers?" Ruth clarified.

"Indeed, they make quite good footwear. I've several pairs of their walking shoes. The story I heard was that Marks convinced Henry Howell to mortgage his London property as well as obtain a huge loan so the two of them could buy the land. Howell moved ahead with the plans and obtained the property because Marks assured him he'd buy into his half as soon as he raised the money by mortgaging some property he owned. But then Cosgrave's decided against building the factory in Leicester and moved it to Melton Mowbray. Unfortunately for Henry Howell, Marks found out about Cosgrave's plans to go to Melton Mowbray and so, of course, he didn't come up with his half of the cost of the land. Howell lost everything. Marks lost nothing."

Ruth stared at her curiously. "You have a remarkable memory."

"I do." Octavia grinned. "But that's not the reason I recall it so vividly. I knew Henry Howell's sister, Maryanne. The London Suffrage Society, that's what our group used to be called, was just getting organized, and Maryanne Howell Collins was one of our supporters. When Marks didn't come through with his half of the money for the loan, Maryanne wasn't shy about voicing her opinion of Jeremy Marks' character. At one point, Maryanne and her husband supported the entire Howell family. But of course, that didn't last long; poor Henry Howell was bankrupted and died soon after. Henry had a son, I think his name was Barton, but when the father died and they lost their home, he started drinking heavily. He stumbled into the Thames one night and drowned." She frowned slightly. "There was a daughter as well. Oh yes, now I remember that bit. She was engaged to be married, but when the Howells lost their money, her fiancé called the wedding called off. That poor family was completely ruined, and they weren't the only ones."

"But unless one believes that vengeance is a dish best served cold," Ruth murmured, "I doubt anyone would wait twenty-five years for retribution."

"True, and there's a good chance all the family is gone now, so I doubt there would be anyone left to exact revenge. Maryanne and her husband moved to York soon after that and no one has heard from her in years. I've no idea what happened to the daughter. But considering the scandal of her family losing everything, if she's even alive, I doubt she stayed in London."

"Do you remember her name?"

Octavia gave a negative shake of her head. "No, but I can ask about and see if I can find out if you'd like."

"Don't bother. It happened a long time ago," Ruth replied. "What about recently? Do you know of anyone else Mr. Marks might have harmed?"

"Alice McElhaney loathed him. They were engaged last year and then they suddenly weren't. She left London for the continent when Marks abruptly ended their engagement. She only got back a few weeks ago. But when she found out he'd become engaged to Hannah Lonsdale, she was furious, and I must say, I'd have been angry, too."

Ruth didn't want to interrupt the flow of information so she merely nodded.

"She's a widow. Her late husband left her well off, but she's nowhere near as wealthy as the Lonsdale family. Once Hannah Lonsdale's old uncles die, she'll inherit even more. She is the only heir. But Mrs. McElhaney didn't let the Lonsdale money stop her from doing everything she could to ruin Jeremy Marks' reputation. She began denouncing his character publicly, especially in places like the West London Archery Club as well as at every dinner party or afternoon tea she's attended."

"And she was at the archery club when he was killed." Ruth thought back to what Luty had told them. "But did she hate him enough to murder him? That's the question."

"He did humiliate her and that wasn't the first time he'd done such a thing." Octavia put her teacup on the table. "Before he married his first wife, I think he was seeing someone else as well, though I can't confirm that tidbit. But I can say that when he met Hannah Lonsdale, the other woman in his life, Alice McElhaney, was out in the cold."

"Gracious, that's brutal." Ruth had already heard this from Mrs. Jeffries at the morning meeting, but it was good manners to respond to Octavia's comment. She didn't want her friend thinking the information she shared wasn't important.

"But it's true."

"I don't doubt you in the least. I know how discreet you are, and everything you tell me is always useful."

"Good. Your inspector makes certain justice is served and that is rare enough in our society, or any society for that matter. But his work is important and I'll do anything I can to help him. If I hear anything else that might be useful, I'll contact you immediately."

"Thank you, that would be wonderful." Ruth hesitated for a moment. Her comment might well sound unkind, but it was pertinent. "Octavia, I do wonder, though, how someone like Jeremy Marks could find two rich women: one he married and one he was engaged with. Yet I've heard he wasn't a very attractive man. Nor does he have a good reputation. So how did he do it? Rich women don't grow on trees and we know women aren't fools."

"I know exactly how he did it. Marks was smart."

"What do you mean?"

Octavia looked thoughtful. "To begin with, he was careful where he did his hunting."

"Hunting?" Ruth put her cup down.

"Wife hunting," she clarified. "He didn't try to storm the bastions of the landed aristocracy or even the new money industrialists. He understood that wouldn't work for someone like him. He did his hunting at places like the West London Archery Club."

"But he's not even a member there now," Ruth replied. "He was there yesterday as Hannah Lonsdale's guest. His own membership had been revoked."

"But he *was* a member there for years," Octavia insisted. "Admittedly, he might have been tossed out recently, but that's where he met his first wife, Elaine Fairfax. Her family had money, but they made it in trade; they weren't landed gentry or aristocrats. Perhaps I'm not explaining very well.

What I'm saying is the world has changed, not as quickly as you and I would like, but in ways that someone like Marks could exploit."

She leaned forward, her expression intense. "I've only just now realized it. Marks is the very embodiment of how society has shifted. Oh, the old money and the aristocrats are still on top, and believe me, it'll be eons before there are any improvements for working people in that quarter. But Marks understood he didn't stand a chance at meeting, let alone marrying, a woman from that class. He concentrated on the places the new money congregated."

"New money?" Ruth thought she understood, but she wanted to make certain. "You mean places like the West London Archery Club."

"Right. He understood that there's plenty of wealth nowadays amongst people who are not and wouldn't ever be accepted as truly upper-class." Octavia grinned. "Small factory owners, successful grocers, cabinet and tool makers, new inventors. In today's world, they make plenty of money, and in their leisure time, they join archery and tennis clubs, bicycle groups, and amateur dramatic societies. From what I've heard about Jeremy Marks, he realized years ago that something fundamental in society had altered and he began frequenting these organizations for the express purpose of finding a rich wife. What's more, he didn't go after beautiful young girls, he went after older ladies, those that thought their chances of marrying had disappeared. Elaine Fairfax was well into her forties when she married him, and Hannah Lonsdale is also close to hitting that mark. The only younger woman I've heard of him courting was Alice McElhaney, and he dropped her quickly when a richer, older woman came along."

Ruth sighed. "That's depressing, isn't it."

"What? That we live in a world where even smart and presumably well-educated women see marriage as the only path to social acceptance and happiness? Of course it's awful, but it's also reality."

"But surely that's what we're working for, a different world. One where everyone's full potential can be realized. Where women can live equally alongside men."

"That's what we want," Octavia declared, "but it will be a long time coming. However, I know this: We'll never get there if we don't begin, and we've begun!"

Witherspoon sent the constables who accompanied him to the West London Archery Club into the common room while he and Constable Barnes went to see Rufus Farley.

"We're here, sir." The inspector stopped in the open doorway of Farley's office.

Farley rose from his chair. "Good. I've let the staff know they're to cooperate fully and answer all your questions."

"Thank you, that should be very helpful." Witherspoon started to walk away, then stopped suddenly. "Mr. Farley, are there any staff members that had problems with Jeremy Marks?"

"Staff members? Certainly not. Why do you ask?"

"A servant holding a grudge isn't entirely unheard of," Barnes put in quickly. "But if you say none of them disliked the man, we'll take your word for it."

Farley shifted uneasily. "I didn't exactly say that. The

truth is the serving staff didn't like him very much. When he was a member, he was always complaining to the staff about something. Either the tea was too strong, not strong enough, the cakes were stale, the filling in the sandwiches too meager and/or the champagne was flat."

"He complained frequently," Witherspoon murmured. "That's interesting to know, but hardly the sort of situation where someone would shoot two arrows into the fellow."

"Are any of the staff archers?" Barnes asked.

"We do allow those that are interested to use the facilities on Wednesday afternoons. We shut early then, but to my knowledge, the only person I've seen take advantage of this is young Mick, he's our footman. But he's just a lad and frankly he's terrible. He never got near hitting the target."

"If you think of anything else that might be useful, please let us know," Witherspoon said. "By the way, is there an empty office or someplace we can use? We've some follow-up interviews today."

"You can use the club secretary's office. It'll be empty today. It's right next to mine and I'll have Mrs. Merchant see that it's unlocked."

"Thank you."

"When do you think you'll be gone?" Farley blurted out. "Oh dear, I didn't mean that the way it sounded. It's just that we've two sets competing today and I don't want there to be any delays. The Novice Men's Longbow didn't get to shoot at all and the Ladies Division still has several of their group that need to finish. We've the national championships coming up soon and those with the highest scores can move on to the regional and then the national competition." He stared at them anxiously. "You do understand. We must get on with it; the scores must be in by next week."

"We'll do our best to stay out of the way of the competition, but my men will be speaking to most of the members today," Witherspoon warned him. "We'll need to make use of your common room."

"Will the members have access to it?" Farley asked.

"They will."

"Then I suppose it'll be alright."

"Is Mrs. McElhaney here this morning?" Witherspoon started for the door again, then stopped.

Farley nodded. "She should be. She's competing today and the ladies are going first."

"She's one of the ladies' champions?" Barnes deliberately used the word "champions" to get a reaction from Rufus Farley and he wasn't disappointed.

"She is. She's a very good archer. She's got a real chance to win one of the national competitions . . ." He broke off as he realized what he'd just said. "But that doesn't mean she had anything to do with Mr. Marks' murder. There are half a dozen women who are as skillful as she is: Miss Lonsdale and Mrs. Merriman, but she isn't competing this time, and also Mrs. Storch and Mrs. Hampton . . . oh dear, I'm just making it worse, aren't I."

"I assure you, Mr. Farley, we'll not be making any arrests just because someone is good at archery," Witherspoon said.

Relieved, Farley pulled a handkerchief out of his coat pocket and mopped his forehead. "That's good to know. If you need me, I'll be out on the archery range."

Witherspoon and Barnes waited till he'd gone before they

went to the common room. The constables were gathered around the table closest to the door. The supplies they'd brought from the station were stacked in the center.

"Let's get started," Witherspoon said as he and Barnes joined the men. "Does everyone understand what we need to do here?"

"I think so, sir," Griffiths said. "We're to speak to everyone at each table and ascertain who was actually at the table when the murder was done."

The inspector nodded approvingly. "That's correct." He pointed to the top paper. One of the circles already had names written on it. "As you see here, I've already filled this one in. At the time of the murder, Emmett Merriman was at a table with a Mr. and Mrs. Belton and Mrs. Storch. Mrs. Storch's companion had been sitting at the table, but she'd been sent off on an errand."

"Her name is Miss Linwood, sir," Constable Parker said helpfully. "According to Mrs. Storch, she took the picnic hamper out to Mrs. Storch's carriage."

"Thank you, Constable, we met the lady yesterday," Witherspoon said. "And by way of illustration on how the system might work, Miss Linwood couldn't confirm that Mr. Merriman was at the table during the pertinent time as she was away herself. My point is this: You might need to ask more than one person at each table for confirmation." He tapped the circle with his index finger. "Once we know for certain that everyone was here, we'll know none of them could have fired the fatal arrows."

"How do we find out who was sitting where?" Griffiths asked. "I mean, we know where some people were sitting from our interviews yesterday, but we don't have the names of everyone at each table."

"That won't be a problem." Barnes nodded toward a middle-aged woman wearing a gray bombazine dress as she stepped into the common room. She was followed by two young women wearing the lavender dress and apron of the serving staff. The older woman paused and surveyed the room, her gaze stopping briefly at the cluster of policemen before she and the two girls moved toward them.

"I'm Mrs. Merchant," she said as she approached Inspector Witherspoon. "I was supervising the common room yesterday and these two"—she nodded at the girls standing behind her—"were serving the sandwiches and either tea or champagne. Mr. Farley said you needed our help."

"We most certainly do," Witherspoon replied.

"We'll do whatever you need to clear this matter up." Mrs. Merchant brushed a lock of brown hair that had slipped out of her topknot away from her eyes. "This is Letty Maddox"—she pointed to the dark-haired young lady—"and this is Emma Sturridge"—she pointed to the other one, a thin girl with dark blonde hair and deep-set brown eyes.

"We appreciate your help." Witherspoon nodded politely and then introduced Barnes and the other constables. "But before I say more, I need to be sure that all three of you were here yesterday when Mr. Marks was murdered."

"If you mean were we all here at three-oh-five yesterday, I can assure you we were. I went downstairs precisely at three to get a tray of cucumber sandwiches. I recall it exactly because the clock was chiming and Mr. Farley had stuck his head in the kitchen to demand we bring up more champagne.

But as my hands were full, I had one of the other girls get it, and by the time it was uncorked and Janet was ready to bring it upstairs, it was three-oh-three. The other girls were already here and busy serving tea. So yes, Inspector, I can confirm all three of us were here in the common room."

"Excellent," Witherspoon said. "Are all three of you familiar with the names of your members?"

"We are," she replied. "I've worked here for six months, and Emma and Letty have been here for over three years. Now, what is it you want us to do?"

He told them, taking his time and ensuring they understood precisely what was needed.

"That shouldn't be difficult, should it, girls," Mrs. Merchant said.

"No, ma'am," Emma Sturridge replied. "I know who was sitting at the tables I served."

"So do I," Letty added. "But there were lots of people that weren't sitting. What about them?"

Witherspoon thought for a moment. "Once you've finished doing the tables, each of you tell the constables the names of the people that weren't seated. Especially, if you noticed anyone coming in or out of the room during that period of time. Those will be the ones we interview again," Witherspoon replied. "That storm yesterday was dreadful, and if the rain had stopped for even a few moments, most people would still be inside. Now, are there any other questions?"

"Do we have any idea where the killer was standing when he shot the arrows?" Constable Parker asked.

"That might be impossible to determine," the inspector said. "Because of the storm, it's not as easy as it should be.

The rain might have stopped when Marks was killed, but the winds were still strong. Mr. Farley says it's a wonder that anyone could shoot an arrow in those conditions and have it hit anything."

"Perhaps the killer is an expert archer," Constable Parker said.

"Or he could have been lucky, but we're going on the assumption he was highly skilled," Witherspoon replied.

"Why don't we just ask everyone if they're an expert archer or not?" Constable Nichols suggested.

"Because half of them will be lyin' through their teeth," Constable Griffiths muttered in a low voice, but he'd spoken during one of the moments when it was quiet, and when he looked at the others, he realized they'd heard every word. "Oh, sorry, sir, I didn't mean to sound disrespectful or flippant. I only meant that people often think they're better at something than they actually are."

"No apology is needed, Constable. You've made a valid point. That, of course, is the main reason we're going to be looking at everyone, regardless of what they claim their skill level might be. We're not just going to take anyone's word for how good they may or may not be. We'll be talking to the members as well as the staff and asking them who they would say was an expert. That will give us a realistic idea of who might have had the skill to send those two arrows into Mr. Marks."

"We're even going to be looking at those that claim they don't do archery at all," Barnes added. "We're not leaving anything to chance. If you're an expert archer who wants to commit murder, would you let the local archery club know how good you might be?"

"You think we might be looking for someone who kept their abilities hidden?" Constable Nichols asked.

"It's a possibility and we've learned from long experience never to dismiss anything out of hand," Barnes replied.

"Any other questions?" When no one spoke, Witherspoon nodded to Constable Griffiths. "You're in charge. We'll be in the secretary's office conducting more interviews." He looked at Mrs. Merchant. "Do you happen to know where Mrs. McElhaney might be?"

"I saw her going upstairs to the Ladies' Day Room a few minutes ago. I'll send one of the girls to tell her you wish to speak with her."

"Thank you, that will be helpful," Witherspoon said as he and Barnes moved toward the corridor.

The secretary's office was much like Rufus Farley's: identical furniture, identical shelving along one of the walls, an empty coat tree in the corner, a chair by the door, and another in front of the desk. But there was a layer of dust on the edge of the shelves, a dead maidenhair fern on the table, and the air was stale from the window being shut all winter.

"Apparently, the secretary hasn't been here in quite some time," Witherspoon commented as he put his bowler on the coat tree.

"I don't think this club is doing all that well." Barnes grabbed the top spindle of the chair by the door and put it next to the desk. "I overheard one of the members say that when Mr. Rogers left, he was the last club secretary, the club didn't replace the position."

There was a brief knock on the door, but before either policeman could respond, it opened and a woman stepped inside. She was dressed in a pale blue blouse and a navy blue tie and skirt. She had a quiver of arrows and an arm guard tucked under one arm. She stood just inside the door, looking at them. "I'm Alice McElhaney. Mrs. Merchant said you wished to speak to me."

"We do, Mrs. McElhaney. We've some questions for you." He tried not to stare. Although she wasn't in the first flush of youthful beauty, she was still a very lovely woman. The inspector thought she must be in her late thirties, with blonde hair worn in an elaborate style that fit perfectly with the jaunty blue hat she wore. Her eyes were blue, her cheekbones high, and her complexion perfect. He gestured at the chair in front of the desk. "Please have a seat."

"I hope this won't take too long. I'd like to practice before I have to compete." She sat down where he'd indicated and put the quiver of arrows and the arm guard on the floor. Straightening, she stared at the two policemen.

"We'll be as quick as possible." Witherspoon took his seat. Constable Barnes was in a chair next to him and already had his little brown notebook and pencil at the ready. "You were friends with Mr. Marks, is that correct?" the inspector began.

"Let's not waste time, Inspector. I'm sure by now you know that we were far more than friends." She smiled wryly. "We were engaged at one time."

Witherspoon cleared his throat. He hated asking women personal, awkward questions; sometimes they cried and he wasn't very good at dealing with that situation. "Yes, we had heard that, Mrs. McElhaney, but we wanted to confirm it with you. When did you and Mr. Marks end your relationship?"

"The same day he asked Hannah Lonsdale to marry him."

"And when would that have been?" Barnes interjected quickly.

"Three months ago. Jeremy sent me a note one day telling me we couldn't marry and asking for my understanding. I thought that was particularly stupid of the man—no woman is ever going to understand being jilted—but then again, Jeremy was very stupid when it came to human relationships."

"Did he say why he wanted to end your engagement?" Witherspoon asked.

She gave a delicate shrug. "The note merely said that he realized we weren't suited to one another, but that was a lie. But that shouldn't have surprised me. I knew he lied, I just didn't think he'd lie to me. That very day, he proposed to Hannah Lonsdale. But I didn't find that out until I got back to London a few weeks ago."

"You only found out he was engaged then?" Witherspoon pressed.

"That's right. When he ended our engagement so abruptly, I went to the continent. A friend had invited me to spend the spring with her at her villa in Florence. Going to Italy seemed a better idea than staying here and enduring pitying comments. When I arrived back from Italy, a friend told me that the day after I left for the continent, their engagement announcement was in *The Times*."

"Did finding that out upset you, Mrs. McElhaney?"

"If by 'upset,' do you mean did I cry and have hysterics?" She laughed. "Hardly, Inspector. I was furious. It became clear he broke off our engagement because he wanted to marry Hannah Lonsdale. I'd have had more respect for him if he'd just told me that to begin with. Instead, that silly ex-

cuse of 'not being suited to one another' was just a convenient lie. But I didn't know that at the time. I'm usually a
confident woman, Inspector, but Jeremy ending the engagement made me doubt myself. I kept wondering what had
gone wrong, what I could have done that upset him so much,
he ended our engagement." She laughed softly. "In one sense,
it was a relief to learn that I'd done nothing wrong; he'd
merely found a richer woman to marry."

"Was yesterday the first time you saw Mr. Marks since
returning from Italy?" Barnes asked.

"Yes, and at first I thought his membership had been reinstated, but one of my friends told me he was only here as
the guest of Miss Lonsdale."

"Did Mr. Marks see you yesterday?" Witherspoon asked.

She shook her head. "No, I deliberately stayed out of his
way until I had a chance to speak to Miss Lonsdale. I knew
if he saw me, he'd go running to her with a pack of lies about
my character and my motives."

Witherspoon stared at her. "Why did you wish to speak
to Miss Lonsdale?"

"I needed to show her what he'd done to me." Her eyes
narrowed. "I knew once she found out what he was really
like, once she'd seen his true character, she'd end it, and I was
right."

"You wanted to hurt him?"

"Of course. I knew she'd be here and I wanted to make
certain I could pay him back for the pain he'd caused me."
She drew back and looked at Witherspoon as if he were a
half-wit. "Don't you understand? Being jilted by someone
like him was embarrassing. I even had acquaintances in Italy
asking me questions. It was awful."

"But you were going to marry him?" Witherspoon was truly confused.

"That's different. Marriage to the man was respectable; publicly having my engagement end in such a manner was humiliating."

"How were you going to show Miss Lonsdale his true character?" Barnes interjected.

"That was the easy part. I showed her the letter Jeremy sent me ending our engagement. It was dated the same day he'd asked her to marry him."

CHAPTER 5

"Now if that's all, Inspector, I must go. I've just enough time to get in my practice shots before I compete." She stood up and started for the door.

"Just one moment," Witherspoon called.

She stopped and turned. "What is it? I've told you everything I know."

The inspector doubted that was true, but he let it go. "Where were you between three o'clock and three fifteen yesterday?"

"You mean when someone killed Jeremy." She tapped her chin thoughtfully. "I was upstairs in the Ladies' Day Room. Now, really, I must go. If you've more questions, you'll have to ask them later."

Neither the inspector nor Constable Barnes said anything as they watched her leave.

Barnes turned to Witherspoon as the door closed behind her. "What do you think, sir?"

"I think that she hated Jeremy Marks but we've no evidence she murdered him," he sighed heavily. "What's more, if she *was* upstairs in the Ladies' Day Room, as she just claimed, then she couldn't have killed Marks. Drat, I wish I'd asked her if anyone saw her when she was up there."

"We can always ask that later," Barnes said. "I wonder, though, if she realized what we were doing."

Witherspoon, who'd started to the door, stopped and looked at the constable. "What do you mean?"

"Just wondering if she noticed the constables working with the common room staff. It wouldn't be hard to guess what we are doing, sir."

"You think she might have seen the constables putting names on the table drawings? But even if she did that, it wouldn't help her. All it would do is give her an excuse *not* to have been in the common room."

"That's true," Barnes muttered. "I suppose I shouldn't worry about it. We'll find out soon enough if she's lying. From what we've been told, there were so many people milling about when Marks was killed that someone is bound to have seen her either in the day room or going up or down the stairs. Shall we go to the common room, sir, and see how the lads are getting along?"

Witherspoon pulled his pocket watch out of his inner coat pocket. "I doubt they'll have much information as yet. Let's give the constables a few more hours to sort out who was where."

"What next, then, sir?"

"Let's pay a visit to Jeremy Marks' solicitor. Perhaps he

can shed a bit more light on who may have wanted the man dead."

Mrs. Goodge put the plate of currant scones on the table and then took her seat. "Don't stand on ceremony, just help yourself, Ida," she instructed her guest.

"I will. You've always made wonderful pastries." Ida Leacock's thin face creased in a wide smile as she reached for the treat. She and the cook had worked together years earlier and had stayed in touch. Ida was a slender woman with curly salt-and-pepper hair piled high in an elaborate style, hazel eyes, and a narrow face. She had left "service" years earlier than Mrs. Goodge and had found success when she married and, with her husband, had opened a tobacconist shop. She was now widowed and owned three tobacconist shops. "Your scones are marvelous."

"I'm so glad you stopped by." Mrs. Goodge stared at her curiously. "I was going to send you a note, but the day got away from me." One of the reasons Mrs. Goodge had renewed her relationship with Ida was because the woman loved gossip. She was smart, and had that rare ability to get anyone to stop and chat with her. She'd helped in a number of the inspector's cases, and for a lady who loved to talk, she could be very discreet.

Ida swallowed the bite she'd put in her mouth and washed it down with a quick sip of tea. "I read about your inspector getting that dreadful case at the West London Archery Club." Ida frowned disapprovingly. "What's the world coming to when you're not even safe on an archery range. The papers said that poor man had two arrows in him."

"That's what the inspector told us." Mrs. Goodge took a scone and put it on the small plate next to her teacup.

"That's why I came," Ida continued. "One of my shops is in Hammersmith and that's close enough to the Marks house that I've picked up a few bits and pieces about the man. I decided to come see you and pass along what I've heard."

"That would be wonderful, Ida. That was so thoughtful." Mrs. Goodge grinned. "Obviously, you know who Jeremy Marks was, then?"

"I do, and from what I know about him, I'm not surprised he was murdered. Mind you, it's never right to kill someone, but to be truthful, Amanda . . ." Ida leaned closer, using Mrs. Goodge's Christian name. "If anyone deserved to be dispatched to meet their maker, it was Jeremy Marks."

"We've heard that more than once. What do you know about him?"

"To begin with, he was quite a ladies' man, if you know what I mean."

Mrs. Goodge nodded, but said nothing.

"Which is odd, because he started gaining weight and losing his hair years ago, but according to what Polly Dumont told me, he's got a way about him. But that's neither here nor there. The truth is, there are several women in London who hate him and when I use the term 'hate,' I'm not exaggerating." She picked up her teacup and took a sip.

"What did he do to them?" Mrs. Goodge had already heard a few bits and pieces about Marks' romantic past, but she wanted to make sure she hadn't missed anything.

Ida put her cup down and leaned closer. "He's a cad, Amanda, a cad. The kind of man who courts women with a bit of money and then drops them if he finds one that is richer."

Mrs. Goodge smiled to hide her disappointment. She already knew this about Jeremy Marks, but didn't want to take a chance on missing something important. "Do you have any names?"

"Do you think I'd bend your ear if I didn't?" Ida laughed. "He's done it twice that I know about, but there are rumors those two aren't the only ones. The first time it happened was a good twenty or so years ago, well before he met and married his wife, Elaine Fairfax. It was a woman named Jeanette Givens. She was from a good family, you know, the kind that are were well off but not wealthy. Then all of a sudden, Marks told Miss Givens, as she was then, that he didn't want to go through with the nuptials and he broke it off."

"He's not the first man in the world to do that," Mrs. Goodge murmured.

"Yes, but he insisted she return the engagement ring he'd given her, and frankly, that's just not done. Most women return them as a matter of course, but Jeanette Givens was furious and told him he'd have to take her to court to get the wretched thing back. He did it."

"He took her to court?"

"That's what he told her he'd do." Ida laughed. "Apparently, he was serious enough about the matter that she gave in, lost her temper, threw the ring at him, and set her cocker spaniel on him. I heard about it from Lottie Yarrow—she was the Givens' housekeeper back then and now lives just across the road from my Hammersmith shop. When Sacha, that's the spaniel, took after Marks, she did quite a bit of damage and Marks was screaming his head off. Lottie ran into the hall to see what was going on and found the dog tearing into Marks' backside as he tried to get the door open."

"Miss Givens didn't call the animal off?"

"No, according to Lottie, she stood in the drawing room door, shouting, 'Get him, Sacha, get him,' and laughing."

"You can't blame her for that. She must have been humiliated," Mrs. Goodge said.

"Being humiliated was the least of her problems," Ida said. "According to Lottie, Miss Givens was worried she might be with child."

Mrs. Goodge was shocked. "She told such a thing to her housekeeper?"

"Of course not. Lottie overheard her telling Jeremy Marks that he had to marry her and that it had to be soon—they weren't going to have time for a big society wedding. She wanted him to take her to Gretna Green and get married right away. That's when Marks told her he didn't want to marry her. You can understand why the young lady was in such a state. She'd been seduced and now abandoned."

"The poor girl."

"Don't waste your sympathy on her. It turns out she wasn't in the family way, and a few months later, she married Thomas Grayson. By all accounts, it was a good marriage, and when he passed away, he left her very well off."

"You said this was twenty years ago?"

"Something like that." Ida took a quick sip of tea. "That's what Lottie said, and she has quite a good memory."

Mrs. Goodge looked thoughtful. "That's a long time ago.

It seems odd that someone would wait that long to get revenge."

"You never know. Sometimes people nurse old grudges for the rest of their lives. But on the other hand, Jeanette Givens ended up with a man who genuinely loved her and gave her a very good life."

"I wonder if she's a member of the West London Archery Club?" Mrs. Goodge murmured.

Ida shrugged. "I've no idea. But according to Lottie, the Graysons lived here in London their entire married life so it doesn't seem logical that Jeanette Givens Grayson waited twenty years to get back at the man, especially as her husband at that time was far better off than Marks. We both know that the rich, if they want to, can be quite ruthless in punishing someone who has wronged them."

Mrs. Goodge nodded in agreement. "Any other names?"

"There was an incident years ago, while Marks was still living at home with his parents. Apparently, he got another girl, a housemaid, 'in the family way,' and of course, you know how those things always go—the girl was chucked out."

Mrs. Goodge was disappointed again—ancient history wasn't going to solve this case—but Ida was such a good source, she didn't want to offend her by ignoring her information. She asked, "I don't suppose you know the girl's name?"

"Actually, I do and we can thank Lottie again. The girl's name was Nora Hartman and it turns out that Lottie's cousin worked at the Marks home when this happened. But I don't think she could be the killer. She'd have had to be there yesterday. The West London Archery Club isn't as conservative and snobbish as some other clubs, but I don't think they'd welcome a servant girl who'd had a child out of wedlock."

The office of Wiley and Upton was located on the quieter end of the Brompton Road. Inspector Witherspoon and Constable Barnes got out of the hansom cab and surveyed the three-story redbrick commercial building. It was a modern building with offices, rather than shops, on the ground floor. They went up the short, broad staircase, through the double doors, and into the lobby.

The floor was polished to a high gloss, and there were two globe chandeliers hanging from the ceiling, a directory on the far-left wall, and a wide staircase leading to the upper floors.

Barnes went to the directory and studied it for a moment. "His office is down the corridor." He pointed past the stairs.

They walked down the hallway until they reached the solicitor's office. Barnes opened the door and the two policemen stepped inside. A dark-haired young man who was sitting at one of the two desks looked up from the open ledger on his desk, his eyes widening at the sight of Constable Barnes. A blond-haired lad with a walrus mustache sat at the other desk.

Shoving his chair back with a clatter, the dark-haired lad leapt to his feet. "May I help you?"

"We'd like to see Miles Wiley. We don't have an appointment but this matter is very important," Witherspoon said.

The young man nodded vigorously as he edged backward toward one of the two closed doors on the back wall. "I'll just let Mr. Wiley know you're here," he said.

"That won't be necessary, Phillips," a tall, gray-haired man said as he stepped into the room. "I've been expecting these gentlemen." He came toward them with his hand extended. "I'm Miles Wiley, Mr. Jeremy Marks' solicitor. I assume he's the reason you're here."

"It is indeed, sir," Witherspoon replied. "I'm Inspector Witherspoon, and this is my colleague, Constable Barnes."

"I'm pleased to meet both of you even under these rather dreadful circumstances." He gestured toward his open office door. "You must have a lot of questions. Let's go to my office."

They followed him inside. Two tall windows let in the spring sunshine. The oak plank wooden floor was covered with an exquisite Oriental rug in sapphire blue and silver, bookcases filled with legal tomes went from floor to ceiling on one wall, while an old-fashioned gray marble fireplace stood opposite it. A portrait of an elderly gentleman in an old-fashioned frock coat and wing-tip collar held pride of place over the mantlepiece. A large desk and chair stood by the windows, in front of which were two leather armchairs.

After closing the door, Wiley went behind his desk and gestured at the armchairs. "Do sit down. Would you like tea?"

"No thank you," Witherspoon replied as he and Barnes took their seats. He waited while Barnes took out his notebook and pencil. Then he said, "As you know, we're here about the murder of Jeremy Marks."

"I read about it in the newspapers and realized you'd need to speak with me." He steepled his fingers together and leaned his elbows on the desk. "I must say I wasn't all that surprised when I read about Jeremy's death."

"How long has Mr. Marks been your client?" Barnes asked.

"Twenty-five years."

"Then you must know him quite well," Witherspoon said.

"I know one very important aspect of the man, but I cannot claim to truly know his character. He has a rather unusual personality."

"In what way?" Witherspoon leaned forward.

"It's difficult to describe, Inspector, but with most of my oldest clients, after a while you begin to understand them as people. You get to know their personalities, their concerns, and the problems they might have with family or friends. But even after twenty-five years, with Mr. Marks, it was always business."

"He didn't like chatting about himself." Barnes looked up from his notebook.

Wiley frowned. "He appeared to be very sociable, very chatty, but once he was gone, you realized he'd told you absolutely nothing about himself unless it had to do with the business matter at hand."

"I think I understand." The inspector nodded. He'd arrested individuals like that. Men and women who seemed to be as open as a Bible on a pulpit lectern, but were just the opposite. "I've dealt with people like that. They appear friendly, but when they've gone, you realize you learned nothing. Which, of course, is a bit of a liability in our line of work."

"In mine as well." Wiley grinned.

"What can you tell me about Mr. Marks?"

"He wasn't a very nice man." Wiley's smile disappeared. "And unfortunately, as his solicitor, it wasn't my place to pass judgments on his actions, unless, of course, they were illegal."

"I take it he always kept to the right side of the law?" Barnes asked.

Wiley nodded. "But that doesn't mean he was always honorable. I drew up the agreements and contracts for all of his business. He always, always insisted that in every Letter of Intent, agreement, or contract, there was essentially an escape clause for himself if things went wrong."

"But surely his associates had solicitors as well," Witherspoon challenged. "Why did they allow such clauses to exist?"

"Not everyone is as careful as Jeremy Marks. Do you know, he's the only client I ever had that read every word of every document pertaining to his business. Most people aren't that diligent and most people tend to take things on trust. That, of course, would be a fatal mistake if one were doing business with Marks. There have been at least five times that he's backed out of business deals with no harm to himself but substantial harm to his partners, suppliers, and vendors. But as you surmised, he always stayed on the right side of the law," he sighed. "As we all know, laws are usually written by greedy, powerful men and they often benefit men like Marks."

"Exactly what kind of business did he do?" Barnes shifted in his chair. "We keep hearing he was a property developer, but was that all he was?"

"He had his fingers in lots of pies, Constable. He invested in real estate, especially the conversion of large homes to flats. That's quite lucrative these days. But prior to that, he bought and sold commercial property as well as investing in a number of overseas enterprises. He's part owner of a tea plantation in India, a cattle ranch in someplace called Montana in the United States, as well as half a dozen other businesses. He's been a very successful businessman, but not a very good human being. Recently, he was engaged to a Miss Hannah Lonsdale."

"We've already spoken to Miss Lonsdale," Witherspoon said. "According to her, she broke off her engagement to Mr. Marks prior to his being murdered."

Wiley looked surprised. "She broke off the engagement, good. His behavior toward the lady was certainly less than honorable."

"How so?"

"After his engagement to Miss Lonsdale, he told me they had agreed to amend their wills to make each other their main heir. That, of course, is often done especially when both parties have no children and substantial estates. I know for a fact that Miss Lonsdale amended her will. When I brought the matter up to Mr. Marks, reminding him that he'd not changed his, he told me he'd wait till after the wedding before making the change."

Barnes stopped writing. "How do you know Miss Lonsdale changed hers?"

"Because I overheard her solicitor complaining about it," Wiley replied. "Please, don't misunderstand. Her lawyer is a good man, not the kind to be talking about his client's personal business. But we were at our club and he was, to use a nautical term, 'three sheets to the wind.' He was quite distraught and upset. Except for some elderly uncles, Miss Lonsdale is alone in the world—her father died several years ago and left her a fortune. He's known her all her life. He told me he'd heard some very unsavory things about Jeremy Marks and he was afraid the man was taking advantage of her. He was opposed to making changes to her estate until she and Marks were legally man and wife. But Miss Lonsdale was adamant she'd keep to their agreement so Mr. Galvan, that's her solicitor, asked me to make certain Mr. Marks lived up to their agreement and made the promised changes himself."

"Did you discuss the matter with him?" Witherspoon stared at him curiously, wondering how far a lawyer could go in making a client adhere to an oral promise.

"I did, and I must say, Jeremy Marks didn't appreciate my questions."

"When did this happen?"

"Last week. As a matter of fact, it was a most uncomfortable discussion, and after it was over, I'd decided I could no longer accept the man as a client. Frankly, I'd had enough of his devious and what I considered to be unethical behavior."

"Did you tell him that?" Barnes flipped onto a clean page of his notebook.

"I did. As I said earlier, it was an awkward conversation but one that was very much needed. I'm no longer a young man desperate for work, Constable. Over the years, Mr. Marks has paid me well, but all things considered, it was time for our association to end."

"Was he upset with you?" Witherspoon eased back in the chair and waited for Wiley's answer.

"He was very annoyed. Then he threatened me." He laughed harshly. "He told me if I mentioned he'd not changed his will leaving his estate to Miss Lonsdale, he'd see I never practiced my profession again. I told him to get out of my office, and that if he ever tried to harm our firm, I'd sue him for everything he owned."

"How did he respond?"

"He left, Inspector, like a dog with his tail between his legs. The one thing Jeremy Marks knows is that I'm one of the best solicitors in London. That's the reason he's paid me so well over the years. Then, of course, he gets murdered and the problem of Jeremy Marks is solved."

Barnes stopped writing and stared at Wiley. "It sounds like it worked out well for you, sir."

Wiley shrugged. "I'd be lying if I don't admit that Marks' death has saved me from what could have been a great deal of inconvenience. But if you're looking to me as the murderer, I've never shot a bow and arrow in my life, and yesterday, I was here all day. You can confirm that with my clerks."

"How valuable is Mr. Marks' estate?" the constable pressed.

"Close to fifty thousand pounds, but most of that is in property and some of that is mortgaged. The actual value of the estate can't be calculated till all the creditors get paid, but I imagine it will still be substantial."

"If you're not his solicitor anymore—" Witherspoon began, only to be interrupted.

"Oh, but I am," Wiley insisted. "I'd not sent out nor received any termination of services correspondence. That's a standard practice at this firm."

"I see," the inspector said. "If Mr. Marks didn't change his will to leave his estate to his fiancée, who did he leave it to? His brother in Wolverhampton?"

Wiley shook his head. "No, the two of them loathed one

another and haven't spoken in years. He left five hundred pounds to his housekeeper and two hundred fifty pounds to the other servants in the household. But the bulk of his estate is going to the Royal Society for the Prevention of Cruelty to Animals. He left instructions that after all the expenses were paid, everything he owned was to be sold and the proceeds given to them."

Surprised, both policemen stared at the solicitor. Witherspoon recovered first. "I'm stunned, Mr. Wiley. From what we know of Jeremy Marks, I'd never have guessed he was an animal lover."

"He's not. It's dogs that he liked," Wiley explained. "He didn't care much for any other animals and he hated cats. But he loved dogs. Apparently, a number of years ago, Marks took to feeding some stray dogs that hung about his neighborhood. One of them died when it ate some bad meat it had actually managed to get out of a butcher box that had been left by the kitchen door at the Marks home."

"Bad meat?" Barnes looked at him curiously.

He laughed. "Marks insisted it wasn't 'bad' meat. He claimed he'd been poisoned. But this was years ago, well before his unethical business practices became well known. At that point in his life, I doubt anyone was out to murder him."

"He told you he thought someone had tried to murder him?" Witherspoon wanted to be sure he understood this.

"He was sure of it, but when I pressed him on the matter and asked him for details of the incident, he admitted that back then there was no one that he could think of who'd want to kill him. From what he told me, it may have been his own fault the meat went bad. He worked what few servants he had so hard that they didn't bother answering the kitchen door when deliveries were made; they let them sit out until late in the day and brought them all in at once."

"What do you think, sir?" Barnes asked the moment he and Witherspoon were in a hansom cab. "Is he a suspect? He could have hired someone to shoot Marks with those arrows."

"Yes, but he struck me as being an excellent solicitor, and a good lawyer knows not to leave a trail when one is committing a crime. Hiring people to commit murder often leads to a very clear path, especially if the hired killers get caught."

"That's true, sir. They chatter like magpies if they're facing the hangman. If Wiley is as good a lawyer as he claims, he'd know that."

"That's what I think as well." The inspector nodded in agreement. "And both of Wiley's clerks verified he was there yesterday, and even if they do work for the man, I doubt the clerks would lie to protect him, not in a murder case."

"Mind you, I do think Wiley is pretendin' to be a better person than he really is."

"What do you mean?"

"He didn't decide to drop Marks as a client until the situation with Miss Lonsdale," Barnes explained. "But he'd worked for Marks for twenty-five years and he admitted that Marks was as tricky and unethical as they come since the beginning."

"Yes, but he also took care to say that Marks always stayed within the law. Furthermore, Wiley claims that he was no longer a young and ambitious solicitor desperate for clients; he's well established now." Witherspoon grabbed the handhold as the hansom swung around the corner.

"I suppose so, sir," Barnes sighed. "And a solicitor's first loyalty is to his client and no one else, so I guess he's no worse than any other lawyer for keepin' Marks as a client as long as he did."

"Don't forget, Constable, that Marks was doing business with men very much like himself, men who could have taken the time to read any and all of the documents drawn up by Wiley on Marks' behalf. He wasn't taking advantage of elderly women or orphans, at least not in his business dealings." He glanced out the window. "Good, we're here."

It was controlled chaos inside the common room. Constable Griffiths was at one of the center aisle tables having what appeared to be a spirited discussion with a serving girl. Constable Nichols was at the next table along with Mrs. Merchant and the other young lady, and Constable McLean was on the other side of Griffiths in deep conversation with Rufus Farley.

Witherspoon headed toward Constable Griffiths while Barnes broke off and went toward Constable McLean on the far side of the room.

Griffiths glanced up as his superior approached. "Hello, sir, I'm glad you're here. We've made progress but we're not finished yet."

"Take the time that you need," Witherspoon said. "We must get this right. Do you have a rough estimate of how many people cannot be accounted for during the time period when Mr. Marks was killed?"

"It's difficult to say, sir. Once we had most of the names on our row of tables, we needed to compare people who Miss Emma"—he nodded at the young maid—"couldn't remember to determine if any of those people had been seen by anyone at the other tables. It gets a bit muddled, sir. That's why we're going through it again."

"Excuse me, Inspector," a timid voice said from behind him. He turned to see the other serving maid, Letty Maddox, standing at the next table. "May I have a word with you, please?" She cast a quick glance at Rufus Farley.

"Of course." He hurried toward her. "Do you have something to tell me?"

"These names." She pointed to the round paper in front of her. "Are they people who were said to be at the table when Mr. Marks was murdered?"

"That's correct," he replied.

An expression of panic crossed her face as footsteps sounded behind her. She looked around and then let out an audible sigh of relief to see it was Constable Barnes. "That's what the young constable told me," Letty said. "But I needed to be certain, sir. This is awkward and I don't mean to imply anything untoward, but one of these people wasn't sitting at this table when that man was killed." She jabbed her finger on the page and pointed at a name.

Witherspoon leaned close enough to read it. Then he looked at the girl. "You're saying that Mr. Merriman wasn't sitting here when it happened?"

She glanced at Farley again and lowered her voice even further. "Not the whole time, sir."

"Are you sure of this, miss? We interviewed Mr. Merriman yesterday, and he assured us he was here during the time in question. We also verified his statement with Mr. and Mrs. Belton. Unfortunately, Mrs. Storch, who was also at the table, had already left by the time we confirmed Mr. Merriman's statement."

"Did Mr. or Mrs. Belton say he'd been seated at their table the entire time?" She crossed her arms over her chest.

It was Barnes who answered. "They both remembered him being there"—the constable frowned—"and Mrs. Belton said that he did leave the table at one point, but he was only gone for a few moments."

Letty looked across at Farley again and then stepped closer to the two policemen. "I'm not one to tell tales out of turn, but Mr. and Mrs. Belton were both drinking the champagne as if it was water." She spoke so softly, Witherspoon cocked his ear toward her to hear better.

"How long do you estimate that Mr. Merriman was away from the table?" Barnes asked quickly. From the way the young maid kept glancing at the club director, it was obvious she wanted to tell the truth but was a bit hampered by the proximity of Rufus Farley. He wouldn't appreciate her offending or disagreeing with an important member.

"A good ten or twelve minutes," she replied. "And he wasn't the only one who was gone. Mrs. Storch's companion, Miss Linwood, was away as well but she was back faster than Mr. Merriman."

"Yes, we've spoken with Miss Linwood," Witherspoon muttered. He gave the room a quick survey, but didn't see the lady. "Actually, we should interview her again."

"Were you in the common room the entire time Mr. Merriman was missing?" Barnes asked.

"Yes, sir, I was. I was working the tea station, sir, and Mrs. Merchant had gone downstairs as we'd run out of hot water so it was just Emma and myself. But both of us were here the whole time."

"Now do be careful, Letty," Rufus Farley said as he approached them. "We don't want the police thinking ill of our guests."

"The young lady is confirming who was or wasn't here during the pertinent time period," Witherspoon said quickly. "And she's been very helpful."

"I'm sure she is, but we must be cautious." Farley straightened his spine and drew in a deep breath. "A number of people cannot be accounted for, but that doesn't mean any of them murdered Mr. Marks."

"Someone did," Barnes said dryly. "And tracking down who was inside, who was outside, or who wasn't anywhere to be seen might help us find the killer."

Farley held up his hand. "I understand that, Constable, but I do think that you ought to check with me before you come to any conclusions. Some of the staff are relatively new and perhaps get a bit confused as to who might be who."

"As soon as we've finished going over the timeline pages, as I like to call them, we'll come to your office so you can have a look as well," Witherspoon replied.

"Thank you, Inspector, that would be very helpful to the club," Farley said. "Now, who is missing from this table?"

"Miss Linwood, and according to this young lady"—he smiled at Letty—"Emmett Merriman wasn't here the whole time, either," Witherspoon said. "We asked him specifically if he'd left the table and he assured us he hadn't."

Farley pulled a handkerchief from his coat pocket and mopped the perspiration off his forehead. "I imagine he simply got a bit confused, Inspector. Most of us aren't used to murder. It's very disconcerting to say the least."

"May we have Mr. Merriman's address?" Barnes asked.

Farley's eyes widened. "Can't you speak to him tomorrow? We're having our annual summer luncheon and everyone will be here."

"And by tomorrow, Emmett Merriman could be across the channel and in France," Barnes said. "Do you know how difficult it is to get foreign governments to cooperate and send witnesses back to England? Good gracious, Mr. Farley, we just want to speak to the man."

By the time they had gone over their timeline pages (as Witherspoon called them) and were gathered outside Farley's office, it was getting quite late in the day. Farley was with the cook, giving what sounded like instructions for tomorrow's luncheon. From the sound of his instructions, it appeared to be a very grand affair.

"Let's hope Emmett Merriman is home," Barnes muttered as they waited for Farley to finish.

"Yes, you're right, I do want to speak with him today," Witherspoon agreed.

"Thank you, Mrs. Leigh," Farley said as the cook left. He waved the two policemen into his office.

They went inside and took the seats in front of his desk while Farley took his own chair. "Now, Inspector, before we take a look at whatever you've come up with, I do want you to understand that Mrs. Merchant has only been with us six months and Letty and Emma, well, they're simply young women and they are easily distracted."

"Are you saying they won't know who is who amongst your members?" Barnes asked.

"I'm not saying that at all," Farley sighed. "I'm just saying you mustn't accept everything you've been told as the Gospel. People make mistakes. Now, what results have you come up with?"

The constable put the two pages down in front of Farley.

"The timelines have led us to two actual lists," the inspector explained. "The list on your right are those names who were not in the common room during the pertinent time period, and the second one is a list of names of people who were moving about, but who couldn't be confirmed to be at any particular table so their whereabouts is still unknown."

Farley picked up the list from his right and read it carefully. "You've six names here. Emmett Merriman, Mrs. Alice McElhaney, Miss Linwood, Steven Marston, Hannah Lonsdale, and Aaron Maypole."

"Can you confirm all of these people were acquainted with the victim?" Witherspoon asked.

Farley gave a negative shake of his head. "Not all of them, Inspector. I don't see that Aaron Maypole has anything to do with the late Jeremy Marks. Mr. Maypole only joined our club just after Christmas. Marks wasn't even a member then."

"He's not a member now," Barnes countered. "I mean, he was here as a guest of Miss Lonsdale."

The director said nothing for a moment, but both policemen noticed a red flush creeping up the man's broad face.

"Mr. Farley, can you confirm that Mr. Marks isn't a member here?" the constable pressed. "You made it quite clear during our initial interview that he was not."

"Look, I didn't mean to lie to you," Farley blurted out. "But the truth is, his membership was reinstated last month at Miss Lonsdale's insistence."

"Why didn't you tell us that?" Witherspoon asked.

"Because the membership committee wanted it to be kept a secret until after Mr. Marks and Miss Lonsdale were married. But, of course, that's not going to happen so I'm telling you the truth now."

"You should have told us immediately, sir," the inspector chided him. "We're not club members who might object to the man's presence." He didn't add that once someone lied to the police, the police tended to take a closer look at him or her.

"I realize that, Inspector, but I didn't really know what to do so I simply kept quiet." He broke off and cleared his throat. "But let's get on with this matter. As I said, I can't confirm that Mr. Maypole even knew Marks."

"Who on this list is the best archer?" the constable asked.

"Alice McElhaney," Farley muttered. "Oh dear, I mean, she's a good archer, but then again so are all the rest of them."

"And the other list, what can you tell us about them?" Witherspoon pressed.

Farley put the first list down and grabbed the second one. "This one has more names on it."

"There's twelve people that can't be accounted for," Barnes said.

"Yes, yes, the ones who were moving about. Frankly, I'm surprised this list is so small. When I stuck my head into the common room, I noticed far more people on their feet and going from table to table."

"True, but during the time Marks was killed, a number of people had sat down to have tea or champagne." The constable pointed to the list in front of Farley. "Do you know if any of those people had a motive for murdering Marks?"

The director studied the names. "I've no idea, Constable. I'm not even certain that most of these people knew Marks. Half of them are simply relatives and friends of the competitors. I can ask about if that would be helpful."

"No, that's alright. We'll interview them anyway." The inspector rose to his feet. "If there's nothing else you can add, we'll be on our way." He glanced at the clock on the director's desk. "We should have enough time to interview Mr. Merriman, but you'll need to give us his address."

Farley yanked open one of the lower draws on his desk and drew out a huge green ledger. Opening it, he went right to a page bookmarked with a thick red ribbon. "Here it is. Mr. Merriman lives at Number Three Ladbroke Crescent."

Barnes wrote down the address, and the two policemen got up to leave and headed for the door.

Witherspoon stopped and turned back to the director. "We'll also want to talk to your staff again, but we've decided to do that after we interview everyone."

"Must you do that, sir? It's very disruptive and tomorrow is our annual luncheon. We're going to be very busy."

"I'm afraid it's necessary. People often forget pertinent details, and after speaking with everyone on the two lists, we may have additional information that might spur someone's memory."

Inspector Nivens closed the file on his desk and relaxed his shoulders against the back of the chair. He let out a sigh and then looked at the stack of cases he'd already read, some of them more than once. He'd been at it since coming in today, going through Witherspoon's cases one by one. But after studying the first twenty murders, he'd realized that he wasn't going to learn much of anything. Oh, he could read between the lines of the reports, but that wouldn't do him any good at all. A turn of a phrase or a constable's comments that clearly showed Witherspoon had help on his homicide cases would not be so obvious to the powers that be. Those people gloried in that charlatan's light, from Chief Superintendent Barrows all the way up to the men running the Home Office. They all loved the publicity that wretched Witherspoon brought with every case he closed. They would never see what he saw in the man's reports. All they would see was a murderer caught, justice served, and the government looking good in the eyes of the public.

Nivens straightened up, focusing his attention on the far wall as he tried to think. Surely there had to be some way to prove the man wasn't what he appeared to be; someone with Witherspoon's limited intellectual capabilities couldn't have solved all those crimes. It simply wasn't possible.

For God's sake, Witherspoon wasn't even particularly well educated, and until he'd inherited a house and a fortune, he was in charge of this place, the records room. Ye gods, it was where one was sent to be punished or shoved to the side because one hadn't done anything genuinely useful in one's career. Yet Witherspoon had gone from here to solving more murders than anyone in the history of the Metropolitan Police.

He looked at the stack of files left to be read and wondered if they would tell him anything he didn't already know. He doubted it. The one thing he had understood by reading the first half of the files was that Witherspoon's ability to solve murders coincided directly with his hiring of Mrs. Hepzibah Jeffries.

But that was also something the powers that be wouldn't care about; even if he could prove that it was that interfering housekeeper and her little band of helpers who solved the murders, Witherspoon would still get the credit.

No, he wasn't going to let that happen. Not now, not this time. He'd worked too hard to get where he was, kowtowed to too many bureaucrats, and put up with enough humiliation to last a lifetime to stop now. He was going to get Inspector Gerald Witherspoon no matter what it cost him.

But how? That was the question.

Nivens leaned his elbows on his desk and rested his chin on his closed fist. Think, man, think, he told himself. He sat there for a long time as one idea after another flew through his mind. He thought back to his most successful moments as a policeman, the best of which was him actually getting back on the force. Of course, getting his position back had involved a huge number of resources, mainly his dear mama and her influence with the Home Secretary. That move had also involved a bit of blackmail; he smiled cynically at the thought that he'd had to pressure a senior officer in order to get this job in the records room. But it had worked. So what if it was politely disguised blackmail? It had gotten him what he wanted, and right now he wanted Witherspoon destroyed.

Maybe it could work again. But to what end? The files hadn't told him anything he didn't already know. So even if he used his network of informants to find out who on the force might have secrets they'd not want spread about, how could that help him ruin that popinjay Witherspoon?

Then it hit him. The only way to bring that fool down, to show the world and the powerful men at the top of the Metropolitan Police Force that Witherspoon wasn't worth their admiration, was to solve his latest case before he did.

Good gracious, the answer was right under his nose all along. Witherspoon had gone from the records rooms to being the darling of the force after solving those Horrible Kensington High Street Murders. He'd stuck his nose into another inspector's case and become the most admired man on the force. Well, not precisely right away; it had taken several cases before the press and everyone else had noticed Witherspoon's accomplishments. But that's how his climb to the top had started. The saintly Inspector Gerald Witherspoon had moved onto another inspector's patch!

If that moron Witherspoon could do such a thing, Nivens knew he could do it as well.

The two policemen walked out of Farley's office, but before they could reach the front door, they were waylaid by Miss Linwood.

"Yoo-hoo, Inspector Witherspoon," she called as she hurried toward them. She was dressed in a white blouse with huge puffy sleeves, a pink cummerbund around her ample waist, and a gray skirt. "I do hope you can spare just a moment. One of those nice young constables said you wanted to speak to me. Is that true?"

Emma, the serving girl, stepped out as well, carrying a stack of serviettes. She darted around Miss Linwood and walked toward the storeroom.

Barnes ducked his head to hide a smile. He'd seen the embarrassment on the inspector's face yesterday as Miss Linwood had gushed about his last case. It wasn't the first time

he'd seen an older woman indulging in a bit of "hero wor-
ship." It happened to policemen occasionally. But he knew it
made Witherspoon very uncomfortable.

"It's true, Miss Linwood"—Barnes gave her a polite
smile—"but just at the moment we're in a bit of a rush. Will
you be here tomorrow for the luncheon?"

"Oh, yes, indeed I will, but I can't imagine why you need
to speak to me? Unfortunately, I didn't even know Mr.
Marks." She kept her eyes on the inspector as she spoke.
"But I'm quite happy to answer your questions. What time
shall I make myself available tomorrow? The luncheon is at
one o'clock but Mrs. Storch and I should be here well before
that. She does like to have time to visit with her friends." She
giggled and clasped her hands together. "I must say, I'm
quite looking forward to it."

From farther down the corridor came the sound of keys
jangling. Witherspoon couldn't quite bring himself to look
at Miss Linwood; the way she was looking at him made him
feel so awkward. He wasn't certain, but he thought she
might be flirting with him. He turned his head and saw
Emma stepping into the storage room.

"We're looking forward to the interview as well." Barnes
turned and headed for the front door. Witherspoon did the
same.

But she followed after them. "Should we set a time, then?
I understand you're both very busy, so perhaps a specific
time will be useful for you?"

"That won't be necessary," the inspector called over his
shoulder. "As you didn't know the man, I'm sure it will only
take a few moments of your time tomorrow. We'll speak to

you then, Miss Linwood. We appreciate your willingness to cooperate."

They'd reached the door, Barnes grabbed the handle, shoved it open, and the two of them dashed outside.

But she caught the door as it closed.

"No appreciation is needed, Inspector." She smiled happily. "Helping you will be one of the greatest honors of my life."

CHAPTER 6

Emmett Merriman lived in a well-maintained home just around the corner from Smythe and Betsy's home. The Merriman house was one of the few that hadn't been broken up into expensive flats. It was a four-story redbrick house with a freshly painted blue front door, gleaming brass coach lamps on each side of the doorframe, and a small but lovely front garden behind a black wrought-iron railing.

Barnes banged the heavy knocker against the wood. A few moments later, a young housemaid opened the door. When she saw the two policemen standing on the stoop, she stared at them for a few moments in stunned surprise. "Oh my goodness, you're the police."

"Yes, miss, we are," Barnes said, "and we'd like to speak with Mr. Merriman if he's here."

"Mr. Merriman," she repeated. "Which one?"

"Carraway, who is at the door?" a man's voice boomed.

"It's the police, sir. They're here to see Mr. Merriman but they've not told me which one it is they need."

"It's Mr. Emmett Merriman," Barnes said quickly.

"Why do they want to speak to him?" There was a thumping sound mixed with footsteps, and a moment later, an elderly, gray-haired man appeared. He was bent forward, resting his thin frame on a cane. A set of tortoiseshell spectacles perched at the top of a long nose and he was dressed quite fashionably in a striped gray vest over a high-collared white shirt with black tie and matching striped gray trousers. He stopped just outside the foyer and stared at the two policemen.

"Mr. Merriman is a witness to a crime," Witherspoon explained. "We need to ask him some questions."

"Should I go get him, sir?" the housemaid asked.

"Yes," Barnes blurted out. "That would be very helpful." The girl started to move.

"Wait a moment," the old gentleman snapped. "Police constables don't give orders in this house."

"We're not trying to give anyone orders," the inspector said softly. "But we do need to speak with Mr. Merriman."

"I'm Mr. Merriman," he replied. "And this is my home."

"Of course this is your home, Papa, and it always will be," Emmett Merriman said as he walked up behind the man.

"It's also my house." The old man turned on his son and banged his cane against the floor. "You keep telling me it's my home, but I say it's my house."

Barnes had had enough. They had too much to do today to waste any more time. He looked at the elder Mr. Merriman. "If you object to Mr. Merriman speaking with us here, he can always accompany us to the station."

"Yes, Papa, that might be better," Merriman agreed. "You mustn't get upset. Remember what the doctor said about your heart."

"That man's a quack. There's nothing wrong with me."

"Papa, you know that Dr. Mainwaring is a superb physician. He's told you time and time again you mustn't be subjected to nervous strain."

"Don't be absurd, Emmett. Allowing two policemen to ask you questions won't cause me any strain whatsoever."

"You're not the only one I'm concerned about." Merriman crossed his arms over his chest. "I don't want to upset Sarah. You know what the doctor said."

"Sarah's upstairs asleep," he protested.

"But she could wake up any moment and I'll not have her distressed by this matter." Merriman uncrossed his arms and stepped around his father. He started toward the coat tree. "It will be better all the way around if I accompany them to the police station. I've always wanted to see what one looked like inside."

"Absolutely not." The old man thumped his cane on the floor with such force, the blue-and-white china umbrella stand next to the door rocked dangerously. "I'll not have the neighbors see you leaving this house in the company of a police constable." He pointed an accusing finger at Barnes. "Your dear mama would be rolling over in her grave at such a spectacle. We'll go into the drawing room and these policemen can ask their questions and be on their way."

Barnes glanced at Witherspoon. He could see the inspector was as surprised by this turn of events as he was. Rarely did anyone from Emmett Merriman's social class volunteer to answer questions in a police station. For a brief second he wondered why, before the obvious reason smacked him in the face. "Excuse me, Mr. Merriman"—the constable directed his attention to the elderly man—"but police interviews are confidential, so we'll need to speak to Mr. Emmett Merriman privately."

"That's correct," Witherspoon interjected, though strictly speaking, there were times when they interviewed witnesses in the presence of others. But the inspector had realized the same thing as the constable. Emmett Merriman didn't want his father listening to their questions or his answers.

"That's ridiculous, my son has nothing to do with that man's death." The elder Mr. Merriman slammed his cane against the floor again. "Why shouldn't I be allowed to be there when you speak to him?"

The housemaid, who'd moved back to the hallway so she could listen, jerked in surprise, noticed Barnes looking her way, and then scurried off.

"Mr. Merriman, taking witness statements is a matter of some importance." Witherspoon racked his brain to come up with a reasonable reply. "Witnesses need to concentrate and we don't like them distracted by others when we're trying to solve a murder."

"It's also a matter of police procedure," Barnes added. "It's important when the case comes to trial that every officer and constable has adhered to the rules."

"You think this case will ever be solved?" The elder Mr. Merriman's expression said that he didn't think it would, but the bluster had gone out of his voice.

"We always solve our cases," Barnes declared. "This one will be no different. Now, it you'll excuse us, Mr. Merriman, we'd like to get to our interview, either here or at the station."

* * *

Constable Griffiths knew that the inspector was counting on him. This wasn't the first time he'd been left in charge, but truth to tell, this was by far the biggest undertaking he'd ever supervised. He was thrilled and a bit intimidated by the task but determined to make his inspector proud. He glanced at the list in his hand. Of the six names, he'd already spoken to four of them, and all four had produced witnesses to where they were during the time period that Marks was murdered. There were only two left, Miss Linwood and Mr. Steven Marston. He'd given Constable Parker the task of tracking down and taking statements from the people on the other list, the ones who'd been milling about but might have still been in the common room.

He glanced up as the common room door opened and Mrs. Merchant stepped inside. She carried a tray of serviette-wrapped silverware. The archery competitions were over and done with yet there were still lots of people here. He was hoping Mrs. Merchant could point out both Miss Linwood and Mr. Marston for him. Griffiths hurried over to her.

"Excuse me, Mrs. Merchant, but is Miss Linwood or Mr. Marston here in the common room?" Constable Griffiths asked.

Mrs. Merchant put the tray on the table, straightened, and turned around to survey the room. "She's just come in, Constable. She's over there by the window." She pointed to the woman sitting alone at a table. "But I don't see Mr. Marston."

"Thank you, ma'am, please let me know if Mr. Marston appears," he said as he moved toward the window table.

Miss Linwood glanced up as he approached. "Did you wish to speak to me?"

"Yes, ma'am," Griffiths replied. He pulled out the chair across from her and sat down. "I need to ask you a few questions. We're trying to verify where everyone was when Mr. Marks was killed."

"That can't be right, Constable. I've just had a word with Inspector Witherspoon and he specifically said he wished to interview me tomorrow," she explained.

Griffiths stared at her in surprise. "He said that he wanted to interview you?"

"Yes." She laughed. "I'm actually very flattered. After all, he is a great detective and I've followed his career ever since I came back to London."

The constable wasn't sure what to do. He'd no wish to offend his senior officer, but the inspector had pointedly told him to try and speak to everyone on his list who hadn't been in the common room when Marks was killed. "I think he'd like me to do the preliminary interview, and then if needed, he'll have a chat with you." He took out his notebook and pencil. "Now, you were sitting at a table with Mrs. Storch, Mr. and Mrs. Belton, and Mr. Merriman, is that correct?"

Her smile had gone. "But he said he wanted to speak to me," she insisted.

"And he will if he has more questions," Griffiths replied. "When did you speak to Inspector Witherspoon?"

"Just a few minutes ago, as he and the other constable were leaving." Her lower lip protruded slightly, making her look like a sulky child. "It is very exciting for me, you understand, the thought of being interviewed by the great detective himself."

"And I'm certain he'll want to speak to you himself," he assured her. He realized the lady was a bit enamored of the inspector. He'd seen it a time or two before. "But why don't you let me ask you a few basic questions?"

She thought for a moment. "Alright, that might be best. That way I'll not waste the inspector's time when he does interview me."

"That's right, Miss Linwood. Now, I understand you're Mrs. Storch's companion?" Griffiths wanted to make sure he had every detail right. Asking all the questions, even the ones they assumed they already knew the answer to, was important.

"Yes, I've worked for Mrs. Storch for over a year now."

"Do you always accompany Mrs. Storch when she comes here?"

"Absolutely, Constable." She smiled and her plain face was suddenly transformed. She looked lovely. "I'm a paid companion. That means I generally accompany Mrs. Storch everywhere except to specific social engagements such as a dinner party or ball."

"Was Mrs. Storch acquainted with Mr. Marks?" Griffiths asked. He had already asked Mrs. Storch that question when he'd taken her statement, but it was always good to double-check.

"I don't think Mrs. Storch knew him well at all," she replied. "He was certainly not a part of her social circle, nor did I ever see her interact with him while here at the club. To be truthful, I've never heard her comment about the man one way or another."

Griffiths nodded. That was exactly what Mrs. Storch herself had said in her statement. "Were you acquainted with Mr. Marks?"

She shook her head. "No, I never met the man. By that I

mean we were never formally introduced. I knew who he was, of course. Mrs. Storch is a very dedicated archer and we're here several afternoons each week so she can practice. You end up knowing most of the other members, at least by sight."

"I see," Griffiths replied. "Miss Linwood, according to others at your table, during the time that Mr. Marks was killed, you left. Where did you go?" Mrs. Storch had stated she'd sent her companion off on an errand and had explained the reason for it. But he was determined to follow Inspector Witherspoon's procedures about taking statements. Get your facts directly from the witness.

"I went down to the kitchen to get the picnic hamper Mrs. Storch had brought," she replied. "When it became apparent the storm wasn't going to let up, Mrs. Storch decided to take the food she'd brought back to her home. The club staff were serving tea, champagne, and sandwiches, so there was no need to waste additional provisions."

"So you carried the hamper out to her carriage?"

"Oh no, it's a huge wicker contraption, and even though I am quite a strong woman, I didn't want to carry that heavy thing. I asked a young kitchen lad to carry it for me."

"He accompanied you from the kitchen to Mrs. Storch's carriage?" Griffiths asked.

"No, just as we got outside, it started to rain again, so I pointed out the Storch carriage and told the lad to put the hamper inside on the floor."

"At that point did you come back inside?"

"No, I ducked under one of the trees out in front so I could shelter from the wet and keep an eye on the boy. I wanted to make certain he put the hamper inside the carriage. It had a number of very expensive food items inside."

"You were afraid the lad would take something?"

"Not specifically, but I was in charge of getting everything back to Mrs. Storch's home and I wanted to be sure the hamper was safely inside her carriage. You do understand, don't you? It was my responsibility."

"I see," Griffiths said. He knew they'd be speaking to the staff at some point, so he made a mental note to be sure to ask the "kitchen lad" to verify Miss Linwood's statement. Still, it wouldn't hurt to ask a bit more right now. "Did anyone see you outside under the tree?"

"I doubt it. It was raining and most people had found some sort of shelter. Even the coachmen weren't to be seen."

"Excuse me, Constable Griffiths," Mrs. Merchant said from behind him. He turned to see her pointing at an elderly gentleman who'd just come into the room. "But that's Mr. Marston."

"Thank you, Mrs. Merchant."

Just at that moment, the old gent happened to glance their way. He saw Mrs. Merchant pointing at him just as Constable Griffiths shoved his chair back and stood up. Mr. Marston turned suddenly and went out the door he'd just entered.

"Thank you, Miss Linwood," Griffiths said quickly. He hurried after the disappearing gentleman. He dodged around an elderly matron, almost slipped on a patch of spilled tea, and made it through the common room door just as Marston was racing out the front entrance.

"Excuse me, sir," Griffiths yelled. "But I'd like to have a word with you."

The constable was sure the man had heard him, because if possible, the old man moved even faster. He leapt down the front stairs and ran toward a hansom cab that was dropping a fare off in front of the club.

Griffiths broke into a run, dashing across the corridor, past the counter, where a rather surprised clerk was taking notes in a ledger, and out the front door. But Mr. Marston was quick; he already had the hansom cab door open.

"Mr. Marston," Griffiths yelled at the top of his lungs. "Please, sir, stop. I need to speak with you."

The cab door closed, and a second later, the horses pulled away from the curb.

Griffiths stopped to catch his breath. What on earth was this about? Why did the old fellow run? He knew the man heard him. Yet he'd taken off like a thief getting caught with his hand in the till.

He sucked a deep breath into his lungs and went back into the club. The clerk at the counter stared at him curiously. Griffiths said, "I take it you work here?"

"I do. I'm Mr. Farley's assistant."

"Can you get me Steven Marston's address, please. I need to speak to him as soon as possible."

Emmett Merriman led them through a set of double doors into a drawing room.

Witherspoon took a quick look around the room while Barnes got his notebook and pencil out of his coat pocket. He was very surprised. From the outside, the Merriman house appeared to be much like his own home, comfortable, prosperous, but certainly not luxurious.

Yet this room was surprisingly ornate; the walls were

painted a pale cream, turquoise drapes topped with elaborate valances framed the three long windows looking out over the garden, and there were at least three marble-topped side tables as well as two carved armoires. A silver-and-blue-striped settee and love seat were in front of the white marble fireplace, and the oak herringbone-patterned floor was covered with an Oriental cream-and-turquoise rug. Above the fireplace was a portrait of a beautiful black-haired woman.

Merriman noticed Witherspoon staring at the painting. "That's my wife. It was done a few months ago."

"It's a lovely painting, Mr. Merriman," Witherspoon replied.

"Thank you, Inspector. That's kind of you to say so. I think she's the loveliest woman in the world, but then I'm prejudiced as I'm her husband. Please, sit down." He gestured toward the settee before taking his own seat in the middle of the love seat.

"Also, I would like to apologize for my father," he continued. "He's from the generation that doesn't understand the world has changed and being seen in the company of a uniformed police officer doesn't end one's social life."

"No apology is necessary, Mr. Merriman. I'm sure Mr. Merriman thought he was protecting your interests. I imagine it's quite frightening for someone when the police show up at their house," Witherspoon said diplomatically, "and he is an elderly gentleman."

"Papa gets quite muddled these days. Despite what he said, this is my house, not his"—he waved his hand around the room—"but when he moved in with Sarah and me, we allowed him to bring a lot of his furniture so he'd feel more at home. I'm not sure that was wise. I think him seeing his things confuses him all the more." He broke off and gave them a strained smile. "Now, why don't you tell me why you're here."

"Mr. Merriman, when we spoke to you on the day Mr. Marks was murdered, you said you were in the common room the entire time."

He inclined his head. "I was."

"But we've now found out that during the most important time period, the ten minutes when we know Mr. Marks was being shot with those arrows, no one can recall seeing you in the common room." Witherspoon watched him carefully. The inspector would be the first to admit he wasn't the best at reading faces, but nonetheless, he felt it was his duty to try. Sometimes it bothered him when the other detectives claimed they could perceive guilt in a suspect by watching how they reacted to questions.

But Merriman's expression didn't change. He merely shrugged. "I can't help what other people have told you, Inspector, but I was in the common room when Jeremy Marks was murdered. I was sitting at the table with Mrs. Storch and Mr. and Mrs. Belton, all of whom I believe have vouched for my presence."

"Mr. and Mrs. Belton were quite drunk, and Mrs. Storch has already told us she was mistaken and that you did leave the table for a period of time," Barnes charged. "The period of time coincides with the time Marks was shot." That wasn't quite true, they hadn't actually spoken to Mrs. Storch as yet, but the constable had decided that Letty Maddox, the serving girl, was a reliable witness.

"We've also been told you're an excellent archer," Witherspoon added. "Which reminds me, sir, why aren't you at the archery club today?"

"I've already competed, Inspector, and I wasn't at the club because my wife isn't feeling well and I didn't want to leave her."

"I'm sorry to hear about your wife, sir. I do hope it's nothing serious."

Merriman smiled. "We're expecting a child. We've been married fifteen years and it's our first. It's a bit of a late-in-life surprise so we're being very careful."

"Congratulations, sir." Witherspoon was genuinely pleased for the man.

Barnes gave him a brief smile and then asked, "Mr. Merriman, where did you go during the minutes you were away from the table?"

Merriman stared at them for a long moment, then he slumped back against the cushion. "Look, this is awkward, but I really can't tell you that. But I assure you, I didn't kill Jeremy Marks."

"Then why won't you tell us where you were?" Barnes persisted.

"Because it involves . . ." He broke off as the door opened and a woman stepped inside.

Both policemen stared at her. The inspector's first thought was that she was as lovely in real life as she was in the portrait. There were a few strands of gray in her black hair and faint lines around her dark brown eyes, but she was blessed with the kind of bone structure that guaranteed she'd be turning heads for many years to come. She was dressed in a pale yellow day dress that couldn't quite hide the bump in her midsection.

"Oh dear, Papa was telling the truth," Sarah Merriman exclaimed. "Do forgive me, gentlemen, I didn't mean to interrupt, but when Papa said the police were here, I was sure he was mistaken." She looked at her husband. "Emmett, darling, I thought you'd already spoken with them."

"I have, dearest. Don't worry about anything." Merriman and both policemen rose to their feet. "This is Inspector Witherspoon and Constable Barnes. They stopped by because there were a couple of matters to clear up."

An expression of alarm crossed her face. "What matters? Just because that horrid man got killed, they can't possibly think you had anything to do with it." She looked at the two policemen. "My husband is a good man. He'd never, ever hurt someone, even someone as awful as Jeremy Marks."

"No, no, dearest, it's nothing like that. They only wanted to ask a few questions about who I'd seen coming and going from the common room." Merriman rushed toward her and grabbed her hands. "You know what the doctor said; you're not to be upset." He looked at Witherspoon, his expression so pained, the inspector made a fast, heartfelt decision.

"Please don't be alarmed, Mrs. Merriman. We're only here because your husband is a good witness. We've been relying on his excellent memory to find out who was missing from the club common room when Mr. Marks was killed. We've no wish to disturb you further so we'll speak to your husband tomorrow." He glanced at Merriman. "Presumably, you'll be in your office, sir?"

"I will, Inspector, and I'll tell my assistant to send you in the moment you arrive."

Mrs. Merriman visibly relaxed. "Thank you, Inspector, that eases my mind."

"Let me walk the gentlemen to the door, dearest." He released her hands. "You go and see if Papa is alright."

Mrs. Merriman nodded politely at the two policemen and left. As soon as the door closed behind her, Merriman said, "Thank you, Inspector. This baby is so important to us, especially Sarah. I think she'd die if something untoward happened. Ever since she heard about Marks' murder, she's been distressed. She remembered how Marks tried to ruin our business years ago."

"We've no wish to cause your wife any further upset, Mr. Merriman, so we'll assume you'll keep your word and be at your office tomorrow?" Witherspoon warned.

"I will be there, and I promise, I'll tell you everything then."

They were silent until they were out of the Merriman house and heading toward the cab stand on the corner.

"What do you think, sir? Should we have a couple of the patrol constables keep an eye on the house?" Barnes suggested. "You know, just in case."

"I was going to propose that myself," Witherspoon said as the constable flagged down a hansom that had just turned the corner. "I doubt Mr. Merriman will try to leave London, but it wouldn't be the first time a suspect attempted to disappear in the night."

Mrs. Jeffries put the feather duster down on a side table and stared at the traffic outside the drawing room window. She'd spent the day doing Phyllis's chores so the girl could be out and about learning something about this case. She liked doing mindless, repetitive tasks when they had a murder; it freed her mind to concentrate on everything they knew thus far.

Jeremy Marks wasn't well liked. But rage wasn't the only reason people were done away with. Sometimes they were in the wrong place at the wrong time, or they'd discovered something about someone that couldn't be allowed to see the light of day. So perhaps the fact that Marks had a long and rich history of dreadful behavior to both his romantic liaisons and his business partners had nothing to do with his being murdered. Perhaps there was another reason. But what could it be? Usually, once she'd figured out the "why" of a murder, it would often point to the "who."

But this murder felt different. She couldn't put her finger on why it felt different, it simply did, and over the years, she had learned to trust her own "inner voice." Something was very odd, and until she could determine what that might be, she had a feeling that this might be the one they and their inspector wouldn't solve.

Mrs. Jeffries caught herself. No, she wouldn't give in to that sort of defeatist thinking. Not this early in the investigation. She grabbed the feather duster from the side table and headed down to the kitchen. It was time to get ready for their afternoon meeting.

Perhaps if they were very lucky, someone had found out something useful about the case.

Hatchet finished his first circle of the common room and leaned against the wall. He'd done his best to pick up a few bits and pieces without having to arouse suspicions here by asking a lot of questions. But despite hovering by tables filled with chattering ladies, eavesdropping on his fellow competitors as they waited to take their turns in the practice barn, and straining to overhear anything the serving staff might be saying to one another, the only thing he'd heard was the same gossip they already knew. Luty wasn't going to be pleased. She had given him strict instructions to pick up as much information and/or new gossip as possible. "If I'm stuck suckin' up to a bunch of borin' old bankers, Hatchet, then you make sure you git us an earful," she had ordered as she'd stepped into her carriage this morning.

He folded his arms over his chest and surveyed the room. Jeremy Marks' murder hadn't kept anyone away. There were only two groups competing today yet the common room was almost full. Small groups clustered near the windows, there were people at every table, and the staff was busy refilling teapots and champagne glasses.

He saw Constable Griffiths at a table with Miss Linwood, Mrs. Storch's companion. She was one of the few who had definitely been outside when Marks was killed. Just then the common room door opened and a slender, white-haired woman stepped into the room.

She smiled broadly when she saw him. "Goodness, Mr. Hatchet, you're just the person I wanted to see. Congratulations on your score. You've improved so much since you first came here."

Irene Thomas was an attractive widow near his own age. He'd seen her watching him as he took his turn and was flattered. It had been a long time since a woman had paid any attention to him and it felt good. But he wouldn't let it go to his head; she was a very nice lady and she was probably just being kind. "Thank you, Mrs. Thomas, even I was surprised by how well I did today. I had several very lucky shots."

"Nonsense"—she leaned closer and tapped him on the arm—"luck had nothing to do with it. You really should consider competing in the regional as well as the national competition."

"Oh, I don't know about that, Mrs. Thomas. I'm only here because my doctor insisted I get regular exercise. Perhaps next year, when I've had more practice." He tried to think of a way to bring the conversation around to Jeremy Marks.

"Don't be so modest, Mr. Hatchet. Your skill level is as good as anyone else in your division."

"That's most kind of you, Mrs. Thomas. I must say, considering what happened, I was a bit apprehensive about today's competition. It's a very odd situation. I mean with Mr. Marks being killed, I thought it might negatively affect the competition."

"Goodness, why?" She looked genuinely confused.

He was tempted to ask her if murder was a regular occurrence at the West London Archery Club but realized she might not appreciate his attempt at humor. "Well, the gentleman lost his life."

"He was no gentleman," she interrupted, "and it isn't as if anyone here actually liked Jeremy Marks. Frankly, most of us were relieved when he was forced to resign his membership. But then he and Hannah Lonsdale became engaged and he was back, much like an obnoxious relative that you can't be rude to but you wish would simply disappear from your life."

"We all know what that's like." Hatchet laughed. "Luckily, I've outlived most of my obnoxious relatives." He saw Mrs. Merchant moving purposefully toward the table where Constable Griffiths and Miss Linwood sat.

"You're very lucky, Mr. Hatchet. One is never supposed

to say it, but mine are alive and well." She grinned. "That's the main reason I take archery so seriously. It gives me a wonderful excuse not to be at home 'receiving.'"

"Very clever of you, Mrs. Thomas." He noticed Mrs. Merchant pointing toward them. He was surprised but then realized she wasn't gesturing at them, but at an elderly man walking quickly in their direction. "Do you happen to know who that gentleman is?" he asked.

She looked over her shoulder as the man reached the door, grabbed the handle, and yanked it open. "That's Mr. Marston. I wonder where he's going in such a hurry."

Marston disappeared into the corridor just as Constable Griffiths stood up and raced after the fellow.

"Goodness, that looks ominous," Mrs. Thomas murmured.

"I wonder what's happening?" Hatchet edged toward the door; he wanted to see exactly what was going on here. He knew that Constable Griffiths wasn't the sort of policeman to charge off half-cocked, so there must be a reason he was chasing after Marston.

"I imagine the constable wants to speak to him," Mrs. Thomas replied as she trailed after Hatchet. "But I've no idea why. He's only recently joined the club and I don't think he even knew Marks."

By this time, Hatchet had reached the door, but instead of going out, he hesitated. He didn't want Griffiths to see he was following him. "He and Jeremy Marks weren't acquainted?"

She shrugged. "I don't think so. I never saw them together."

"It does make one curious," Hatchet said. "I wonder why the constable appeared to be pursuing the gentleman?"

"He must have had a reason. But I can't imagine what it could be. Then again, Marston's a curious fellow."

"In what way?" Hatchet threw caution to the winds. It was apparent to him that Mrs. Thomas loved a good gossip.

"Mr. Marston is a very nice man but he tends to keep to himself. Also, he's an excellent archer, but he seems to have no interest in competing. Dorian Fordham told me that when Marston first joined the club, everyone in the Men's First Division had heart palpitations when they saw how good he was at hitting the target. Bull's-eyes every time. But much to the delight of the Men's First Division, he didn't enter this year's competition."

"You mean the one we're playing now?" Hatchet's gaze was caught by Miss Linwood as she pushed her chair back from the table and stood up. Ye gods, she was as tall as he was.

"Yes."

"Are you acquainted with Miss Linwood?"

She looked surprised by the sudden change in conversation. "I've met her, of course. Mrs. Storch and I have known one another for years and Miss Linwood is her companion. She seems a very pleasant person, but I can't say I know her well." She drew back and gave him a long, assessing stare. "Why do you ask?"

"Oh, I was just curious." Hatchet smiled self-consciously. He didn't want his questions to arouse suspicion. A good gossip was one thing, but too many pointed inquiries could lead to trouble.

"Really?" She stared at him, her expression skeptical. "I don't suppose your questions have anything to do with the fact that Dorian Fordham told me he overheard you and your . . . uh . . . Mrs. Crookshank."

"My employer," he interjected. "Yes, as Miss Linwood is Mrs. Storch's employee, I work for Mrs. Crookshank."

She nodded nonchalantly. "Well, Dorian overheard you speaking to the policeman in charge of the murder," she said. "Apparently, you and Mrs. Crookshank know him quite well. I wondered if you were doing a bit of investigating on his behalf."

Hatchet realized this woman was smart and trying to deny it would be pointless. "Alright, I'll admit that I am keeping my ears open and I'm hoping to pass along any information that might be useful."

She gave a full-throated laugh. "In that case, you can pass this along to Inspector Witherington . . ."

"Witherspoon," he corrected, "but do go on, I didn't mean to interrupt."

"Perhaps you haven't heard this, but Hannah Lonsdale and Marks had a dreadful row just before he was killed."

"I've heard that as well."

"And Miss Lonsdale was supposed to have left the club right after she competed." Mrs. Thomas paused and took a deep breath. "But I'll wager you didn't know that she didn't leave. One of the kitchen girls claims they saw her standing on the far side of the practice room. She was watching Marks and laughing."

"Do you know which kitchen girl witnessed this?"

"I don't."

"It shouldn't be hard to find out who it was," he murmured.

"I wouldn't count on that," she said. "Those girls want to keep their positions. Causing problems for the club or the members can result in being unemployed without a reference."

When Constable Barnes and Inspector Witherspoon arrived back at the archery club, the competition was finished.

Witherspoon whipped off his bowler hat as they entered the common room. "The place has emptied out." He looked around, hoping to find Hatchet and have a quick word with him. But he was nowhere to be seen.

Constable Griffiths, who was at the table closest to the door, stacking the timeline pages, hurried over to them. "I'm glad you're back, sir. We've finished with most of the secondary interviews."

"Excellent. What have you found out?"

Griffiths yanked his notebook, a twin to the one Barnes carried, out of his pocket and flipped it open. "I spoke with Mr. Maypole and he said he didn't know Jeremy Marks. He was in the lavatory when Marks was murdered and we were able to confirm that he is telling the truth. Sally Emerson, one of the housemaids, was cleaning the corridor floor outside the lavatory because so much water and dirt had been tracked inside."

"What about Miss Linwood?" Barnes asked.

"Miss Linwood said she was under a tree when Marks was murdered and that she had the footman carry a picnic hamper to the Storch carriage," Griffiths reported. He told them what she'd told him. "But I haven't confirmed that she was really there. The footman—he's really just a lad, sir— verified he took the hamper out to the Storch carriage."

"Miss Linwood was under one of the trees out front because she wanted to keep the rain out." Barnes frowned. "That's surprising. Considering how much lightning was overhead, it sounds dangerous. I'm surprised anyone would do that."

"She said she didn't want to get wet, sir," Griffiths replied. "But something else happened, something really strange." He told them how he'd asked Mrs. Merchant to point out Steven Marston and how the man had made a run for it.

"Are you certain about that?" Barnes pressed. "You're sure he wasn't just a half-deaf old man who didn't realize you were trying to speak to him?"

"No, sir, I know he heard me. I called out to him two or three times, and every time I did, he ran faster." He broke off and took a deep breath. "I took it upon myself to get the man's address and I sent Constable Pritchett there to keep an eye on the place. I hope that was alright, sir. But his behavior was so suspicious, I didn't want to risk him making a run for it, sir." He looked at the inspector, his expression anxious.

"Good thinking, Constable. That's precisely what you should have done. Did you give Constable Pritchett instructions as to how long he was to stay?"

Griffiths nodded. "I told him to stay and keep watch until I had a chance to report to you."

"Where does the man live?" Barnes asked.

"Close to the station, sir, on Ladbroke Road. He's got the bottom floor flat at Number Twelve."

"Then let's have the lads at the station keep an eye on the place," Witherspoon said. "If they see any movement or someone leaving with luggage, raise the alarm."

"Yes, sir."

"What about Mrs. McElhaney? Were you able to confirm she was in the Ladies' Day Room when Marks was killed?" Witherspoon asked.

"No, sir, no one saw her go upstairs or into the room, but we've still to speak to the staff," Griffiths replied.

"We'll ask if any of them can confirm her movements," Barnes muttered. "What else?"

"Constable Parker has confirmed that nine of the twelve people who weren't at a table were in the building. Most of them were with friends or just milling about. We're still trying to track down the movements of the last three people on the second list," Griffiths continued. "But they're not here today. Shall we get started speaking to the staff?"

"No, it's getting late and I don't want to hold them up. We'll speak with them first thing tomorrow."

Betsy was the only one missing from their afternoon meeting. "I made her stay 'ome to get some rest," Smythe explained as he took his seat. "She's exhausted and the little one isn't 'elpin' much. She's runnin' poor Betsy off 'er feet."

"Oh dear, I'm so sorry to hear that. Let's hope she feels better tomorrow." Mrs. Jeffries poured a cup of tea and handed it to Smythe. "Did you have any success today?"

"Not really." He nodded his thanks and took a quick sip. "None of the hansom drivers had much to tell me, but one of the carriage blokes told me he'd seen a big fellow runnin' toward the carriage 'ouse on that abandoned property next to the archery club."

"What time did he see him?" Mrs. Goodge asked.

"Around the time of the murder," Smythe replied. "But

I'd not put too much stock in it. The driver said it was probably a tramp lookin' to get out of the wet. The man was 'oldin' an old blanket or somethin' over 'imself as he ran, and when I asked the driver if he saw the fellow carryin' a bow and arrow, he said no."

"I wonder why that property is still so neglected," Mrs. Jeffries murmured. "Surely whoever owns it could make a fortune developing the place."

"It ain't bein' developed 'cause there's a family squabble. The original family that owned it more or less died out twenty-five years ago and the house went to a distant cousin," Luty said. "He lived there for some years but didn't have the cash to keep the house or the grounds up. He died a few years back and it passed on to another set of cousins. They've been fightin' over it ever since." Luty shrugged. "And that's about the only new thing I learned today. I tell ya, the only bits and pieces I heard from them borin' old bankers was stuff we already knew! But tomorrow I'm goin' to see someone who might have somethin' useful to tell me." She glanced at Hatchet. "You probably found out plenty today, didn't ya? I can tell by that smirk you've been tryin' to hide."

"Nonsense, madam, smirking is both undignified and pointless. But you are correct. My efforts today were more fruitful than yours." He gave her a cheeky grin and looked at the others around the table. "If there's no objection, I can complete my report fairly quickly." He paused for a moment and then told them he'd had the same problem as Luty, mainly that despite his best efforts, the only things he'd heard when eavesdropping were facts or gossip they already knew. Then he told them about seeing Constable Griffiths speaking to Miss Linwood and, most important, how the constable had chased after a man named Steven Marston.

"Cor blimey," Wiggins exclaimed when Hatchet paused to take a breath, "I wonder if he's the old gent Janet Marshall mentioned?"

"What old gent?" Phyllis asked.

"It's what I 'eard today. Janet, she's one of the serving girls, told me there was two old dears 'avin' an argument about some old fellow at the club that one of 'em insisted was someone she'd known years earlier. Janet wasn't sure what the name was, she thought it was Stewart Miller, but that's close enough to Steven Marston that I think we need to look into this fellow."

"Was that all this 'Janet' had to tell you?" Phyllis demanded.

"Pretty much." Wiggins grinned. "But she did say that me givin' 'er a couple of shillin's would put her cousin's nose out of joint!"

"I'm sure Constable Griffiths will tell the inspector about this, but just in case, we'll be sure to mention Mr. Marston to Constable Barnes in the morning." Mrs. Jeffries looked at Hatchet. "Is that all?"

"Mrs. Thomas did say one other thing," Hatchet continued. "Apparently, Hannah Lonsdale didn't go home right after she'd ended her engagement to Marks. One of the serving girls was overheard saying she saw Miss Lonsdale on the far side of the practice barn when Marks was outside searching the grounds in front of the targets and she was laughing at him."

"Which means she might have been there when the murder was committed," Phyllis muttered. "Or perhaps she nipped into the practice barn, grabbed a bow, and shot him herself."

"That's very possible, but perhaps we should confirm that she was there before we jump to any conclusions," Mrs. Jeffries warned.

"That should be easy enough to find out," Wiggins countered. "All we got to do is ask her coachmen when he took 'er 'ome."

"That might or might not work," Phyllis said. "We don't know if Miss Lonsdale's servants will lie for her."

"This is a murder investigation," Mrs. Jeffries reminded them. "Even a devoted servant might not want to lie to protect their master or mistress."

"No, but they might lie to protect their job," Phyllis murmured softly. "But I agree, Mrs. Jeffries, there must be some way to confirm where she was when he was killed." She smiled ruefully and shook her head. "At least we've learned something useful today. I didn't find out a ruddy thing."

"Don't take it 'ard." Wiggins gave her a sympathetic smile. "You could put what little I found out in a thimble and still have room for your finger."

Ruth glanced at the carriage clock on the pine sideboard. "I found out a few interesting tidbits." She paused a moment and then told them everything she'd learned from Octavia. She was careful not to leave out anything, no matter how unimportant it might sound. They had learned long ago that it was often the small, inconsequential-seeming detail that pointed to the killer. When she'd finished, she picked up her teacup, took a sip, and sat back.

"I'll go next," Mrs. Goodge volunteered. She told them about her visit with Ida Leacock. Like Ruth, the cook took her time and ensured she didn't omit anything. "So it seems Jeremy Marks wasn't just a cad once, he was a cad twice," she finished.

"But only one of them paid the price for his behavior." Ruth looked disgusted. "Jeanette Givens wasn't with child and went on to have a decent marriage, but that poor housemaid was tossed into the street. That's dreadful."

"It is awful," Mrs. Jeffries agreed. "As Mrs. Goodge has said, both the incidents happened years ago. But as the saying goes, 'Sometimes vengeance is a dish best served cold.'"

CHAPTER 7

Mrs. Jeffries hurried up to her room, went inside, and crossed to her desk. She had just enough time to make a few notes before the inspector arrived home. It was a practice she'd started two years earlier when she'd realized her memory wasn't as sharp as it had once been.

Yanking out her chair, she sat down and opened the drawer. She took out a sheet of paper and grabbed the pen from the plain brass inkwell set. She began writing, taking her time and making certain she wrote every pertinent detail in simple sentences. She wrote for a good twenty minutes, and when she was done, she put the pen back and read her words. Satisfied, she smiled. Whether they knew it or not, they'd learned a number of things today, and once she added what the inspector and Constable Barnes might have to say, perhaps she'd soon have some idea about who murdered Jeremy Marks.

She put her notes away, taking care to place them under the delicate stationery box in her desk drawer. It wouldn't do to have anyone see what she'd written. Once the case was concluded, she'd burn everything. It was the best way she'd found to protect the inspector.

She wouldn't put it past that obnoxious Inspector Nivens to break into the house in search of proof for his ridiculous theory. She laughed as the thought came into her head. Nivens was right, of course. Inspector Witherspoon did have help solving his cases, but that wasn't any of Nivens' business. She was firmly convinced that, even without their assistance, their dear inspector would still have solved far more cases than that incompetent fool.

Still, it was important to take precautions. A shaft of guilt speared through her, but she fought it back. She hadn't wanted the others distracted, so when Constable Barnes told her the blackguard had used his mother's influence to get reinstated to the Metropolitan Police, she'd kept that information to herself. She'd asked the constable to stay silent on the matter as well.

Yet Nivens coming back to the force hadn't worried her until Barnes told her where Nivens was assigned. He had Witherspoon's old position; he was in charge of the records room. Mrs. Jeffries knew what that meant; she had no doubt that Nivens had connived to get the position. He was going to use Witherspoon's old cases against him or at least he'd try. If Nivens had enough influence to get back on the force, he also had the power to get assigned where he wanted. He'd chosen the records room. Nigel Nivens wasn't giving up.

Once she'd put her notes away, Mrs. Jeffries went downstairs. As she reached the foyer, she heard a hansom draw up outside. A few moments later, she heard the inspector's key in the front door and he stepped inside.

"Gracious, sir, I didn't expect you this early." She reached for the bowler hat he'd just taken off. "I thought with the case you'd be a bit late."

"Everyone at the archery club had scattered to the four winds so I couldn't continue taking statements. Mind you, it worked out nicely. Constable Barnes and I went to the station so that I could send in a preliminary report to Chief Superintendent Barrows."

"This soon, sir?" she asked. "It's only been two days since Mr. Marks was murdered."

"Barrows made it clear he wanted to be kept informed." Witherspoon shrugged. "I've no idea why. Additionally, it allowed us to assign some constables to keep watch on two places."

"Keep watch?" she repeated.

"I'll tell you all about it over a glass of sherry. Have we time before dinner?"

"Of course, sir."

Five minutes later he was ensconced in his favorite chair and she'd poured both of them a drink. "Now, sir, do tell me everything."

He took a sip of his sherry. "To begin with, I came up with a way to use my 'timeline,' so to speak." He told her exactly what he'd done and how it appeared to be working very well. "As a matter of fact, it was because of my 'timeline' sheets that we learned that one person who we thought was in the common room during the pertinent time actually wasn't there." He gave her all the details they'd heard from Letty Maddox.

"Goodness, sir, surely Emmett Merriman must have realized someone would have known he wasn't where he claimed he'd been when Marks was murdered."

"I suspect he was counting on the fact that there were so many people hanging about the room. Nonetheless, thanks to Miss Maddox, we went and had a word with him." He told her about the interview with Merriman, and as was his habit, he made sure to leave nothing out. "Of course, after both Constable Barnes and I realized Mrs. Merriman was in a very delicate condition, we left. We didn't want to upset the lady further. Which is the reason we're having the constables on patrol as well as several others keep an eye on the Merriman house. At the first sign that the man is trying to make a run for it, they'll raise the alarm."

"You said there were two places you wanted watched?"

"I'll get to that, Mrs. Jeffries." He took another drink. "I don't want to get ahead of myself. Oh dear, I think I already have. Before we interviewed Merriman, we had a word with Alice McElhaney." He told her everything he'd heard from her. "Mind you, when we asked her where she was when Marks was killed, she claimed she was upstairs in the Ladies' Day Room. We haven't been able to confirm that, but we'll be speaking to the club staff tomorrow, and hopefully, if she really was there, someone will have seen her going up the stairs or into the room."

"She must have really hated Marks to go to such lengths."

"She didn't even try to hide it and she was delighted she'd caused Hannah Lonsdale to call off their engagement." He shook his head. "I must say, Mrs. Jeffries, matters of the heart can be so very complex. I'm so very grateful to have someone as sensible and good in my life as my dear Ruth."

"I imagine Lady Cannonberry is equally happy that you're in her life, sir," Mrs. Jeffries said. "Exactly where in the building is the Ladies' Day Room? Does it overlook the archery range?" She wanted to make this point. Witherspoon had already mentioned so many of the principals in this case were excellent archers and that included both Miss Lonsdale and Mrs. McElhaney. Marks had a history of disreputable behavior, but most of his transgressions were in the past. Only Hannah Lonsdale and Alice McElhaney were recent recipients of his odious actions.

Witherspoon frowned thoughtfully. "I don't know, but now that you've mentioned it, I shall make certain to have a good look at the room. If it does overlook the archery range, we'll have another word with Mrs. McElhaney. After taking her statement, we paid a visit to Marks' solicitor."

"I take it Mrs. McElhaney's home isn't one of the ones you're having watched tonight?"

He chuckled, thoroughly enjoying himself. "Now, now, now, Mrs. Jeffries, all in good time, but no, she isn't. We did learn some remarkable information from Mr. Miles Wiley." He told her what the lawyer had passed along to him.

Mrs. Jeffries listened carefully and was quite stunned when Witherspoon told her the bulk of Marks' estate was going to the Royal Society for the Prevention of Cruelty to Animals. "Mr. Marks was an animal lover?" she exclaimed.

"Only dogs." The inspector told her the rest, including the fact that a stray dog had once died by eating the meat meant for Jeremy Marks. "Apparently not only has he always been fond of dogs, but he credited the death of that poor animal with saving his life. He claimed someone was trying to poison him."

"How long ago was this?"

"Wiley didn't say exactly, but he did say it was a long time ago. After leaving Wiley's office, we went to interview Merriman again and you know what happened there." He drained his glass. "Should we have another?"

"Absolutely, sir." She got up and poured them each another sherry. Her mind was working furiously. She couldn't reconcile that horrid man leaving a huge fortune to the RSPCA. Especially as he'd been attacked by a spaniel when he'd broken his first engagement to Jeanette Givens. "Then it appears that Jeremy Marks knew he had lethal enemies." She handed Witherspoon his glass.

"He must have. After leaving the Merriman house, we went back to the archery club, but by then, most of the members had left. Constables Griffiths and Parker had done a fine job of tracking down the people who were either definitely not in the common room or weren't at a specific table when Marks was murdered."

She sipped her sherry as he gave her the remaining details. When he reached the part where Constable Griffiths raced out of the room in pursuit of Steven Marston, she took special note of what he said. When he stopped to take a quick sip, she said, "Let me guess, sir. Mr. Marston lives close by and he's the other one you're having the constables keep under watch."

Witherspoon laughed in delight. "You have been listening!"

As soon as the kitchen was tidy and the house quiet, Mrs. Jeffries hurried up to her room. As she'd done earlier, she pulled out her notes and then added the new information

Witherspoon had shared to what she already had. Then she read through it all, twice. She put the pages back in their hiding place and turned to the window. The twilight was gone and now darkness had descended. She went over the facts as she remembered them while she got ready for bed, but once she slid under the covers, sleep eluded her.

She spent a restless night, got up earlier than usual, and went down to the kitchen. Mrs. Goodge was at the cooker frying the bacon, Phyllis was setting the table, and Wiggins had taken Fred for his morning walk.

By the time Constable Barnes arrived, the household had finished breakfast and the kitchen was ready for their morning meeting. Barnes drank his tea and listened as Mrs. Goodge and Mrs. Jeffries passed along everything the others had found out the day before.

"Was the source sure about Hannah Lonsdale being at the club when Marks was killed?" he asked when they'd finished.

"Definitely," the cook replied, "but as Hatchet heard this second or third hand, I'd say it would be best to check with the serving girls. Supposedly it was one of them that spotted Miss Lonsdale."

"The inspector said you'd be interviewing the staff this morning," Mrs. Jeffries reminded him. "Perhaps you'll be able to verify the information."

"If the girl really was there, she might have noticed the direction the arrows came from." Barnes put his mug on the table and got up. "That might be useful. Time to go. We've an enormous amount of ground to cover today. I shall see you two ladies tomorrow."

He disappeared up the stairs, and a few moments later,

they heard the two policemen going out the front door. Five minutes after that, the others trickled in for their morning meeting.

Smythe was the last one to arrive. "Betsy's seein' the mid-wife this mornin'," he explained. "After that, she's goin' to the dressmaker's to get her clothes let out some, but she told me to tell everyone she'll be here this afternoon."

"That's good to hear, Smythe," Mrs. Jeffries replied. "I do hope that means she's feeling better."

He grinned. "She's had a good night's sleep and the little one is behavin' as well."

The morning meeting didn't take long. Mrs. Jeffries and Mrs. Goodge took turns reporting what they'd learned from the inspector and Constable Barnes. As soon as they were done, Mrs. Jeffries did something she had often cautioned them not to do. She knew she was taking a big risk here, but her "inner voice," as she liked to call it, was screaming that it was the only way to solve this case.

She took a deep breath before she spoke. "I know this is going to sound very strange, but today, I think it would be wise for all of us to concentrate on Hannah Lonsdale and Alice McElhaney."

There was a long moment of stunned silence then they all began to speak at once.

"Cor blimey, I don't understand," Wiggins exclaimed. "We never do things like that this early in the investigation."

"What on earth are you on about, Hepzibah?" Mrs. Goodge was so shocked, she used Mrs. Jeffries' given name in front of the others.

"Do you think that's wise?" Ruth murmured. "We still don't have much information about this case."

"Is there a reason you think we should concentrate on those two women?" Phyllis asked.

"Nells bells, I ain't ever heard you say something like this so early in a case," Luty charged.

"Yes, yes, I know it's strange, but hear me out." Mrs. Jeffries held up her hand for silence. "Last night, something occurred to me. There are only two people who have recently been hurt by Jeremy Marks' odious behavior."

"Hannah Lonsdale and Alice McElhaney." Phyllis smiled as she nodded in agreement. "I see what you're saying, Mrs. Jeffries. The rest of the ones that hated him were from a long time ago."

"That's correct. All the other negative stories come from years ago. One must then ask oneself, why?"

"Maybe people wised up that he couldn't be trusted," Luty suggested. "Even dumb people ain't stupid enough to keep doin' business with someone who crosses 'em at the first sign of trouble."

"That's precisely what I think, Luty," Mrs. Jeffries replied. "But before we can concentrate on his past, we have to be sure that his present circumstance isn't a factor in his murder."

"So how do we do that?" Hatchet asked. "If we find these two women are innocent of the crime, what then?"

"Then we keep on looking." Mrs. Jeffries glanced at Smythe. "I know you're going to see your best source today, right?" She waited a moment as he nodded in agreement. "Good, then find out if there have been any recent business scandals with the man. Something that might have happened in the last few years."

"Alright, that should be easy enough," Smythe said.

Mrs. Jeffries looked at Luty. "Ask your banker friend the same thing."

Luty laughed. "If anyone knows about recent scandals, it'll be John Widdowes, and if he don't know, his wife Chloe will!"

"I've a source I can tap as well," Hatchet murmured.

"And I can have another go at the staff at the archery club," Wiggins said. "Servants are smart; someone will have seen somethin' useful."

"I've a few sources that might help." Ruth looked uncertain. "Fingers crossed that someone knows something."

As the meeting broke up, no one noticed that Phyllis remained silent.

"Now that we know Steven Marston is still in his flat, let's hope Emmett Merriman really is in here this morning," Barnes said to the inspector as the hansom cab pulled up in front of Merriman's company. They had gone to the Ladbroke Road Station after leaving the inspector's home and were glad to hear the constables keeping watch on Steven Marston's flat reported the gentleman was still inside.

They had also decided that they'd postpone talking to the club staff until after the day's luncheon. Barnes knew that much of the information he'd learned from Mrs. Jeffries and Mrs. Goodge might be confirmed by one of the club servants. To that end, he'd pointed out that if they interviewed both Merriman and Steven Marston, they'd be able to take their time this afternoon interviewing the serving staff and anyone else who worked at the archery club.

Emmett Merriman's place of business was located on the ground floor of a commercial building on the Brompton

Road. They stepped through the front door and stopped to take stock. The smell of sawdust and the pounding of hammers filled the air. Men in heavy aprons worked around tables planing wood, tapping nails, sawing two-by-fours, and drilling holes. Unfinished cabinets, cupboards, and drawers were scattered along the back wall. Cupboard doors, some bare wood, some stained, some with brass or iron handles, were lined up against a railing that spanned one wall to another.

Barnes walked up to a blond giant of a fellow screwing metal brackets onto a cabinet. "Excuse me, but we'd like to see Mr. Merriman."

The blond giant raised his eyebrows as he took in the constable's uniform. "His office is over there." He jerked his thumb toward a door opposite them.

"Ta," the constable said as they crossed the room. Barnes knocked, and a moment later, the door flew open and Emmett Merriman stood there. "Ah, excellent, you're here. I was wondering where you were." He stepped back, holding the door wide and waving them inside.

"I've been waiting for you." He gestured at two chairs in front of his desk. "I'm so very grateful you didn't upset my Sarah."

"How is your wife today?" Witherspoon asked as he and Barnes took their seats.

He smiled gratefully. "She's good, and according to the physician, all is well. I'm quite happy to answer all of your questions, Inspector."

"That would be very helpful, Mr. Merriman," Witherspoon said. "First of all, I want to remind you that we've a credible witness who claimed you weren't in the common room when Mr. Marks was murdered. Where did you go when you left the common room?"

Merriman looked down at the floor and then lifted his chin. "I had to meet someone, Inspector."

"Who did you meet?" Barnes asked softly.

"Oh Lord, this is so hard, Constable. Must you really know the name? I've no wish to harm the lady or her reputation."

"You met a woman?" Barnes glanced at the inspector.

But Witherspoon's gaze was fixed on Merriman. "Mr. Merriman, are you saying what I think you're saying?"

"I'm not proud of my behavior, Inspector. But sometimes all human beings do foolish things and make stupid, ridiculous decisions." He swallowed heavily and then sighed. "My wife is a wonderful, delightful woman, practically a saint. She never gets angry, she never gets shrewish or nagging, but sometimes perfection is difficult to live up to."

Witherspoon had no idea what the man was talking about. His own relationship with his dear Ruth was such that he couldn't fathom looking at another woman when she was in his life.

"Go on," Barnes pressed. "Tell us the rest."

Merriman closed his eyes for a brief moment. "As I'm sure you've deduced, I've done something incredibly foolish, so foolish and stupid that I'm terrified I'm going to lose everything. By everything, I mean my beloved wife and even perhaps our child."

"Go on," the constable prodded. "We need to know everything."

"It's not an original story, Constable." He smiled cynically. "Sarah and I had been married a long time and I'd reached the point in my marriage where I was bored. God forgive me, I was too idiotic to realize what I was risking. The lady in question is a decent, kind woman and is trapped in a miserable marriage. I've no wish to make her life worse, Inspector."

"Where did you meet her?" Barnes asked.

He laughed harshly. "Where do you think? At the archery club, and that's the irony of it. I only joined the club to please Sarah, but by joining, I have done something that will hurt her greatly if she finds out."

"We need the lady's name," Witherspoon stated.

"Is that really necessary?"

"I'm afraid it is," the inspector replied. "We'll do our best to be discreet as we've no wish to cause her any harm."

Merriman looked away, sighed, and then turned back to face them. "Her name is Angela Harland. She'll be at the club luncheon today. You can speak to her then. But do be careful; her husband might be there as well."

Witherspoon nodded. "Is Mrs. Harland a good archer?"

"She is, but she had nothing to do with Marks' murder. She didn't even know him well. Besides, she was with me when the murder happened."

"We'll need to confirm that, sir," Barnes told him. "If you were with the lady, someone must have seen you."

"No one saw us," Merriman insisted. "We went to a great deal of trouble not to be seen."

"There were dozens of people moving about the place when it happened," Witherspoon reminded him. "I'd not be too sure you were as discreet as you think you might have been. Now, according to our witness, you were away from the common room for ten or twelve minutes, so that means

you must have stayed on the club premises. Where, specifically, on the grounds did you meet?"

"We went upstairs, Inspector, to the attic. We didn't have
much time, so I told Angela that now the baby was coming,
we couldn't see each other anymore. The truth is, even before Sarah and I knew we were expecting a child, I'd decided
to end it. As I said, despite my wretched behavior, I love my
wife more than anything."

"Did Jeremy Marks know you'd broken your marriage
vows?" Barnes kept his gaze on Merriman's face. He wasn't
disappointed by the man's reaction.

His mouth gaped open and his eyes widened in stunned
shock. "Why . . . why are you asking that?"

"Because your wife is more than a few months along, sir,
and you only now thought to break it off with Mrs. Harland? Why did you wait so long?"

"I didn't wait too long, I tell you, I love my wife. Sarah
is . . . is . . . oh, blast and damn, I don't know if the bastard
knew or not. But Angela told me he'd made some odd comments to her in front of Michael, that's her husband, and I
couldn't take the chance that Marks had seen us together."

"And that's when you decided to break it off with the
lady, when you thought Marks was onto you?" the constable
charged.

"No, no, that's not the way it happened. I know this
makes us both look dreadfully guilty, but it's the truth.
You've got to believe me. We had nothing to do with Jeremy
Marks' death."

"When you went up to the attic, did either of you happen
to look out the window?" Witherspoon asked.

He shook his head. "I didn't. My mind was on other matters."

"Did you see anyone going in or out of the Ladies' Day Room?" Barnes asked.

"I don't remember. I was in a hurry, Constable, and I wanted to get the matter over with and get back downstairs. Angela made some comment about something she'd seen, but frankly, I wasn't paying attention."

Inspector Nivens put the file down on his desk and smiled. It had taken a bit of time, but it had been worth it. Sitting back, he stared at the shafts of sunlight coming through the narrow windows running along the top of the wall. The records room was on the lower ground floor so it tended to be very gloomy down here. But he wasn't in the least gloomy, not now. He'd finally realized what he needed to do.

He'd got his hands on the Horrible Kensington High Street Murders report. It hadn't been filed with the rest of Witherspoon's cases because the case belonged to another officer; Inspector Thomas Knatchbull.

The report itself made for interesting reading. It was obvious from everything Knatchbull wrote that he didn't have a clue who had murdered the three victims. But then Witherspoon had subtly begun interjecting himself into the matter—asking questions, dropping clues, pointing Knatchbull in the right direction, and then, at the very last moment, Witherspoon had arrested the perpetrator. Knatchbull claimed he accepted Witherspoon's help in the interests of cooperation and justice, but it was obvious that was a lie.

Witherspoon might have made the arrest, but it was

Knatchbull who got the credit for it, at least in the newspapers. But everyone important at the Home Office and Scotland Yard had realized it was Witherspoon who'd solved the
crime. What's more, he'd solved it *before* it had become another Ripper case.

Nivens knew what to do now. He got up from his chair,
stretched, and straightened his tie. Hurrying to the coat
tree, he grabbed his hat just as his assistant, Constable Quigley, stepped through the door.

"I'm going out for a few hours." Nivens nodded at the file
on his desk. "Make sure you put that back where it belongs."

"I don't understand it, Constable," Witherspoon muttered
for the third time. "How on earth could Merriman betray
his wife in such a manner? If one cares about someone, one
cares, and that should be the end of the matter."

"Yes, sir, that's certainly the way it ought to be." Barnes
glanced at the inspector. Witherspoon looked puzzled, as if
he couldn't understand how anyone could be unfaithful to
someone they loved. Yet his apparent confusion about Merriman's lack of fidelity hadn't stopped him from believing
Merriman to some extent. He'd not said so specifically,
but the constable was fairly good at reading the man and he
had the impression the inspector was taking Merriman at
face value. He glanced out the window as the hansom
cab drew up in front of Number 12 Ladbroke Road. "We're
here, sir."

They got out of the hansom and Witherspoon waited
while Barnes settled up with the driver. Marston lived in the
ground-floor flat of a three-story red-brown brick building.
A black wrought-iron fence enclosed a small garden crammed

with half a dozen overgrown bushes on one side of the garden and a short hedge running underneath the front window.

Opening the gate, they went up the short walkway and Barnes tried the knob. The front door opened onto a gloomy, dimly lighted foyer across from a steep staircase leading to the upper floors. On one side of the foyer was a door. Barnes banged on it, and a moment later, it opened.

A balding man of late middle age stared out at them. Spectacles covered his watery hazel eyes, his clothes were rumpled as if he'd slept in them, and he was holding a bottle of whisky in his right hand. "Come in, gentlemen, I've been expecting you." He stepped back and waved them inside.

"Are you Steven Marston?" Barnes asked as they entered the flat.

"That's my stage name, so yes, I am."

"Stage name?" Witherspoon repeated as he followed the constable across the threshold. "Are you an actor?"

"I was. I'm retired now." Marston lifted the bottle to his mouth and took a swig. "Do make yourselves comfortable."

Witherspoon took a moment to look at his surroundings. Seascapes, landscapes, and portraits crowded the cream-colored walls, an overstuffed easy chair was on one side of the fireplace, and a gray horsehair settee was in front of it. A side table covered with a purple fringed runner and topped with knickknacks, figurines, and stacks of magazines was next to the settee. The floor was covered with a fading Oriental rug and there was a bookcase topped with more periodicals and newspapers against the far wall.

"Do sit down, gentleman." Marston plopped down in the overstuffed chair. "I'm not going anywhere, and as I said, I've been expecting you."

Barnes and Witherspoon both took a seat on the settee. The constable pulled out his notebook and pencil. As soon as the inspector saw that he was at the ready, he said, "I'm Inspector Witherspoon, and this is Constable Barnes."

"I know who you are." He raised the bottle to his mouth and took a drink.

"Why did you run from Constable Griffiths yesterday?"

Marston stared at him and then carefully leaned forward and put the whisky bottle on the floor. "Why do you think? I didn't want to speak to him."

"But why didn't you want to speak to him?" the constable asked. "Have you done something wrong?"

"We've all done something wrong, Constable. The question you should be asking is have I broken the law?"

"Have you?" Witherspoon interjected.

"Not at all, Inspector. As I imagine you've learned, my real name isn't Steven Marston. It's Stephen Mueller. I had to change my name and leave the country after Jeremy Marks ruined me."

The inspector struggled to keep his expression under control. They knew no such thing but it wouldn't do to make that obvious. "Your real name is Stephen Mueller?"

"Yes."

"And I take it you knew Jeremy Marks?"

"I did, more's the pity, but luckily, so much time had passed since dear old Jeremy saw me last that he didn't recognize me. Then, of course, the stupid fool got chucked out of the club."

"Mr. Mueller, why don't you just start at the beginning and tell us everything?" Barnes suggested.

Marston gave him a sour smile, reached down, and grabbed

the whisky. He took a long drink, almost draining the remainder of the bottle. "I imagine that would be best. But where to begin, that's the question."

"Try the beginning," the inspector said. "When did you meet Jeremy Marks?"

"It was over fifteen years ago." He burped slightly. "I was a much younger person then, Inspector. Even in middle age, I had a full head of black hair and no spectacles. I was a fine figure of a man, as the saying goes. But years of hard luck and being on the road ages a man before his time. However, I digress. Back then, I was a businessman."

He paused for a moment. "Our family owned a substantial number of properties in North London, Islington to be exact. But we hit some tough times and we were looking to turn most of the properties into flats. I made inquiries within the property community, but at that time, unfortunately, most everyone knew our company was in rather dire straits. The only person who considered partnering with us was Jeremy Marks. His own reputation wasn't good, but we were desperate, so I contacted him and we came up with a business plan."

"Let me guess," Barnes murmured. "You mortgaged everything, he risked nothing, and then he pulled out of the deal when things started to go bad."

"That's exactly what happened and the awful part of it was that I only had myself to blame."

Witherspoon leaned forward. "What do you mean?"

"My father and brother were against doing business with Marks, but I thought I could handle him. Our only hope was to get as many of the homes converted into flats as fast as possible so that we had adequate cash to service our debt."

"Go on," Witherspoon pressed.

"The whole project was a dreadful disaster from the start," he continued. "I mortgaged everything, but before we even started redoing the first property, the roof collapsed and the project cost increased tenfold. That's when Jeremy pulled out." He looked disgusted. "I knew what Marks was, but I ignored both my instincts and the people who'd tried to warn me about him. I'd heard what he'd done to Henry Howell ten years earlier but I'd deluded myself into thinking I was too smart to let it happen to me."

"Henry Howell?" the inspector repeated. He looked at Barnes. "That sounds familiar. Have we heard that name before?"

Barnes had definitely heard that name, but as it had come from Mrs. Jeffries, he had to think fast. "I heard it in passing, sir, you know gossip, and I probably mentioned him when we were discussing the victim's past."

Witherspoon nodded and then looked at Marston. "Do go on, sir. What happened after Marks pulled out of the deal?"

"What do you think? We lost everything. We defaulted on our loans, my father and brother never forgave me, all our friends deserted us, and my mother died of a broken heart. My reputation was so destroyed, I had to leave the country. I went to the United States, California to be exact, because I wanted to start over. But that was nothing more than a pipe dream; with modern communication methods, my infamy preceded me. I couldn't get even get a job as clerk in a mining camp. I was alone, broke, and desperate. But luckily, just when I was at my worst, my ability to speak fluent French got me a job with a traveling vaudeville show that was going to Quebec. Over the years I became quite a good performer and I stayed with them until I came back to England last year."

"Are you an expert archer, Mr. Marston?" Barnes asked. He'd already heard this as well.

Marston smiled proudly. "I am. I took it up in California because I knew Jeremy loved it and I had plans to make the man pay for what he'd done to me and my family."

"And did you make him pay by putting two arrows into him?" Barnes persisted.

"No, someone else had that privilege." He shrugged.

"If you're such a good archer, why didn't you compete?"

"I didn't want a written record of my expertise, Inspector," he explained. "Surely you can understand that. I knew that people had seen me shoot, but as long as there was nothing in writing, I could always claim they were mistaken and that I wasn't as good as they thought."

Witherspoon was confused. The man was practically admitting to the murder; he had motive, means, and surely, the opportunity, so why be so forthcoming now? "Why did you join the West London Archery Club? Was it for the express purpose of meeting Jeremy Marks again?"

"It was. You see, I'd kept my eye on good old Jeremy over the years. I knew that archery was the only activity he liked and that he was a member here. But alas, right after I joined, he was chucked out."

"Why didn't you leave then?" Barnes flipped to a clean page in his notebook.

"Because I knew he'd be back and I planned on killing him." He took another swig from the bottle. "But I never had the chance."

*   *   *

"This is what I was on about." The gardener's helper at the West London Archery Club pointed at the burlap bag spread out on the ground next to a huge pile of broken branches, weeds, leaves, and the other debris deposited by the storm. "This old sack won't 'old much of anything and Mr. Sherrod wants all this stuff off the lawn before the luncheon today. Ruddy storm made a right old mess of the whole place but at least yesterday all I had to do was clear the leavin's off the archery range."

"It must be difficult for you." Phyllis nodded sympathetically. "Especially if you're the one who gets blamed when the, uh . . . what did you call them?"

"Tarps, when the tarps go missing, Mr. Sherrod always claims it was because I didn't store 'em properly. But no matter where I put the ruddy things, someone moves 'em, and now I've got all this stuff to clear up. Mr. Sherrod goes mad when there's anything left on the lawn."

"Why would anyone move a tarp?" she asked. She didn't really care. One part of her decided it was her own fault for trespassing onto Wiggins' patch. But she'd been so desperate to find out any information, and so grateful he'd talk to her, that she'd already wasted a good half hour. He'd been the only person she'd seen when she arrived earlier today, and she'd jumped at the chance to see if he knew anything. His name was Jamie Gunn and he looked to be about seventeen, with dark hair underneath his flat cap, a ruddy complexion, blue eyes, and a prominent nose.

"Who knows why any of these toffs do anything." He gestured toward the club proper, his expression disgusted. "All I know is now it's goin' to take more than one trip to get this mess out of sight." He shook his head in disbelief. "And I know where I put the tarp. It was right inside the barn. I shoved it behind the door just after the storm hit because I knew I'd have a lot of cleanin' up to do. But someone must 'ave moved it. Still, complainin' about it ain't goin' to help."

"How far do you have to move it?"

He pointed to a spot near the crumbling fence separating the club from its run-down neighbor. "There's a hole there that we use for composting. Anyway, it was nice speakin' to ya, miss. I'm sorry your cousin isn't here."

She had given him a story that she was here looking for a cousin that the family had lost contact with but which she'd heard was working in the kitchen. "That's alright, and thank you for trying to help me. I'll be going now." She turned and moved along the side of the building, moving quickly so if someone in the kitchen saw her feet moving past the row of windows, she'd be around the front of the place before anyone could catch her.

Thus far, she had seen only two police constables but they'd gone inside without seeing her, and it was still early enough that most of the club members weren't there yet. Rounding the corner, she stumbled to a halt as she ran smack into Wiggins.

He stood there with his arms folded across his chest and a frown on his normally placid face. "What are you doin' 'ere?"

"Well, I'm, uh . . . uh . . ."

"You know this is my patch, don't ya? I'm the one that's supposed to be makin' contact with the staff 'ere, not you."

"I just happened to be close by and I ran into that gardener's lad . . ."

"You didn't run into anyone. I've been watchin' ya for the last half hour," he snapped.

Phyllis could tell he was really angry, and she didn't much blame him. "Look, I didn't come here to show you up or anything like that. It's just that for the past two days I've gone to every shop between Holland Park and Hammersmith and I've not found out one thing we didn't already know."

"So because you couldn't find out anything on your patch, you decided to invade mine? That's not fair now, is it."

Her shoulders slumped and she looked down at her feet. "You're right, I'm sorry, but I just hate showing up with nothing to report again. It makes me feel like such a failure." She raised her chin, but he wasn't looking at her; he was staring over her shoulder with a stunned expression on his face. Suddenly, he grabbed her wrist in a viselike grip and took off running.

"What's wrong?" she gasped as she stumbled and then quickly regained her feet.

"Cor blimey, it's him. Move faster, we can't let him see us." He increased his speed, dragging her behind him as they raced toward the main road.

"Him who?" Her breathing was now so heavy, she could barely get the words out. "What's going on?"

"Oh no." Wiggins came to an abrupt halt, causing her to slam into his back.

"Ouch," she yelped. "Please tell me what's going on?"

"Blast a Spaniard." He glanced over his shoulder. Inspector Nigel Nivens was heading in their direction, but he'd stopped, turned, and was staring at something on the archery range.

"Good gracious, what's he doing here?"

"Maybe he's a member," Wiggins hissed. "But we can't let him catch us and we can't go 'round the front."

"What'll we do, then?"

He started to run, pulling her after him. "Come on, we've got to get to the carriage house."

"But he'll see us." She pointed in Nivens' direction.

"As long as we keep our backs to 'im, all he'll see is two young people larkin' about." Wiggins sincerely hoped that would be the case.

They raced across the grass, reaching the low wall. Wiggins dropped her wrist, leapt over it, and then helped her clamber across the crumbling stone. "This way." He kept his voice low, grabbed her hand again, and yanked her toward the carriage house entry. They dodged around trees, she stumbled twice, and both times Wiggins kept her on her feet.

When they'd reached the safety of the narrow porch, Wiggins slipped behind her and gave her a gentle shove. She lifted her hands defensively as she moved toward the door; he was right behind her.

The door flew open and they stumbled inside.

"Keep moving," he ordered. "Get over to the window and get ready to jump out if I shout."

"Alright." She turned and saw him at the door, his attention focused on the archery club. Then she did as he told her and headed for the window. "Should I climb up?"

He shook his head. "Nah, we're okay. Nivens didn't see us."

"Why is Inspector Nivens here? Do you really think he's a member?"

"I doubt it, but I suppose it's possible." Wiggins looked confused. "I mean, 'e's not even on the force anymore so there's naught he can do to our inspector. But we'll give it a few minutes before we try and leave. I don't know why 'e's 'ere, but I still don't want 'im seein' either of us."

"He knows us by sight, doesn't he." Phyllis recalled the time Nivens had come to Upper Edmonton Gardens to ask for their help. He'd seen all their faces then.

"That's right and I don't trust 'im any further than I could throw 'im. But as we're stuck for a while, why don't you tell me what that lad was tellin' you?"

"He didn't tell me much of anything," she admitted. "Look, I am sorry. I had no right coming here when I knew you were."

"I'll get over it." Wiggins laughed. "Seems like you went to a lot of trouble for nothing."

"Well, the lad did tell me that someone had moved his tarps. He was really annoyed about it as well." She told him everything she'd heard from Jamie Gunn. "But you're right, it was a lot of trouble for learning nothing."

Wiggins thought for a moment. "How big was this tarp?"

"He didn't say. Why?"

"Let's have a look around," he suggested. "There's a staircase there." He moved across the kitchen to the door in the middle of the wall. "There's another room."

"You've been here before." She followed after him. "What's up there?"

"I don't know, but I have an idea." He crossed the short space, yanked open the door, and started up the stairs.

"Be careful. These stairs might be rotted." But she followed him.

The stairs led to a hallway, off of which was a bedroom. They stood at the open doorway and stared inside at a rusted iron bed frame, a moldy mattress, and a green leather chair with stuffing coming out in half a dozen spots.

Wiggins surveyed the room, but it was Phyllis who spotted it.

"Look." She pointed to a spot beneath the window and what looked like a crumpled brown-gray blanket. "It's a tarp. Now, why would someone pinch Jamie's tarp and just leave it up here?"

The moment the words left her mouth, she knew why the tarp was here, and when she saw Wiggins' expression, she knew he did as well. "Oh Lord, of course that's why it's here."

He grinned. "That's right. The killer used the tarp to keep the wet off him."

CHAPTER 8

"Mr. Marston, do you understand what you're saying?" Witherspoon asked.

"I understand exactly what I'm saying." Marston broke off as he was racked by a cough. He yanked a handkerchief from his trouser pocket and blew into it. "I freely admit I came here to murder the man, but as I said, someone beat me to him."

"Do you expect us to believe that?" Barnes charged. "Where were you when Marks was killed?"

Marston smiled slightly. "I was upstairs, Constable. I went to the lounge upstairs."

"Why did you go there?" Witherspoon asked. He now realized that he and Barnes should have already gone to the upper rooms. That way they'd have some sense of where the Ladies' Day Room and the lounge might be. More important, they'd know if anyone there could have seen what was happening outside when Marks was murdered.

"I needed privacy and I knew that most people were going to stay close to the common room in case the competition resumed."

"Privacy? What for?" Barnes demanded.

Marston balled the handkerchief up and stuffed it back in his pocket. "I have a medical condition and I went up there to give myself a shot of morphine. I have cancer; it's terminal. You can go ahead and arrest me, but it will be a miracle if I live long enough to face trial and you'll have let the real killer get away with it. But perhaps that's not such a bad thing. God knows whoever killed Marks did the rest of the world a favor."

Witherspoon glanced at the constable and then back to Marston.

"But if you don't believe me," Marston continued, "you can speak to my physician. His name is Hamish McDowell and his office is on Harley Street. I've already given him permission to discuss my condition with the police. I've not much longer to live. I'll be lucky if I have two months."

"Rest assured we will check with your doctor, Mr. Marston," Witherspoon said. "When you went upstairs, did you see anyone going in or out of the Ladies' Day Room?"

"The door was open and I glanced inside, but there was no one there." He yanked the handkerchief out again as he went into another coughing fit.

The inspector waited until the coughing passed and Marston was able to catch his breath. "What time was this?"

"Just after three o'clock."

"You're certain the Ladies' Day Room was empty," Barnes pressed.

"I am. I looked inside because there isn't a door on the

lounge, which is just across from the Ladies' Day Room, and as I said, I needed privacy. Giving oneself an injection isn't very nice and I didn't particularly want any witnesses."

"I don't suppose you happened to look out the window?" Barnes muttered.

"Actually, I was standing by the window when I filled the syringe. Even with spectacles, my eyesight isn't what it used to be and I needed the light."

"Which direction were you facing? The archery range or the front of the club?" Barnes asked.

"The front."

"Did you see anyone outside? Anything that struck you as suspicious?" Witherspoon asked.

"No, the only thing I saw was Mrs. Storch's companion. I think her name is Miss Linwood."

"What was she doing?"

"Nothing noteworthy, Inspector. She was just walking rather quickly. Actually, it was more like a run than a walk. It had started to rain again and I imagine she didn't want to get wet." He started coughing again. This time he shoved the handkerchief to his mouth and hacked directly into it.

Witherspoon could see bloodstains on it. He rose to his feet. "Mr. Marston, if you think of anything else that might help us, please contact us."

Marston looked surprised. "You believe me, then?"

"To be honest, sir, I don't know, but one thing I do know is that when one is going to meet one's maker, one usually, though not always, tells the truth."

The Dirty Duck Pub wasn't open, but that didn't stop Smythe from going inside. He needed to see the owner, Blimpey

Groggins. Blimpey was in his usual seat at a table in front of the unlighted fireplace. He was a portly man with ginger hair, a ruddy complexion, and a ready smile. His man-of-all-work, Eldon, was drying a tray of glasses at the bar. Eldon waved as Smythe crossed the room. "Ya need somethin'?" he called.

"Nah, I'm alright, I just want to 'ave a word with the guv."

Blimpey put down his newspaper as Smythe approached. "I've been expectin' ya. I know your inspector caught the Marks murder so I thought you'd be here yesterday."

"Betsy isn't feelin' well and I wanted to stay close to 'ome. But she's better today and I've found out sweet sod-all about this murder."

"I'm sorry your lady is feelin' poorly," Blimpey replied. "You give 'er my best regards. Now, I'm guessin' you're wantin' to know what I know about Jeremy Marks."

"I don't suppose you know who killed 'im?"

It wasn't as outrageous a question as it sounded. Blimpey Groggins wasn't just a pub owner, he bought and sold information. His clients ran the gamut from businesspeople to politicians and anyone else with the money to afford his exorbitant fees. He had sources at the docks, every insurance company, the newspapers, the banks, the hospitals, and some whispered that he had a contact at Buckingham Palace.

"I leave that sort of thing to the police." Blimpey grinned. "But there's plenty here in London that 'ated the man."

"We've found that out." Smythe yanked out a stool and sat down. "What can ya tell me that I don't already know?"

"Did ya know that someone's been tryin' to kill 'im for years?"

"Years?" Smythe repeated.

Blimpey nodded. "That's right. Accordin' to my source, Marks claimed someone's been out to get 'im for a long, long time. The first attempt was poison."

"We 'eard about that one," Smythe muttered.

"But did ya know that, a few years later, Marks claimed that someone took a shotgun to him when he was comin' out of a funeral at Saint John's Church."

"Which Saint John's Church? London's got 'alf a dozen of 'em."

"Saint John-at-Hampstead," Blimpey said. "Whoever it was missed him but killed a stained-glass window. But looks like someone figured out 'ow to finally get it right, since Marks is dead."

"That doesn't mean it was the same person who's been tryin' to get 'im. From what we've 'eard, he's been makin' enemies for years." Smythe sighed. "Especially amongst his former business partners. But what I want to know now is who he's partnered with 'in the last few years."

"No one," Blimpey replied. "He's crossed his partners too many times. He's had to finance everything on his own for the past fifteen years. Mind you, that also means he didn't 'ave to share the lolly with anyone."

Smythe frowned. "You sure about that?"

"Don't insult me. 'Course I'm sure. No one would part-ner with 'im, and his reputation was so bad, most of the banks wouldn't touch him, either. The only thing that saved his bacon all these years was marryin' well. But his wife, a member of the Fairfax family, passed away, and from what I know, all he got out of 'er estate was a life-long interest in livin' in her home. Why do ya think he got engaged to Hannah Lonsdale? It wasn't because he was in love with the lady. He needed her money."

"So you're tellin' me that Marks hasn't been involved in any scandals or troubles for the past fifteen years?"

"The only thing he's done recently was break off his engagement to Alice McElhaney so he could propose to Hannah Lonsdale."

"Yeah, we 'eard about that as well. Mrs. McElhaney wasn't real 'appy about it, either. That must be humiliating for a lady. She took off for the continent rather than stay in London."

"True." Blimpey leaned closer. "But I'll bet you didn't know that before she left for Italy, she made a few inquiries about 'irin' someone to kill Marks."

"Do you believe him, Constable?" Witherspoon asked as the hansom cab pulled up in front of the West London Archery Club.

Barnes was surprised by the question. The inspector hadn't said much since they'd left Marston's flat and he wondered what was going through his mind. It wasn't often that Witherspoon was so silent and the constable didn't quite understand it. "I do, sir. Why? Don't you?"

The inspector sighed. "I've been thinking about it ever since he told us. It would certainly be a convenient excuse for his actions."

"Agreed, sir, but just because it might be a convenient excuse, that doesn't mean it isn't true."

"And he only has two months to live," Witherspoon murmured.

Barnes reached over and opened the hansom cab door. "We're here, sir."

Witherspoon stepped out of the cab. He stood on the pavement and waited while the constable dealt with the driver. When Barnes joined him, he noticed the inspector was staring off into the distance.

"Is everything alright, sir?" Barnes asked.

Witherspoon exhaled a deep breath. "It's fine, Constable. It's just that I don't think it will be necessary to speak to his doctor. I've seen this before. He's dying."

"But surely we should at least send a constable to double-check, sir? He claims he gave his physician permission to verify his illness."

"Yes, I suppose you're correct; we need to confirm it. But I know I'm right. There was something about his coloring . . . his complexion, the watery blue eyes. My mother . . . she looked much like Mr. Marston in the month before she died. It was cancer, Constable, and that's one of the reasons I feel so badly. The poor fellow is in for a dreadful, painful time of it." He gave a small, barely perceptive shake. "But that's long in the past. Come on, let's get started. The first thing we need to do is take a look at the Ladies' Day Room and the attic." He pulled his pocket watch out of his waistcoat. "It's half-past one; the luncheon should be almost over. We ought to have time to nip upstairs before we speak to Angela Harland and the staff."

But before they could make their way down the corridor to the staircase, they were waylaid by Rufus Farley. "Gracious, Inspector, how much longer are you and your men going to be on the premises? It's causing us a great deal of inconvenience."

"Mr. Farley, we're doing the best we can, but this is a murder investigation." Witherspoon took off his bowler. "We're hoping to finish our inquiries today, but we still must interview your staff."

"Must you, Inspector?" Farley looked like he was going to cry. "We'll be announcing the names of those archers that qualified for the regionals in two days and the Board would like it to be a festive occasion."

"You didn't announce them at the luncheon today?" Barnes asked.

"We never announce at the luncheon. It's supposed to be a cheerful time when all rivalry is put aside. No, the official announcement is made at our monthly meeting in two days, and frankly, we're hoping this matter can be resolved by then." His eyes widened as Constable Griffiths and Constable Pritchett stepped inside. "Oh dear, there's more of you?"

"The constables are here to help us speak to your staff," Barnes interjected. "If you'll excuse me, I'll get them started." He broke off and went toward the two policemen.

"We'll be as discreet and quick as possible, Mr. Farley, but we will be here for a few more hours. If you'd like to lodge a complaint, you can contact Chief Superintendent Barrows at Scotland Yard. Now, if you'll excuse me, Constable Barnes and I need to go upstairs for a few moments."

"It's been far too long, Hatchet." Myra Manley ushered him into her elegant Mayfair drawing room. "It's wonderful to see you. Gerald will be delighted. We were just talking about you."

"I hope you were saying something nice." Hatchet adored

the Manleys. They were both good friends as well as an excellent source of information. Gerald was an artist who was by far the best portrait painter of his generation, and Myra was an intelligent, perceptive woman from one of the wealthiest families in England. She was middle-aged, slender, and at first glance would be seen as slightly plain. But there was something compelling in her face, something almost luminous in her hazel eyes.

"We always speak well of you." Gerald rose from the settee and crossed the room to greet him. "We were hoping you'd stop by. We read in the newspaper that your inspector is in charge of the Jeremy Marks murder."

He was a man in his early fifties with black hair threaded with gray, blue eyes, and the kind of bone structure that had matrons staring at him for inappropriately long periods of time.

The two of them had found one another late in life; she'd been a fortyish spinster and he had just ended a lengthy liaison with an older woman who'd kept him well supplied with paints and brushes. It was a relationship that should have been doomed, but they were devoted to one another.

"He is," Hatchet replied.

"Do sit down," Myra said. "Have you time for coffee?"

"That sounds lovely." Hatchet sat down on the chair opposite the settee.

Myra rang for the butler and then joined her husband on the settee. They spent the next few minutes catching up, but the moment the coffee was served and the drawing room door closed behind the butler, Gerald said, "Alright, now that we know what we've all done and where we've all been, let's get right to it."

Hatchet reached for his coffee cup. "What can you tell me about Jeremy Marks?"

"You probably already know he was a cad and not to be trusted." Myra paused, and when he nodded, she continued, "But he wasn't just a wretched person; he was responsible for the deaths of most of the Howell family. I knew them, you see."

"They were friends?"

"Not close friends, but I knew them socially. After Marks reneged on some sort of a business deal, the father died. I can't remember how but I do remember that the son drowned. Poor Cornelia, she was the daughter, she was left destitute and homeless. The worst of it was her fiancé broke their engagement. I was at the dressmaker's shop when Cornelia came in to tell them she no longer needed her wedding dress or trousseau."

"That must have been very awkward," Gerald said.

"You'd think so, but in actuality, it was one of the most bizarre incidents I've ever seen."

Gerald grinned wickedly. "Do tell, darling."

"The woman that charged into Didier's Dressmakers that morning seemed a far different person from the one I'd known."

Fascinated, Hatchet leaned toward her. "Different how?"

Myra glanced at her husband for a brief moment. "By any standard, Cornelia Howell was an awkward woman. She was taller than most men and stout. At social engagements, she'd hide behind a potted fern rather than be noticed. But she was of the class and background where a woman had little choice about her own life, so appearing in society was a sacred duty if one were to find a husband."

"I do hope you're being sarcastic, darling." Gerald stared at his wife; his smile was gone.

"I was, my dearest. You know that I don't hold those ridiculous beliefs. But you need to understand what she had been like to see how truly strange the incident at the dressmaker's was. Cornelia, like myself at one time, was marked as a spinster. That's one of the bonds that drew us together when we happened to be at the same social function."

"I don't like you speaking about yourself in such a manner," Gerald muttered. "You're beautiful and you were never socially backward or inept."

"Thank you, my love. I never believed it about myself, either, but that's neither here nor there. Cornelia fell in love with a well-suited young man, and by all accounts, he was very much in love with her. But when the Howells were swindled by Jeremy Marks, her fiancé's father made him break off the engagement."

"Why didn't he tell his old man to go to Hades?" Gerald asked.

"Because his father threatened to cut him off. He had no other way to make a living, so he ended things with Cornelia. His family made certain everyone in society knew the engagement was over. Everyone also knew that the Howells were now penniless."

"That probably didn't make the dressmaker happy," Hatchet said.

"Indeed, French dressmakers aren't known for taking a loss on their goods and services. That's why when Cornelia came in that day, the whole room went quiet. But this wasn't the woman who'd tried to hide at balls and dinner parties; she marched in with her back straight and her head high. She went right to Madame Didier, the owner, and said she no longer needed the wedding dress or the trousseau."

"Why haven't you told me this before?" Gerald frowned playfully at his wife. "You know how I love a good tale."

"I thought I had."

"What happened next?" Hatchet had no idea if this story had anything to do with Marks' murder, but he wanted to hear the rest.

"Madame Didier suggested they go into her office and discuss the matter. But Cornelia wouldn't hear of it. She said there was nothing to discuss, she had no money to pay for the goods, and if Madame Didier wanted restitution, she should send the bill to Jeremy Marks. Then she turned and left."

"Do you know what happened to her?" Hatchet asked. Something nudged the back of his mind, but it was gone before he could grasp it.

"She left London soon after the incident at Didier's. She took a position as a paid companion to the wealthy widow of a botanist in Edinburgh. Then I heard she came back to London but didn't stay long." Myra shook her head. "After that, I don't know what happened to her."

"What a strange story." Hatchet remembered Mrs. Jeffries' instructions. "I hope things ended happily for the lady. I don't suppose either of you know anything about Alice McElhaney or Hannah Lonsdale?"

"Hannah Lonsdale was engaged to Marks, wasn't she?" Myra murmured.

"Yes, but we've heard she broke the engagement less than an hour before he was shot," Hatcher replied.

"I've heard she's an excellent archer," Myra said. "I don't

know anything about Alice McElhaney. Are they both suspects?"

"I think so but I don't know if the inspector has his eye on them as yet," he admitted honestly.

"Oh, I don't know about that." Myra laughed. "I know he has a lot of assistance, but I suspect your inspector knows what he's doing."

"I've told the lads to start the staff interviews in the kitchen," Barnes informed Witherspoon as they reached the second floor of the club. "And I've asked Mrs. Merchant to tell Mrs. Harland we'd like to speak to her if she's still here."

They moved down the carpeted hallway, passing what had once been bedrooms but were now something entirely different. There were carved wooden signs on each doorway.

The first one said LIBRARY, across from that the sign read GENTLEMEN'S DRESSING ROOM, and next to that the sign LADIES' DRESSING ROOM.

The Ladies' Day Room and the lounge were both at the end of the corridor. "Let's do this one first." Witherspoon rapped on the door of the Ladies' Day Room and they stepped inside. It was simply furnished with a green settee and two matching overstuffed chairs. Lime-colored curtains framed the two windows and there was a green-and-gold-patterned rug on the floor. An armoire with a mirror stood between the windows and opposite that was a pale green marble fireplace.

"Let's see what you can view from the windows." Barnes hurried to the one on the left while Witherspoon went to the right.

"There's a good view of the archery range here," the constable said. "But I think you must have a better one."

"I do," the inspector replied. "You can see the end of the practice room from this one."

"What do you think, sir?" Barnes asked. "Do we believe Mrs. McElhaney or Steven Marston?"

"That's the question, isn't it," Witherspoon sighed. "I'm leaning toward Marston. He's no reason that we know of to lie and say Mrs. McElhaney wasn't in here."

"I agree, sir. If he was lying to us, it would have been easier just to go along with us when we asked him if he'd seen her." Barnes stared at the inspector. But finally, he couldn't help himself. "You seem to believe Marston. But why do you believe him, sir? Because he brought up memories of your mother's passing?"

The inspector nodded. "Not just the memories, Constable, but a hard truth I learned when I was taking care of her. The dying don't lie unless it's to protect someone they love."

"I imagine that's why we take death bed confessions so seriously, sir."

"Mr. Marston appears to be alone in the world, so if he claims he didn't kill Jeremy Marks, I believe him."

"Then we'll need to have another chat with Alice McElhaney," Barnes concluded. "Because I believe Marston, too. Shall we take a look at the lounge, sir?"

They crossed the hall to the lounge. Like the Ladies' Day Room, it was simply furnished with horsehair sofas, several chairs, and a desk. Both windows there overlooked the front of the club, not the archery range.

"Marston said the only person he saw was Mrs. Storch's

companion, Miss Linwood, and that she was walking rather quickly. Perhaps we ought to have a word with her, sir," Barnes suggested. "She might have seen something."

"But surely if she had, she'd have come forward by now." Witherspoon moved toward the door.

Barnes grinned. "Not necessarily, sir. She's quite an admirer of yours, sir, and she's probably holding on to any information she might have to impress you."

Surprised by the comment, the inspector gaped at Barnes as a blush crept up his cheeks. "Surely not, Constable. What's more, I think Miss Linwood was merely being polite when she made that comment about following my cases. We've made it very clear to everyone that if they've seen or know anything, they must tell us."

"True, sir, but it wouldn't hurt to have a brief word with her before we interview Angela Harland and the staff."

He nodded quickly and then headed for the door. "Yes, well, let's get downstairs, and if Miss Linwood is still here, we'll ask her."

Miss Linwood was indeed still on the premises. As a matter of fact, she was waiting for them at the foot of the staircase. "Oh, Inspector," she called cheerfully. "Mr. Farley told me you'd gone upstairs. I've already spoken to that nice Constable Griffiths, but he said you'd need to speak to me as well so I decided to wait here for you."

"Thank you, Miss Linwood, that was very thoughtful of you." Witherspoon surveyed the corridor. Except for the three of them, it was empty. He decided this was as good a place as any to interview the lady. "I don't have many questions. I know Mrs. Storch sent you on an errand during the time period when Mr. Marks was killed."

"That's right." She nodded enthusiastically. "I supervised the footman taking Mrs. Storch's hamper out to the carriage."

"But you didn't go to the carriage yourself, correct?" Barnes said. He'd heard this before from Constable Griffiths, but in keeping with the inspector's methods, it never hurt to hear it directly from the witness. Sometimes they added a pertinent fact or two to their original statement.

"Correct. Frankly that hamper is dreadfully heavy and I was afraid I'd get soaked. I didn't want to get too wet, you see. I'm prone to chest colds. But my worst fear was that I'd drop the thing and that crock of foie gras would come flying out and dash itself into a hundred pieces."

"How did you supervise the lad if you didn't go to the carriage?" Barnes asked. Nothing new yet, but he was a patient man.

"I went under one of the willow trees," she explained. "It was quite dry under there. I could see the footman the whole time."

"How long were you there?" Witherspoon added.

"Perhaps five or six minutes, I'm not sure. But Mrs. Storch's carriage was the last one and it took the footman time to get there and get the hamper inside it."

The inspector nodded encouragingly. "What did you do after that?"

"I came back inside."

"Did you see or hear anything unusual while you were outside?" Barnes asked.

"No, not really." She frowned slightly. "Well, I'm not certain, Constable, but I think I heard one of the upstairs windows squeaking open. But I can't be sure. It was during one of those lulls in the storm and the only reason it struck me is because last week Mrs. Storch and I were in the Ladies' Day Room. It was a dreadfully warm day and Mrs. Storch asked me to open the window, which I did, and they're so old, they make a terrible screeching noise. But the sound was faint and I'm not really certain that was what I heard."

Barnes nodded. Finally, something they hadn't heard before. "Where were you when this happened?"

"I was walking towards the front door."

"Thank you, Miss Linwood," Witherspoon said. "Your assistance is very valuable."

"Really, Inspector. I'm so delighted. It's an honor to have helped you, sir. But I must go. Mrs. Storch will no doubt be ready to leave by now." She smiled broadly and gave a jaunty wave as she left.

As soon as she was out of earshot, Barnes looked at Witherspoon. "That confirms what Marston said about seeing her from the lounge window. But do you think you can hear a window open from outside like that? The Ladies' Day Room faces the archery range, not the front of the building."

"She didn't say she heard that specific window open," Witherspoon pointed out. "She merely said that she knew the windows screeched loudly because she'd opened that one in the Ladies' Day Room herself."

"And the implication is that all the windows are old and they probably all make a racket," Barnes said. "I suppose it's possible. But still, if you don't mind my saying so, I think she really wanted to impress you, sir. I'm not saying she didn't hear *something* but I'd take it with a grain of salt."

Witherspoon laughed. "I'd come to the same conclusion myself. Let's go see if Mrs. Harland awaits us."

The common room was quiet when they went inside. The luncheon was over and most but not all of the members had gone. A couple of men were standing by the entrance chatting, and there was a group of three ladies sitting at the table closest to the door. At the far end of the room, Constable Griffiths was sitting with a blonde-haired serving girl. He had his notebook open and was scribbling away as the lass spoke.

There was a brown-haired woman sitting at a table next to the window. She glanced up as the two policemen came into the room. Getting up, she walked toward them. "My name is Angela Harland. I understand you wish to speak to me."

She was slender and petite in stature with a smooth complexion and eyes so dark brown, they looked almost black.

Witherspoon, concerned for the lady's safety, looked toward the cluster of men by the door. Enraged husbands could do a lot of damage, and though he didn't condone adultery or any of that sort of nonsense, he wouldn't stand by and let a woman be harmed, not even by her own husband.

"Don't worry, Inspector, my husband is at his office." She smiled. "Emmett sent me a note, so I know you want to speak with me. He also said you were a true gentleman and that I could trust you and Constable Barnes."

"We appreciate this must be very difficult for you." Witherspoon gestured at the table where she'd been sitting and the three of them sat down.

Witherspoon waited till Barnes had his notebook and pencil ready before he spoke. "Mrs. Harland, uh, Mr. Merriman said that you were with him during the time period when Jeremy Marks was killed. Is that correct?"

"It is." She swallowed nervously.

"Where exactly did the two of you go?" Barnes wanted to see how much her story matched Merriman's. She'd already admitted he'd sent her a note and he wondered if that note had contained any details of his interview.

"We went upstairs to the attic, Constable."

"Why the attic? Why not one of the upstairs rooms?"

"The upstairs rooms can be used by any of the members. Emmett said he had something to tell me that required privacy." She crossed her arms over her chest. "There were far too many members so we went to the attic."

"I take it anyone can get into the attic?" Witherspoon wanted to avoid asking the awkward questions for as long as possible. He knew his duty and he was going to get to them eventually, but there was always the possibility that Constable Barnes might ask them first.

"Oh no, the doors to both the attic and the box rooms are locked, but Emmett knew where the attic keys are kept. Mrs. Merriman's uncle is a director. The keys are kept in the club secretary's office and that's usually unlocked."

Barnes' brows drew together. He distinctly remembered Rufus Farley telling them when they asked for a private place to conduct interviews that he'd ensure Mrs. Merchant unlocked the door for them.

"Are you certain about that, Mrs. Harland?" Witherspoon asked. "Mr. Farley had to have Mrs. Merchant unlock it for us when we began conducting interviews. We used that room."

She shrugged. "I don't know anything about what Mr. Farley may have told you, Inspector, but that room is rarely, if ever, locked."

Witherspoon made a mental note to speak to Farley or, even better, directly to Mrs. Merchant. He cleared his throat. "Uh, what time did you and Mr. Merriman go upstairs?"

"It was three o'clock or thereabouts. I was upset, Inspector, so I didn't notice the exact time."

"Had Mr. Marks come through the common room and gone outside before you and Mr. Merriman went to the attic?" Barnes asked.

"I don't recall seeing him," she replied. "But then again, as I've told you, I was feeling quite anxious and the only person I was looking at was Emmett."

"Why were you upset?" Witherspoon thought he knew, but one had to ask these sorts of questions.

"Because I knew that Emmett was going to end things between us." She uncrossed her arms and looked Witherspoon directly in the eye. "I'm in love with him, you see. I know it's wrong and I know he's not in love with me, but I still didn't want it to end."

"How long have you been seeing one another?" The constable looked up from his notebook.

"Is that relevant? Emmett said you needed me to confirm that we'd been together when Marks was murdered. We were." She started to get up.

"Just a moment, Mrs. Harland," Witherspoon said quickly.

She sank back into her seat and looked at him expectantly. "Is there something else? I don't mind answering questions that have to do with proving we've nothing to do with Jeremy Marks' death, but I object to discussing my relationship with Emmett Merriman."

"Understood, Mrs. Harland," Witherspoon agreed. He wanted her cooperation and she didn't need to know that they asked questions about her relationship with Merriman in order to ascertain if she'd lie for him. But he'd deal with that issue later. Right now, he had more questions. "We'll stick to the subject at hand as long as we're sure you're not trying to hide pertinent information from us."

She crossed her arms again. "In other words, as long as you're sure I'm not lying to protect my lover?"

Witherspoon could feel a blush climbing his cheeks. But luckily, Constable Barnes took matters in hand.

"Are you, Mrs. Harland?" Barnes asked softly.

"No, I didn't like Jeremy Marks, but I don't approve of murder and I know that neither of us had anything to do with his death."

"How long were you and Mr. Merriman in the attic?" Witherspoon asked.

"Not long, perhaps ten minutes or so." She looked down at the table. "It didn't take long for Emmett to break the news to me. I knew it was coming, you see. Once I found out that Sarah, Mrs. Merriman, was expecting a child, I knew it was just a matter of time before he ended it."

"I take it he ended things, then." Witherspoon stared at her sympathetically.

"He was never in love with me." She looked down at the table, her voice so low, they could barely hear her. "But if I hadn't had him in my life these past few months, I don't know what I'd have done." She took a deep breath and raised her chin. "Do either of you know what it's like to be married to someone you hate? I do and I'd not wish it on my worst enemy."

"Your husband is cruel?" The inspector hoped that wasn't the case.

"He doesn't beat me or anything like that; he's just a cold, heartless man who has a need to control everything, including me."

Witherspoon didn't like where this conversation was going. "Mr. Merriman said that you'd mentioned that Mr. Marks had made some odd remarks to you. Is that correct?"

"That's right." She frowned. "I can't recall his exact words, but he implied he knew about Emmett and myself."

"Can you paraphrase what Marks said to you?"

"It was something like, 'Isn't it sad that your husband isn't here very often, Mrs. Harland. But perhaps that's the way you prefer it?'"

"And you took that to mean he knew about you and Mr. Merriman," Barnes pressed.

"I did. Not because of the words themselves, Constable, but because of the way he said them. He had a horrible expression on his face, a dreadful, smirking smile that made my skin crawl."

"Is there a window in the attic?"

She seemed surprised by the question. "Yes, we were sitting just next to it."

"When you were there, did you see anything untoward? Anything that struck you as odd?" Witherspoon asked.

"I didn't see who shot those arrows at Jeremy Marks, but I did see someone running. They were holding something over themselves, a blanket or something like that."

"Was it raining at that time?"

"I'm not sure. I just assumed it had started again, because whoever it was held it as if to keep the wet out. But they weren't on the club premises; they were on the other side of the wall moving towards that old carriage house."

"Thank you, Mrs. Harland." Witherspoon rose to his feet, signaling the interview was over. Barnes closed his notebook and got up as well.

She stood along with the men. "If you've more questions for me, I'd appreciate it if you could ask them here. Please don't come to my home."

"Of course, Mrs. Harland, we've no wish to cause you any further distress," Witherspoon assured her.

"Good day, Inspector, Constable." She nodded and moved to the door, getting there just as Hilda Storch came into the room.

"There's Mrs. Storch," Barnes said. "If you don't mind, sir, I'd like to have a quick word with her."

"Excellent idea, Constable. Perhaps she'll confirm the time frame Merriman was gone. I'll go down to the kitchen and see how the staff interviews are coming along." He headed for the corridor as the constable moved to intercept the older woman.

"Mrs. Storch, may I have a quick word with you?" he asked as he waylaid her.

She was a plump, gray-haired woman carrying a quiver of arrows and holding a bow. She stared at him in surprise. 'I've already spoken to you lot."

"Yes, but I've several more questions for you, please." He gestured at an empty table. "It won't take long."

"Yes, I suppose. I've got to wait for Miss Linwood anyway and I've no idea where she's gone." She put her quiver and bow on the table and took a seat.

Barnes sat down as well. "I just need you to confirm that Mr. Merriman was gone during the time frame that Mr. Marks was murdered?"

"He was gone. I was a bit muddled when the constable first asked me who was where at that time. I'd sent Miss Linwood to the kitchen to get the hamper and I'd had a glass of champagne, but I most certainly wasn't drunk. It was only after Miss Linwood and I went home that I realized he'd been gone for some time. Naturally, one doesn't like to associate oneself with something as dreadful as a murder, but human nature being what it is, of course we talked about it." She laughed. "Let me be truthful, Constable, that's all we talked about all the way home and during dinner that evening."

"That's only natural, Mrs. Storch," Barnes said. "Miss Linwood told us she's been in your employ for a year, is that right?"

"It is and she's been a godsend! Since my late husband died, I've been very lonely but I'd resisted getting a paid companion. However, my son insisted. He didn't want me on my own all the time and he'd heard about Miss Linwood from Mrs. McCray. She's the widow of the famous Dr. Landon McCray; he invented McCray's Vermin Solution. Miss Linwood was her companion years ago in Scotland. She came highly recommended and she's been a wonderful friend to me. But you're not concerned with the interesting life my companion has led; do go on with your questions."

Barnes couldn't imagine how "interesting" a paid companion's life might be nor did he care. He went on to the next question. "How did Mr. Merriman seem when he arrived back at your table?"

"How did he seem?" she repeated. "Well, I didn't notice at first, but Miss Linwood mentioned he seemed a bit upset.

She said his hands were shaking when he picked up his teacup."

"But you didn't notice anything untoward," Barnes pressed. "Please try to remember, Mrs. Storch. It could be very important."

Unlike Inspector Witherspoon, the constable was a tad more cynical about Mrs. Harland and Emmett Merriman. The two of them had a strong motive for wanting Marks dead; a cruel husband learning of her infidelity could make her life an absolute misery, and Merriman was so besotted with the thought of having a child, he'd not do anything to upset his lovely, pregnant wife.

Mrs. Storch looked thoughtful, then she gave a negative shake of her head. "No, I'm sorry, I didn't notice anything odd at all."

"Now, don't be nervous, miss." Witherspoon smiled at Gracie Benton, one of the kitchen girls. She was a tall girl with a blotchy complexion and brown hair. "Just tell me what you saw when Mr. Marks was outside the common room."

"I've already told that policeman." She pointed to Constable Parker. "I don't want to get into trouble. I need my wages and Mr. Farley won't like me tellin' tales out of turn, especially if it's about Miss Lonsdale. Her uncle is one of the club's directors."

"Telling the truth isn't the same as telling tales," the inspector explained patiently. "I understand you don't want to risk losing your position. But this is a very serious case. Mr. Marks was murdered. Surely you'd not want a murderer to get away with the crime."

She bit her lip and nodded. "Murder is a sin, Inspector. I go to church on Sundays and I know that. Besides, I've already told the other constable, so there's no reason not to tell you as well. Mrs. Leigh sent me upstairs to see if we needed more sandwiches in the dining room. When I got up there, Mrs. Merchant said we didn't but she needed sugar and that's kept in the storage room. But Mr. Farley had her keys so I went to track him down and get the sugar for her. He wasn't in his office but Sally was just goin' upstairs to clean and she told me she saw Mr. Farley outside. I hurried out and had a good look about the place, I went around the whole building, but I couldn't see him anywhere. But I did see Mr. Marks walkin' about in front of the targets and I also saw Miss Lonsdale. She was standin' there laughing."

"Standing where?"

"Just on the other side of the practice room. She was watching Mr. Marks."

"Are you certain it was Miss Lonsdale?"

"There's nothin' wrong with my eyes, sir. I know what I saw."

Nivens kept his gaze on the front door of the archery club as he rounded the corner and headed toward the range. Witherspoon and Barnes were both still inside and that was fine with him. As long as they were there, they couldn't catch sight of him. He wanted to have one last look at the range, the targets, and the surrounding area.

He frowned and wished he'd been faster earlier. Blast, he was almost certain he'd seen people running through the copse of trees on the property next door. Unfortunately, a constable had come out onto the range just then, so he hadn't been able to have a good look around, and by now, whoever it had been was probably gone.

He stopped when he reached the spot where the archers took their places to shoot. Frowning, he realized the targets were actually quite a long way off. So surely that meant whoever killed Marks had to be really good at archery? He wished he could get his hands on Constable Barnes' notebook; the man wrote everything down. Either that or get ahold of one of Witherspoon's tiresome "timelines." As much as he hated to admit it, tiresome as they were, they were quite useful.

Nivens spent another few minutes examining the area and then went back to the front of the club and headed toward the weeping willow trees. It was a good place to conceal himself. When Witherspoon and Barnes came outside, he was going to follow them and see where they went next and who they might be speaking with.

CHAPTER 9

Everyone was on time for their afternoon meeting. Betsy came as well but she didn't have Amanda with her. "I know we promised to bring her," she explained, "but she needed a nap, and now that she's down to one little sleep a day, she's a handful if she misses it."

"We'll see her soon," Luty reassured Betsy. "Don't you be frettin' none about us. Not in your condition. We're all just wantin' you to rest up and git ready for the new baby. How much longer?"

"The midwife says another couple of weeks." Betsy slid into the chair next to Smythe. "I'm not sure I'm going to last that long. I've had to take more of my dresses in to be let out."

"You'll do fine, Betsy. It's not much longer." Ruth gave her a sympathetic smile.

"I know, I shouldn't complain, but I just want it over with."

"That's understandable." Mrs. Goodge put a plate of currant scones on the table next to the teapot.

"Shall we get started?" Mrs. Jeffries took her seat, waited a moment, and then asked, "Who would like to go first?"

"I'll have a go," Smythe offered. "I 'ad a word with one of my main sources and I found out a right interestin' bit about Jeremy Marks." He told what he'd heard from Blimpey before looking at Mrs. Jeffries. "Marks 'asn't been able to find anyone to go into business with him for years," he explained. "Not even the banks would touch him. Looks like the only people 'e's harmed in the past few years are the two ladies, Hannah Lonsdale and Alice McElhaney."

"It appears so," Mrs. Jeffries murmured. She knew she should be pleased that her assumption about the case was correct, but there was something troubling in the back of her mind. It was something she'd heard, a casual remark that one of them had shared, but now she couldn't recall exactly what it was. "Nonetheless, we'll keep on digging. Did you find out anything else?"

Smythe grinned. "I've saved the best for last. My source claims that before Mrs. McElhaney left London, she was lookin' to hire someone to kill Marks."

Mrs. Goodge gasped. "No, I don't believe it. How would a woman like her even know where to look for a . . . what do they call it, a hired killer?"

"Cor blimey, was your source sure?" Wiggins felt like Smythe had just stolen his thunder. He and Phyllis had discussed seeing Inspector Nivens at the club, and both of them had thought that news would be what surprised everyone.

"He was," Smythe confirmed. "Mrs. McElhaney had a friend who is a bit of a gambler. You know what I mean; 'e's one of them toffs that seems like he's a tough one, but it's all an act. He told her he couldn't do it and didn't know anyone who would. At that point, she seemed to 'ave given up and gone to Italy."

"How did your source find out?" Phyllis asked.

"The gambler told my source. He thought it was funny and was 'avin' a bit of a laugh at 'er expense. But what it did show me was that Alice McElhaney wasn't above doin' murder."

"That's exactly what it tells us about her," Mrs. Jeffries agreed. She knew who Smythe's source was, and she also knew that if Blimpey Groggins shared the information, he took it seriously. "Did you learn anything else?"

Smythe shook his head. "That's all from me. But I'll get out tomorrow and do a bit of snoopin' at the pubs near the archery club."

"I'll go next," Hatchet offered. "But after hearing from Smythe, I'm afraid my information is interesting, but not particularly useful. Still, as Mrs. Jeffries often tells us, anything we learn needs to be shared." He told them what he'd heard from Myra Manley. "But this happened twenty-five years ago and the last my source had heard of Cornelia Howell, the poor woman had taken a position in Scotland."

"Now that's a right sad tale," Luty muttered. "But at least you found out something. I went to see my source today, and he and his wife went off on a trip to Paris. They ain't comin' back until next week. But I ain't givin' up. I've got a couple more people to see tomorrow."

"I'll go next." Wiggins glanced at Phyllis. She gave him

an encouraging smile. He cleared his throat and told them about their joint effort at the club. He told them about racing across the grounds to escape getting caught, but he was deliberately vague about who was chasing after them. He was saving that for the end. "And I'm glad Phyllis showed up, because if she 'adn't, we'd not 'ave 'ad to make a run for it to that carriage 'ouse. That's where we found the tarp."

"Why do you think that's important?" Ruth asked. "Perhaps that tarp had been there for some time. Do we know if it has anything to do with the murder?"

"We don't know for sure, but I think it does because it was still wet." Wiggins reached for a scone. "Not on the top, but inside the creases and the folds, there was a lot of water. The only time we've 'ad rain recently was the storm when Marks was killed." He looked at Phyllis and then took a deep breath. "But that's not all. The reason we had to run for the carriage 'ouse was because someone else was there and it was someone we didn't want seein' us. It was Inspector Nivens."

There was a moment of stunned silence. "Good Lord," Luty cried. "That varmint is snoopin' around the archery club? Why?"

"Is he a member?" Hatchet asked.

"I don't think so, but I didn't 'ang about to ask 'im." He looked at Mrs. Jeffries. "Can you ask the inspector what's goin' on? Nivens isn't even on the force."

Mrs. Jeffries sighed heavily. She'd known this day was coming, but she'd hoped to put it off a bit longer. "I'm afraid he is back on the force. I've no idea how he managed it, but he was reinstated some months ago. The inspector didn't mention it and I only found out myself recently."

"Why didn't you say anything?" Mrs. Goodge demanded.

"I didn't think he'd be a problem for us. He's been assigned to the records room. Oh dear, I'm so sorry, but frankly, I was hoping that as he wasn't assigned to a station and therefore wouldn't be working on current cases, we could safely ignore him. But apparently, if you saw him at the club, I was sadly mistaken."

"You should have said something," Wiggins argued. "That man's poison to our inspector. 'E's been out to ruin 'im for years."

"We deserve to know what's goin' on," Luty agreed. "You shoulda told us."

"Really, Mrs. Jeffries, you did take rather a lot upon yourself," Hatchet complained.

"Yes, yes, I know, you're all right, I shouldn't have kept silent. I just didn't want any of you worrying about that odious, horrible man. For years now, every time we've had a case, we've been looking over our shoulders and wondering if that dreadful man was watching us. I thought it would be so much easier to get out and about if we didn't have to be worried about him catching us out. I am sorry, I should have realized he'd reappear in our lives. It was a stupid lapse in judgment on my part. I hope you'll forgive me."

"There's nothing to forgive, Mrs. Jeffries," Betsy declared. "You did what you thought was right at the time." She looked at the others around the table. "I say we stop finding fault and try to figure out why Nigel Nivens came to the archery club today. I know I've not done my part on this one, but I've done enough in the past to have my say. Mrs. Jeffries is right—if we'd known he was back on the force, we'd have worried ourselves silly. In the years before he got chucked out of the police, he was watching us every time the inspector caught a case. Mrs. Jeffries was hoping to make it easier for us, that's all."

"Thank you, Betsy." The housekeeper smiled. "That's very nice of you, but I shouldn't have taken it upon myself to stay silent. I'll never do it again. Though we aren't blood, we are a family and I had no right to make a decision that affects all of us."

"I'm sorry I said anything to ya, Mrs. Jeffries. Betsy's right, you've been watchin' out for us for a long time now." Wiggins reached for another scone. "As to why was Nivens snoopin' around the archery club, I reckon it's because 'e knew our inspector 'ad the case."

"I suspect you're right." Mrs. Jeffries poured herself another cup of tea. "I have a nasty suspicion he's going through all of Inspector Witherspoon's case files."

"Will he be able to find anything untoward about Gerald?" Ruth stared at her with an anxious expression.

Mrs. Jeffries shook her head. "I doubt it. Constable Barnes once told me he goes over the reports before they're sent in and makes certain there's no mention of 'outside' assistance."

"Then what's the man doing?" Hatchet cried.

"I can't say for certain"—she added some milk to her tea—"but I wonder if he may be imitating our inspector. If you'll recall, when Inspector Witherspoon was in charge of the records room, he got involved in those Horrible Kensington High Street Murders."

"That was before I was involved here." Ruth stared at Mrs. Jeffries. "But I remember it. That was the first time Gerald solved a murder, right?"

"That's correct, but even though he figured it out, the inspector who was officially on the case received the credit."

"Maybe Nivens is wantin' to do the same thing. Blast a Spaniard, Mrs. Jeffries, our inspector stuck his oar in on that one, but it wasn't 'is case. But the brass at Scotland Yard took notice of our inspector," Smythe reminded them, "and he was out of the records room in two shakes of a lamb's tail and sent to the Ladbroke Road Station."

"Where he's now solved more homicides than any detective in the history of the Metropolitan Police Force," Mrs. Jeffries said.

"And that's what's stickin' in Nivens' craw." Luty snorted faintly. "But no matter what he does, he'll never be as good as Inspector Witherspoon. Nivens might have more ambition than blood in his veins, but the difference is, Nivens is a fool and our inspector ain't."

Witherspoon was exhausted by the time he walked in the front door of Upper Edmonton Gardens. "Gracious, Mrs. Jeffries," he said as he handed her his bowler, "I've learned so much today, my head is spinning."

She felt very much the same, but she could hardly say so. "Really, sir, that must mean you're close to catching the culprit."

He gave a self-deprecating laugh. "If only that were true. The fact is, I'm a bit muddled over this one. Shall we have a drink before dinner?"

"Of course, sir." She hurried down the hall to his study, dashed in, and made her way to the mahogany cupboard. She could hear the inspector settling into his old leather chair as she poured their sherry.

Since the afternoon meeting with the others, she'd wondered what, if anything, she ought to say to the inspector. Surely he knew that Nivens was back on the force, but he'd not said a word. She'd found out from Constable Barnes.

She wondered why Inspector Witherspoon had kept silent. Then she'd worried that perhaps he didn't know. It wasn't out of the realm of possibility; Witherspoon wasn't ambitious and he was very naive about office politics. It would never occur to him to worry about Nigel Nivens unless someone dangled the man right under his nose, and perhaps no one had mentioned it to him. It was possible, she thought as she took her seat, but not likely.

Still, she had to do something. Nivens was at the archery club and she was angry at herself. She should have realized exactly what the blackguard was up to when she first heard he was back on the force. She'd been far too complacent about the situation and she vowed never to do it again.

Witherspoon took a sip of his sherry, closed his eyes, and leaned his head back against the chair.

"You look tired, sir."

"I'm fine, Mrs. Jeffries, just mulling over everything we learned today. It started off well enough." He took another fast sip. "Both Steven Marston and Emmett Merriman stayed put in their residences. We went to Mr. Merriman's workplace first." He told her everything he and Barnes had learned, including the fact that Emmett Merriman was unfaithful to his wife. "At first, Mr. Merriman didn't want to divulge the lady's name, but we insisted."

"Were you able to get confirmation from her?" Mrs. Jeffries asked.

"Yes, later that day. She verified they were together and

told us what she'd seen from the attic window," he continued. He took his time and used the conversation as a way of reminding himself of the events of the day. His conversations with Mrs. Jeffries were very helpful in keeping his mind focused on the case.

But by the time he'd finished speaking, her head was spinning as well. When he'd sipped the rest of his sherry and gone into the dining room for dinner, she did her best to recall every single thing he'd told her. But it wasn't easy. As soon as she'd taken his meal to him, she hurried upstairs and once again wrote up everything he'd said.

Frowning, she read through it and realized that, despite all the words written on the page, despite the ideas, theories, facts, and bits of gossip, she had no idea who had murdered Jeremy Marks.

When Constable Barnes stepped into the kitchen the next morning, Mrs. Jeffries was ready. She'd spent a restless night but decided that, at her age, missing a little sleep wasn't going to kill her.

"Sit down, Constable," Mrs. Goodge commanded. "We've lots to tell you and I've a feelin' you've plenty to tell us."

"I do. That's why I came a few minutes early." He nodded his thanks as Mrs. Jeffries handed him his tea mug.

"Did you know that Inspector Nivens was at the club yesterday?" Mrs. Jeffries asked.

Barnes gaped at her. "Nivens? At the club? Good Lord, why was he there? He's in charge of the records room."

"We were hoping you could tell us," she replied. "But I've a feeling that if you can't, it's because he's taking a leaf out of Inspector Witherspoon's book."

His brows drew together in confusion for a few moments and then he nodded. "I get it, Mrs. Jeffries. You think he's going to interfere in Inspector Witherspoon's case?"

"I do," she admitted. "I think he took the position in the records room so he could go over Inspector Witherspoon's cases, and when that didn't work, I think he pulled the Horrible Kensington High Street file so he could see how it all began. I think he's planning on imitating our inspector. I don't recall the name of the inspector who was actually credited—"

"Inspector Thomas Knatchbull," he interrupted her. "He had the case and got the credit for the arrest."

"But it was Inspector Witherspoon's career that bloomed," she said. "And I think that's exactly what Nivens is trying to do."

Barnes stared at her curiously. "You don't think Nivens is trying to destroy Inspector Witherspoon?"

"Oh, I do, but he's not very good at it. Nonetheless, I told you about him so you could keep an eye out. But as Mrs. Goodge said, we've much to tell you and we hope you've something to tell us as well."

"Thanks for the warning. I'll keep an eye out for Nivens. I take it the inspector told you about our meeting with Emmett Merriman?"

"He did," Mrs. Jeffries replied. "Why? The inspector seemed relieved that Mrs. Harland verified they were together when Marks was murdered."

"That was my impression as well, but our inspector is one of nature's gentlemen. I'm not. I'm a bit more cynical."

"Meaning you think they were lying?" Mrs. Goodge asked.

"I'm not sure." He tapped his finger on the rim of his mug. "The two of them have a compelling reason to want Marks out of the way. Mrs. Harland claimed her husband was cold and heartless, the kind of man who could make a woman's life a misery. Emmett Merriman is besotted with the idea of having a child and he'll not want to do anything to cause his wife to lose the baby."

"The inspector did tell me that Mrs. Harland implied Marks knew about them. But we've no evidence he was a blackmailer," Mrs. Jeffries said.

"True, but I'm still keeping my eye on those two. Mind you, they're not the only ones. We're going to have another word with Mrs. McElhaney and Miss Lonsdale today. Both of them lied to us about where they were when Marks was killed."

"And they're both excellent archers." Mrs. Jeffries looked at Barnes curiously. "You know those two out and out lied, yet you seem more suspicious of Emmett Merriman and Mrs. Harland. Why?"

"To be truthful, I don't know," he admitted. "But there's something about Merriman's manner that bothers me."

"Is it possible you're prejudiced against him because he's unfaithful to his wife?" Mrs. Jeffries eyed him speculatively. "You're a very moral person, Constable. But just because Merriman is a cheating husband, that doesn't mean he's a killer."

"I know that, Mrs. Jeffries." He leaned forward, his expression troubled. "I've asked myself the same question. You're right, his behavior offends me. For God's sake, I've been married for over forty years myself, I know that even the happiest of couples can get bored with each other, but you know what, most of us don't. I wouldn't ever do such a thing. I'd never risk hurting my wife. Yet Merriman claims he loves his more than anything, but I don't believe him. That's not the only reason. When I had a word with Mrs. Storch, she said that when Merriman returned to the table, Miss Linwood, that's her companion, commented later that Merriman's hands were shaking when he picked up his tea-cup." He broke off and sighed. "But you're right. I'll not let my dislike of him blind me and we'll get this case sorted eventually."

"Did this Mrs. Storch have anything else to say?" Mrs. Goodge asked.

Barnes told them the rest of his conversation with the lady, then broke off with a smile. "I think Miss Linwood is very taken with our inspector; she's always finding excuses to speak to him and make it clear she thinks highly of him."

"Does it make him blush?" Mrs. Jeffries chuckled.

"Yes, but I pretend not to notice."

Mrs. Jeffries and Mrs. Goodge passed along everything they'd heard from Barnes at their morning meeting. Then the housekeeper brought them up to speed on what she'd learned from the inspector. When she'd finished, she took a deep breath and reached for her teacup. "Honestly, I've no idea what to make of this case. We've so much information, but none of it makes any sense."

"You always say that, Mrs. Jeffries," Phyllis said cheer-fully. "But you'll suss it out; you always do. You've already pointed us in the right direction. Marks hasn't had any busi-ness partners to mess about in years, so whoever murdered him must be someone he's harmed recently."

"That should narrow it down some," Hatchet said.

"I certainly hope so," Mrs. Jeffries said slowly. But something tugged at the back of her mind again. It was a wisp of a comment or an idea. But then it was gone as soon as it came. "What is everyone going to do today?"

"As we're taking a closer look at Emmett Merriman and Mrs. Harland, I'll have a go at them." Phyllis looked at Wiggins. "You don't object if I try to find one of their servants, do you? I've not had any luck with the merchants or the shop clerks."

"Go ahead. I thought I'd have a go at Miss Lonsdale's or Mrs. McElhaney's staff."

"What about Mrs. Storch and Miss Linwood?" Betsy asked.

"Why them two?" Luty demanded. "Mrs. Storch was sitting in the common room when Marks was killed and her companion was watchin' a footman carry a picnic basket out to the carriage."

"That's right. Mrs. Storch never left the table," Betsy muttered. "But I think we ought to take another look at this Miss Linwood. She was one of the few that wasn't in the common room, and if they weren't there, we ought to have a good look at them."

"But neither of them even knew Marks very well," Ruth pointed out.

"That's what they say, but do we really know it's true?" Betsy argued. "Look, I know you all believe I'm not thinking properly because of this." She patted her stomach. "But one thing I've learned from our past cases is that we've got to keep our minds open to any and all possibilities. I say anyone who wasn't seen in the common room is someone we should take a long, hard look at. As a matter of fact, I'm going to do that today."

"Thank you, Betsy." Mrs. Jeffries smiled gratefully. "You've made an important point and I think you ought to see what you can learn about Miss Linwood."

"Not just her," Betsy declared. "That Mr. Marston needs looking at, too."

"That's an excellent idea," Mrs. Jeffries replied. She looked at the faces around the table. "Right then, let's get to it. I've a feeling we might be running out of time on this one."

"Mr. Farley will not be happy to see us," Barnes muttered as he and Witherspoon went into the archery club.

"Be that as it may, Constable, there are staff members we must interview again. Constable Griffiths and Constable Parker both made a point of saying they think we ought to speak with Mrs. Merchant and Mick Marshall again."

They had gone to the station to look over the statements the constables had taken from the staff yesterday. Only two had been tagged for a second interview.

"Let's hope this won't take long." Barnes led the way toward Farley's office. "We've got Miss Lonsdale and Mrs. McElhaney to interview again."

"And we've got to go to the Yard," Witherspoon sighed. "Why on earth Chief Superintendent Barrows wants us there is beyond me. I sent him a progress report yesterday."

They reached Farley's office and the door was open. Farley was behind his desk, and as predicted, he wasn't pleased to see them. "What are you doing here?" He rose from his chair.

"We've two more interviews, Mr. Farley. We'd like to

speak to Mick Marshall and Mrs. Merchant. Is that possible?"

"It is. They're downstairs. Is that all you'll be doing?"

"Yes, sir, we'll just have a quick word with them and then we'll be on our way. Don't trouble yourself by coming with us. We know the way."

When they reached the kitchen, Mrs. Merchant and the cook were talking. She frowned when she saw them. "Mr. Farley didn't tell us you'd be here today."

"No, ma'am, he didn't know," Witherspoon said. "We've two more interviews."

"But the constables spoke to everyone yesterday," she protested. "We've so much to do, Inspector. The monthly meeting is tomorrow and we've a whole luncheon to plan for the members."

"This won't take long," he assured her. "We need to speak with you and with Mick Marshall. I believe he's the footman."

"Why do you need me again?" She gave an exasperated sigh. "I've already answered all the constable's questions."

"We've more to ask you, Mrs. Merchant. Shall we go upstairs to the common room?"

Resigned, she nodded and turned to Mrs. Leigh. "Where's Mick?"

"In the practice room," the cook replied. "I sent him up there to tidy up before tomorrow. You know how the directors always like to have a look about the place. I'll send one of the girls after him."

"That's not necessary." Barnes was already on the move. "I'll speak to the lad up there."

A few moments later, Witherspoon and Mrs. Merchant

were sitting at a table. "Alright, Inspector, as I said, I'm busy, so please get on with it."

"You spoke to Constable Griffiths yesterday, correct?"

"That's right."

"You said you were either here or in the kitchen during the time period Mr. Marks was shot. Is that correct?"

She said nothing for a moment. "That's right. What of it?"

"But that's not true, is it? According to several other witnesses, when you left the common room, you didn't go to the kitchen. We've witnesses that say you didn't get there until almost three ten." Constable Griffiths had compared Mrs. Merchant's statement to those of the other girls in the kitchen. Both of them said she hadn't come into the kitchen until a good ten minutes past three. "Where were you?"

"Right here, Inspector." She waved her hand around the room. "I might have muddled the time frame, but I was up here until I had to run downstairs for more champagne. Now, I don't care what Gracie or Janet might have said. They're both good girls but they're wrong. I was either here or I was in the kitchen." She got up. "Now, unless you've more questions, I need to get back to work."

Witherspoon inclined his head. For some reason, he believed her. "Thank you, Mrs. Merchant. If I have anything further, I know where you'll be."

Downstairs in the old butler's pantry, Mick Marshall, aged sixteen, stared expectantly at Constable Barnes. "It was just like I told that other policeman. After I put the hamper in Mrs. Storch's carriage, I went to thank Miss Linwood. She gave me a shillin' and she'd said she was goin' to be under one of the willow trees to stay out of the wet if it started rainin'. But when I went up there, she wasn't there at all."

"Why did you want to see her again?" Barnes asked.

He shrugged. "Just to say thanks again. Some of the people 'ere are right good at crossin' your palm with a coin or two when you do 'em a favor. She was like that, and well, I wanted her to know I was grateful. You know, so that in the future, she'd remember me. That way, if she needed somethin', she'd think of me."

"And cross your palm with a coin or two." Barnes chuckled. The lad was smart. "But she wasn't where she said she'd be."

"Nah, I reckon she just went back inside. The wind was up somethin' fierce, and even though it weren't right overhead, there was lightnin'. Standin' under a tree is dangerous. Even I know that."

"At least now that answers one question I had about Miss Linwood. She wasn't stupid enough to stand under a tree during a lightning storm," Barnes said as he climbed out of the hansom. Witherspoon followed him.

"I'm not going to say our detour to the club was a complete waste of time," the inspector said. "But it does rather feel like it might have been."

"I don't think so, sir. We did confirm that Mrs. Merchant is telling the truth."

"I suppose that's one way of looking at the situation." Witherspoon started up the walkway to the Lonsdale home.

Barnes hurried after him. "Why do you believe her?"

"Because she has no reason to lie." Witherspoon climbed the stairs. "But more importantly, she only started working at the club six months ago and Marks wasn't in attendance there for most of that time. What she said made sense—she was running up and down trying to take care of everything. I don't think she had time to do anything but supervise the common room."

Barnes nodded in agreement. He knocked on the door and the butler answered. "We'd like to speak to Miss Lonsdale. Is she at home?"

"She's in the drawing room." He stepped back and waved them inside. "Wait here and I'll announce you."

A few moments later, he returned and led them to the drawing room. Hannah Lonsdale was sitting on the settee. She put the book she'd been reading on the cushion next to her. "Why are you here?"

"We've some questions to ask you," Witherspoon replied.

She shrugged. "Sit down, then, and let's get this over with."

Witherspoon took a seat in one of the chairs while Barnes took a spot on the love seat. When they were settled, Witherspoon said, "Miss Lonsdale, you told us that other than going to Mr. Marks' home to return his engagement ring, you then came straight home."

"I know what I told you."

"But we've a witness that claims you were seen at the archery club during the time that Marks was murdered."

"Your witness is mistaken."

"Nonsense, Miss Lonsdale," Barnes interjected. "They were very sure of what they'd seen and they have no reason to lie."

"Don't be absurd. I don't talk nonsense," she snapped.

But Barnes ignored her outrage. "You were outside at the far corner of the practice room. From there you watched

Jeremy Marks walking in front of the targets. He was apparently looking for arrows."

She crossed her arms over her chest and glared at them. Then she gave a short, harsh laugh. "He wasn't looking for arrows. He was looking for an emerald-and-diamond bracelet."

"How do you know?"

"Because he'd given it to me as an engagement present, and I told him I'd lost it when I was shooting. I hadn't, of course, but I wanted to watch him try to find it."

"You admit you were there?" Witherspoon charged.

"Yes, I was there. There's no point in lying about it now, Inspector. Someone obviously spotted me. After I arrived home, the rain began to let up and I knew that Jeremy would go out to the range to try and find the bracelet. It's very valuable. I was angry and hurt and I wanted to watch him make a complete fool of himself. So I went back to the club."

"How did you get there?" Barnes asked.

"I walked, Constable. I told my staff I wasn't to be disturbed and went to my study. As soon as everyone was busy, I took an umbrella and left the house."

"What time did you arrive back at the club?"

"I don't know the exact time, but it was probably just after three because I wasn't there very long before Jeremy came racing out of the practice room and began searching the ground for the bracelet."

"You were there when he was killed?" Witherspoon watched her carefully.

"I was, but I didn't kill him."

"Did you see who did?" Barnes asked.

"No, the storm had moved on a little, but the sky had

darkened and it was hard to see anything. One moment he was walking up and down the range, holding the lamp close to the ground, and the next, he was lying there with two arrows sticking out of him."

Witherspoon leaned forward. "Could you tell what direction the arrows might have come from?"

"Oh yes, they were fired from the direction of that old carriage house," she said.

"You're sure about that?" Barnes pressed.

"I am. But the direction is the only thing I can tell you. It happened so fast, I couldn't see who it was that murdered him."

"How do we know you didn't kill him?" Barnes accused. "You've admitted you were there and you were angry enough at Marks to go back to the club so you could watch him make a fool of himself."

"If you'll ask whoever saw me standing there, they'll tell you I didn't have a bow with me," she snapped. "What's more, I didn't want him dead. I had other plans. I was going to ruin him financially."

"You were going to ruin him?" the inspector repeated. "How?"

"I just told you, Inspector." She glared at him. "Financially. The moment I realized that he was marrying me for my money, I decided to take away the one thing that was important to him: his business. He couldn't get partners anymore and I knew the last thing he'd ever do is use his own money to finance his ventures. He was planning on using mine."

"His solicitor said he's got quite a large estate, so why would he need yours?" The constable stared at her skeptically.

"Because most of his property is mortgaged to the hilt."

She smiled. "He had such a dreadful reputation, he couldn't get loans from a reputable bank. When he began courting me, I had my business manager look into buying up some of Jeremy's loans. In other words, Constable, I had him right where I wanted him. All I had to do was call in some of the notes and he'd be ruined." She smiled. "Why would I kill him when it would be so much more satisfying to watch him lose everything?"

"Oh my gracious, I've been such an idiot," Mrs. Jeffries declared. "How could I not see it?"

"See what?" Mrs. Goodge demanded. The two women were alone in the kitchen getting ready to have their morning tea. "You've been muttering to yourself for five minutes, Hepzibah. What's the matter?"

"McCray's Vermin Solution," she murmured. "That's what Constable Barnes said this morning. But what if it's just a coincidence? Lots of people go to Scotland. What if I'm wrong?"

"Wrong about what?" The cook frowned at her. "What are you goin' on about? Come on, don't keep it to yourself. Talk to me."

She clasped her hands together. "But I could be so very wrong, and if I am, I might be stirring up a hornet's nest and we can't risk that with Nigel Nivens snooping about."

"You've sussed it out, haven't you?"

"I might have, but there's so little real evidence that I could easily be mistaken," she admitted. "Did you happen to hear where Hatchet was going today?"

"I don't think he mentioned it." Mrs. Goodge put her elbow on the table and rested her chin on her fist. "Why?"

"Because if I'm right, it's going to be one of his sources that can confirm it. But if we don't see him until our afternoon meeting, it'll be tomorrow before anything can be confirmed."

"You mean like the identity of the killer?"

Mrs. Jeffries nodded as she stood up. "I'm going to Luty's. With any luck, either Luty or Hatchet might be there."

"Sit back down, Hepzibah," Mrs. Goodge ordered. "You know as well as I do that both of them will be out on the hunt."

Mrs. Jeffries started to argue, but then thought the better of it. "Oh, Amanda, I hate it when you're right. I'll just have to wait for him. I suppose there's no rush. If I'm right, the killer is quite sure they're safe. But I do hope that everyone gets here on time today!"

"Hell hath no fury like a woman scorned," Witherspoon murmured. He and Barnes were in a hansom on their way to the McElhaney home.

"You can say that again, sir." Barnes grabbed the handhold by the window as the wheels hit a pothole. "If she was telling us the truth, her plans to ruin him were almost as bad as murdering the man."

"I'm not sure what to believe," Witherspoon said ruefully. "But she was correct about one matter: Even though she was seen there, she wasn't seen holding a bow."

"Which means we can't prove she shot him." He let go of the handhold as the hansom pulled to the curb and stopped.

"But we'll keep an eye on the lady." Witherspoon opened the door and stepped out. He stared at the McElhaney home while he waited for Barnes.

It was a well-kept four-story redbrick house at the end of a tree-lined street. The two policemen went up the paved walkway and through the white-painted wrought-iron fence. To their right was a steep staircase leading to the lower ground floor. They climbed the short flight of stairs and the constable banged the heavy metal knocker against the door.

When it opened, a young red-haired housemaid stared at them in alarm. "Oh dear, you're the police."

Witherspoon gave her a reassuring smile. "We'd like to speak with Mrs. McElhaney. Is she home?"

"She's in the drawing room, sir. If you'll wait, I'll tell her you're here." With that, she slammed the door shut.

Surprised, the constable stared at the closed door. "She could have invited us into the foyer," he complained.

"I imagine she was a bit startled," Witherspoon murmured. "We'll give her a few moments, and if she doesn't come back, we'll try again . . ." He broke off as the door opened.

"Come on in, then." The maid stepped back and waved them inside. "It's this way." She led them through the small foyer and past the staircase toward a set of double doors. "Go on in." She pointed impatiently. "She's waitin' for you."

They stepped into the drawing room. The floor was polished oak and the walls were covered with a yellow-and-cream-patterned wallpaper. A white marble fireplace topped with a gold-framed mirror stood at one end of the room. Portraits of women and men in old-fashioned clothing hung on the walls, and a huge fern stood between the two windows overlooking the garden. French provincial coral-and-cream upholstered sofas and chairs were grouped in front of the unlighted fireplace.

Alice McElhaney sat in one of the chairs. "What are you doing here? I've already told you everything I know."

"I'm sure you think you have, Mrs. McElhaney," Witherspoon began.

"I know I have," she interrupted. "Now what do you want? I'm very busy today."

Barnes had had enough. "We're busy as well, Mrs. McElhaney. In case you've forgotten, we're trying to catch a killer. I think that's a bit more important than any of your plans for the day."

She gasped at him in surprise. "How dare you speak to me like that."

"I meant no disrespect," the constable assured her, though it was an outright lie; he was deliberately trying to rattle her. He knew the reason Hannah Lonsdale had admitted she'd been at the club when Marks was murdered was because he and the inspector had been a bit more forceful with her than she'd expected. Being a bit less deferential to the upper classes always ruffled them. "But the fastest way to get rid of us so you can go about your day is to answer our questions."

She shrugged. "Alright, go ahead."

Witherspoon cleared his throat. "You told us that during the time when Marks was murdered, you were upstairs in the Ladies' Day Room."

"That's where I was."

"We have a witness that says you were not," the inspector replied.

"I don't care what anyone says, I was upstairs in the Day Room," she insisted. "Whoever says I wasn't is lying."

"I doubt it, Mrs. McElhaney. This witness has no reason to say anything that isn't true."

She got up, walked to the window, and stared out at the garden. "I didn't kill Jeremy Marks. I loathed the man and I freely admit I did everything to ruin his engagement to Hannah Lonsdale, but I had nothing to do with his murder."

"Then just tell us the truth," Witherspoon exclaimed. "You weren't in the Day Room. Where were you?"

She turned to face them. "I was in the Ladies' Day Room, but I needed to go outside, so I went down the stairs and out the little side door to the lawn."

"But that door leads to the entryway to the practice room," Witherspoon pointed out.

She shook her head. "There's another smaller one on the other side of the staircase. It leads outside. That's where I went but I stayed close to the building because I didn't want anyone to see me."

"Why didn't you want anyone to see you?" Barnes asked.

She smiled slowly. "Because if they had, I'd be tossed out of the club. You see, Constable, they don't allow women to smoke on the premises of the West London Archery Club."

CHAPTER 10

"You're going to wear a hole in the floor if you keep that up," Mrs. Goodge warned. "You've not sat down for over an hour. For goodness' sakes, Hepzibah, they'll get here when they get here."

"Yes, yes, I know I'm being ridiculous." Mrs. Jeffries stopped and glared at the clock on the pine sideboard. "But I can't help it. Usually, when I have a theory about the case, I've more evidence than I do now. All I've got is a comment that Constable Barnes made this morning and a few other facts. Facts that I could be misinterpreting completely. Yet I have a feeling I'm right."

"You've not been wrong yet," the cook replied. "Come and have a sit down. You need to save your strength."

Mrs. Jeffries laughed. "Save my strength? What on earth do you mean?"

"Don't be daft, Hepzibah. You know exactly what I mean.

Once you figure it out, you'll not rest until it's finished. We'll all be at sixes and sevens and you'll have the men out doing all sorts of interesting things."

Just then they heard the back door open and Fred, who was sleeping on the rug by the cooker, got up and raced down the back hall with his tail wagging. "'Ello, old boy, I'll take you for walkies in just a bit."

"It's early for him to be back," Mrs. Goodge muttered.

"Cor blimey, I've 'ad the worst day," Wiggins announced as he and Fred came into the kitchen. "You'd think with the sun shining and the weather bein' nice that a servant or two would stick their noses outside. But no, I couldn't find any-one that'd give so much as the time of day."

"Are you alright? What happened?" Mrs. Goodge went to the cooker and put the flame under the kettle.

"I'm fine, Mrs. Goodge," Wiggins sighed heavily. "But I didn't find out much of anything. First of all, I went to the Lonsdale house, and blow me down, before I could even find the servants' entrance, I 'ad to make a run for it. When that didn't work out, I went to the McElhaney home. At least there I found the servants' door, but that didn't do me any good because no one came outside. I stayed as long as I could, you know, pretendin' I was lookin' for an address while I kept an eye on the place, but again, not so much as a door opened. Then, wouldn't you know it, Inspector With-erspoon and Barnes showed up again."

"What did you do then?" Mrs. Goodge went to the side-board, grabbed the small teapot off the shelf and the tea tin. She added two teaspoons of tea to the pot and went back to the cooker just as the kettle whistled.

"There was nothin' I could do but get away before they

saw me. It was only half eleven and I didn't want to come 'ome right then. It was too early."

"You must have gone somewhere else." Mrs. Jeffries looked at the carriage clock on the sideboard and saw that it was already past three.

Fred butted his head against Wiggins' legs in a bid for more attention. Wiggins reached down and stroked him, then took his usual spot at the kitchen table. "I 'ad Mrs. Storch's address with me and I thought, why not go there? She didn't live far and that Miss Linwood was one of the ones that was outside when Marks was killed."

Mrs. Goodge poured the water into the pot and then sat down next to the footman. "You were going to try and speak to Miss Linwood?"

"Nah, I didn't think someone like 'er would be easy to get chattin', but I was thinkin' that if she saw something, she might have mentioned it to one of the other servants. You know how people like to say things that make 'em seem important."

"Did you make contact with anyone?" Mrs. Jeffries sat down as well.

"I took my time gettin' to the Storch house. There wasn't any 'urry; it's not like I'd 'ad much luck. The Storch place is one of them big houses on Holland Road so I 'ung about a bit and then I saw a housemaid come out. I managed to get chattin' with the lass. Her name is Annabelle and she told me she was on 'er way to the station as it was her afternoon out. Bein' as I didn't have anythin' else to do, I walked her there."

"Did she tell you anything useful?" Mrs. Goodge glanced at the clock to see if the tea had steeped long enough.

"Not really. It took me a while to get the subject 'round to Marks' murder. Even then, the only thing she said was that Mrs. Storch and Miss Linwood were both there when he was killed. Actually, Annabelle talked more about Miss Linwood than the murder. She is right impressed with the lady."

"Why would anyone be impressed with a rich woman's paid companion?" Mrs. Goodge wrinkled her nose. "When I was in service, I met many paid companions, and for the most part, they were timid women from the upper class whose families had lost everything. I used to feel sorry for them; they usually had to put up with silly nonsense from everyone in the household. They were like the governess, not really servant or mistress. Most of them spent their days fetching and carrying and doing whatever they were told. It was awful to watch."

"What did Annabelle tell you about Miss Linwood?" Mrs. Jeffries prodded.

"Only that the lady was friends with an Indian chief and they still wrote each other. She was real impressed with that bit."

"Where would Miss Linwood meet an Indian chief?" the cook demanded.

"She lived in Canada before she became Mrs. Storch's companion," Wiggins replied. "She went there with a rich Canadian lady who lived on a big estate outside Toronto. Then Annabelle went on and on about Miss Linwood. She said she knew 'ow to mix potions and that she'd made Annabelle one that cleared up the spots on her face. But what really made her take notice was the time Miss Linwood killed a rat with her slingshot."

"Slingshot?" Mrs. Jeffries wanted to be sure she understood. "You mean like the one David used to kill Goliath?"

"I'm guessin' it was one like that." Wiggins laughed. "She didn't really say much about the weapon itself, but she claimed she'd seen Miss Linwood use it. This big rat waddled in from the communal gardens and was 'elpin' itself to the birdseed that Mrs. Storch put out for the wrens and the swifts. Annabelle said the rat weren't in the least scared of humans but all of them was scared of the rat so Miss Linwood rushed up to her room and come down with her slingshot. She grabbed a rock, put it in the slingshot, and killed the rat."

Mrs. Goodge eyed him skeptically. "I've never heard of such a thing. Was this Annabelle person telling the truth or just making bits up to impress *you*?"

Wiggins laughed again. "Could be, because I know she liked me. But I think she was tellin' the truth."

Mrs. Jeffries' mind was racing furiously. But she had to know more. "Is it possible for you to see this girl again?"

"I think so. Like I said, she liked me. She kept askin' me where I lived and what I did."

"What'd you tell her?" the cook asked.

"I said I was a reporter for the *Echo* and that my name was Arthur Harley-Jones," he replied. "It's what I usually tell people when I'm out on the 'unt." He turned to Mrs. Jeffries. "She said she'd be comin' back to the Storch house on the five o'clock train. So I might be able to find her when she comes out of the station. But what is it you want me to ask?"

"Find out how long Miss Linwood was in Canada and if that was where she learned how to use a slingshot," Mrs. Jeffries told him. She gave him a list of other questions as well.

"Alright, she likes to chat so that shouldn't be 'ard," he said, but his expression was troubled.

"Is there something wrong with speaking to her again?" Mrs. Jeffries asked.

He looked embarrassed. "This is 'ard to say, but the truth is, I don't just *think* she liked me, I know she did. If I see 'er again, she might think I like 'er, you know, in a romantic sort of way. I don't like messin' girls about like that, Mrs. Jeffries. It's not right."

"I agree, it isn't right. But this young lady may have information that will help find Jeremy Marks' killer."

"I know," he protested. "I'm goin' to do it, but I wish there was another way."

"So do I, Wiggins, so do I."

Before the others arrived for their afternoon meeting, Wiggins left for the station to find Annabelle. He told Mrs. Jeffries and the cook he wanted to be there in case she took an earlier train back to London.

After he was gone, Fred went back to sleep on the rug by the cooker while Mrs. Jeffries and Mrs. Goodge got things ready.

Smythe, Betsy, and Amanda arrived first. Smythe, who'd been carrying their daughter, put her down and she raced into Mrs. Goodge's arms yelling, "Goma, Goma, gimme hug."

Goma was the name she used for Mrs. Goodge, her godmother. She referred to Luty, her other godmother, as "Gama." The inspector was the third godparent and she called him "Papapapa."

"Of course, my sweetness." The cook enveloped her in a huge embrace, and when she released her, she said, "Would

you like a treat, my pet? I've made some lovely treacle tarts."
She glanced at Betsy, who gave her permission with a nod.

"Want one, Goma, yeth, yeth."

Mrs. Goodge took the biggest tart off the plate she'd just
put on the table, grabbed one of the serviettes from the stack,
wrapped the pastry in the cloth, and handed it to the toddler.
"There now, you enjoy it, love. Do you want to go to Goma's
room and play with the toys?" The cook kept half a dozen
toys in her quarters for the child.

"Yeth, Goma, yeth, yeth." Mrs. Goodge laughed, then
took her hand and led her toward her room.

"Don't be climbing on Goma's bed or opening the ward-
robe or her drawers," Betsy called as the two of them disappeared. "Honestly, she's into everything these days."

"How are you feeling, Betsy?" Mrs. Jeffries asked.

"I'm fine." She took her usual spot at the table and
reached for a tart. "I should wait for the others, but they
look so delicious, I can't resist."

"Eat as much as you like." Mrs. Jeffries took her seat as
well. "Mrs. Goodge made plenty."

For the next ten minutes the others trickled in and took
their seats. Ruth was the last to arrive. As soon as she was
settled, Mrs. Jeffries said, "Let's get started."

"Shouldn't we wait for Wiggins?" Phyllis asked.

"He said he might be late," she replied. "But he might get
back before the meeting ends, and if he doesn't, one of us
will tell him what we discussed."

The cups were placed in a semicircle around the big
brown teapot. Phyllis picked the pot up and began to pour.
"Did he say where he was going?"

"Mrs. Jeffries sent him to the station to pick up more information," Mrs. Goodge said as she came into the room after checking on Amanda.

"Pick up what information?" Luty demanded. She'd gone with the cook to see Amanda. She hurried to the table and sat down next to Hatchet.

"She's got it sussed out," Mrs. Goodge told them as she took her own seat. "But she'll not say much until she's got everything sorted in her head."

"The only reason I keep my own counsel at this point is because I'm not sure I'm right," the housekeeper defended herself. "I have been wrong on occasion."

"Not really," Phyllis reminded her. "You always say that but you're always right."

"She was wrong once." Mrs. Goodge laughed. "But even when she was mistaken, she pointed our inspector in the right direction and he caught the killer."

Surprised, Phyllis stared at the cook. "What case was that?"

Mrs. Goodge waved her hand dismissively. "It was a long time ago—one of our earlier ones but I don't recall all the details. I think it might have been the Horsley case."

"I remember that one." Smythe grinned. "It was a nasty one."

"And it taught me a very valuable lesson," Mrs. Jeffries said. "It's the reason I no longer say very much about who the murderer might be until I'm absolutely certain."

"That's understandable," Phyllis said.

There was a general murmur of agreement around the table, then Luty said, "I might as well go first. My report won't take long."

Hatchet snickered. "Oh dear, madam, was it another bad day for you?"

The two of them were very competitive. Sometimes it spilled over into out-and-out warfare between them as they tried to outdo one another in the search for clues.

Luty's eyes narrowed. "It weren't a bad day. I did find out a pertinent fact or two and what I found out is important. Probably better than anythin' you heard today."

"Really, madam," he goaded her. "I await your report."

"Yes, Luty," Mrs. Jeffries said quickly. "Do tell us."

She turned her attention away from her butler. "My source is still out of town and the others I tried to find today didn't have much to say. So I went to Saint John's Church in Hampstead."

"Isn't that the place where Marks said someone tried to shoot him?" Betsy asked. She'd missed most of their meetings, but Smythe had kept her fully apprised of the situation.

"Yup, that's the spot. It's a beautiful church. I had a chat with the preacher."

Hatchet interrupted. "Vicar, madam. He's referred to as a vicar in this country."

"Preacher, vicar, what in the name of Sam Hill is the difference?" She glared at him.

"Preacher makes him sound like one of those itinerate pastors that crop up so frequently in the churches of the more rural parts of the United States," he explained. "Vicars are highly educated men, most of whom read Latin, Greek, and often Hebrew. Furthermore, it is the term that is most often used here in England."

"America has plenty of educated clergy," Luty shot back.

"It's just different than here. Hold your peace until I'm finished, and when it's your turn, you can say whatever the dickens you want. Now, as I was sayin' before I was interrupted . . ." She shot him another frown. "I had me a right nice chat with the vicar. Nice fellow, been there a long while. He told me that, ten years ago, someone did shoot out one of the church windows. Happened right after a funeral for a man named John Crawley."

"Did he remember what this Mr. Crawley did for a living?" Mrs. Jeffries asked.

Luty chuckled. "He was a businessman, one of the first that started turning some of the big houses in this part of London into flats. You know, a property developer."

"Did he do business with Marks?" Ruth asked.

"Doubt it," Smythe answered. "Sorry, Luty, didn't mean to stick my oar in your river. It's just that my source said Marks hasn't had a business partner for the past fifteen years."

"Maybe they partnered prior to that time frame." Mrs. Jeffries reached for a tart.

"The vicar didn't remember many details about the fellow," Luty said. "Only that the window had been shot out as the mourners were leavin' the church. But it sounds to me like whoever shot out the window was aimin' for Marks and missed."

"Only if we know for sure Marks was one of the mourners," Betsy pointed out.

"We do." Luty shot Hatchet a triumphant grin. "Crawley had no family so the guest book they always have people sign as they're going into the funeral was still at the church.

Marks' name was in it. By the way, his handwriting was terrible."

"Good gracious, madam, that must have cost you an arm and a leg." Hatchet snickered again.

"I'll admit I made a hefty donation to compensate the vicar for his trouble. It took a couple of hours to find the guest book."

"So we know that Marks wasn't mistaken. Someone could well have tried to kill him ten years ago." Mrs. Jeffries wished she'd asked Wiggins to find out another fact. But it was too late now.

"And when you add that to the poisoned dog incident," Phyllis added, "it looks like someone really was out to murder him."

"If it was the same person," Betsy murmured. "Marks made enemies all the time. It's not impossible the attempts on his life were done by different people."

"That's a good point." Mrs. Jeffries frowned thoughtfully for a moment and then looked at Luty. "Anything else?"

"Just one thing: The vicar said that after the window was shot out, the church received a generous donation to pay for gettin' it fixed."

"Who sent the money?" Smythe asked.

"It was an anonymous donation."

"That's unfortunate," Mrs. Jeffries said. "Who would like to go next?"

"I'll do my bit next," Phyllis offered. "It won't take long. I tried all the merchants and shop clerks again—this time I used Hannah Lonsdale's and Alice McElhaney's names. But the only thing I heard was that Mrs. McElhaney was thinking of joining a shooting club. Apparently, she likes shooting guns as well as shooting arrows."

"I'll take my turn now if no one minds." Ruth smiled at Phyllis. "My report is even shorter than yours. I've found out nothing but I'm going to a dinner party tonight and fully intend to drop Jeremy Marks' name and see what happens."

"That sounds like an excellent plan." Mrs. Jeffries nodded approvingly.

"My turn." Smythe raised his hand to his mouth to cover a yawn. "Sorry, just a tad tired. That's what 'avin' a little one does to a body."

"It's going to get worse before it gets better." Betsy patted her stomach.

"The babes are worth it." He smiled at his wife and then back at the others. "I spoke to some hansom drivers and a couple of the private carriage drivers that were at the club on the day of the murder."

"How did you find them?" Hatchet asked curiously. "There isn't anything going on at the club today."

"Yeah, I found that out after I wasted time goin' there. But then I went to Howards'. There aren't many stables left in this part of London and I was pretty sure that someone from the club used Howards'. Turns out I was right. Mrs. Storch and Mr. Pollard stable their horses and store their carriages there. Mrs. Storch's driver said the footman from the club put the hamper back in the Storch carriage and Mr. Pollard's driver told me that he saw Hannah Lonsdale when she came back to the club that day. He knew 'er by sight and he saw her walkin' around the side of the building to the far corner of the practice room."

"Was she carrying anything with her?" Mrs. Jeffries asked.

"You mean like a bow and arrow." He smiled as he shook his head. "Nah, I asked the bloke and he said all she had with her was a great big black umbrella."

"He's sure it was an umbrella?" She pressed.

"I asked and he was." Smythe struggled to stifle another yawn.

"Hey, I'm the one that's supposed to be tired." Betsy poked him in the ribs with her elbow. "But as we're almost finished, it's my turn. I'll go next." The expressions on the faces around the table ranged from curious to doubtful. "Yes, yes, I know I've not really been part of this case, but Smythe has kept me informed and today I had a bit of luck. I went to Lanier's dressmaking shop. When I got there, I had a word with Nanette Lanier. You know what she's like—she loves gossiping so I thought I'd see if she knew anything."

"How is she these days?" Mrs. Goodge asked.

Nanette Lanier had been involved in one of their older cases and they all liked her. Betsy had used her as a source a number of times and she was smart and very discreet.

"She's fine. But as I was sayin', I asked her about Jeremy Marks. She told me that one of the seamstresses in her shop used to work for Didier's Dressmakers."

"I remember that place," Mrs. Goodge exclaimed. "Years ago it was one of the most exclusive shops in London."

"It went out of business when Madam Didier passed away. She was the owner. But it's been gone for a long time now. One of Nanette's seamstresses worked there. A few weeks back, she insisted that she'd seen a woman who had been a customer at Didier's—and that the woman she'd seen had come into Didier's years and years back and caused a scene." Betsy paused, more for dramatic effect than anything else. "She refused to pay for a wedding gown and trousseau she'd ordered."

"In other words, Nanette confirmed what Hatchet told us." Mrs. Jeffries let out the breath she realized she'd been holding. She looked at him. "Your source told much the same thing."

"And I don't believe in that kind of coincidence," Hatchet murmured.

"Neither do I," Mrs. Jeffries replied.

"Nanette said that the seamstress claimed the woman who'd made the terrible scene at Didier's had come into Nanette's shop. But don't get too excited. Nanette also said that Miss Grant, that's the seamstress, 'is quite old and she seems to be going senile,'" Betsy explained. "Nanette says that every time an older customer comes into the shop, Miss Grant is positive it's someone from her past."

"But she's still working for Nanette," Phyllis protested. "So she can't be too far gone."

"I asked that very thing." Betsy shrugged. "Nanette said Miss Grant is still a very talented seamstress. Her eyes are still sharp and her hands nimble, but she can't find her way to the shop or to her home on her own. Her brother brings her in the morning and comes in the evening to take her back."

"The poor woman," Ruth murmured sympathetically. "Why is she still working?"

"Because she has to," Phyllis muttered. "The poor have to work until the day they die. That's the way of things here."

Ruth sighed heavily. "I know, and it's sad. But that's one of the issues women will take care of when we get full rights. We'll insist that society do a better job of taking care of the old, the sick, and the infirm. We'll make certain that no one has to spend their old age just trying to keep food on their table and a roof over their heads."

Wiggins arrived back after the household, save Witherspoon, had eaten their suppers. Mrs. Goodge took his food out of the warming oven. "You must be starvin'." She put his plate of roast beef, potatoes, and carrots in front of him.

"Ta, Mrs. Goodge, I'm famished. Sorry it took so long to get 'ome, but I walked Annabelle back to the Storch house and she's not a fast one. Truth is, she walks about as slow as anyone I've ever seen."

Mrs. Jeffries glanced at Mrs. Goodge with a knowing smile. "Of course she took her time, Wiggins. Girls sometimes do that when they want to be with a young man," Mrs. Jeffries said. "But I am sorry. It must have been awkward for you."

Wiggins chewed the tender beef and swallowed. "It's alright, Mrs. Jeffries. She's a nice girl, and actually, I quite liked her. Once she started chattin', she's interestin'. Especially when she started talkin' about something other than Miss Linwood."

"Who is interesting?" Phyllis came into the kitchen and went to the pine sideboard to get the inspector's tray.

"Annabelle." He took a forkful of carrots. "I found out a lot from 'er." He shoved the vegetables in his mouth and chewed.

Phyllis put the tray on the far end of the table and loaded it up with the salt cellar, the pepper pot, cutlery, a serviette, and a wineglass. She glanced at Wiggins. "Are you going to tell us what she said or not?"

"Give the lad a moment to get some food in his stomach." Mrs. Goodge sat down next to Wiggins. "He's been on the hunt all day."

Phyllis shrugged apologetically. "Sorry, I'm just in a hurry to find out what she told you."

"It's alright." He reached for his beer glass and took a quick sip. "She was right surprised to see me, but pleased, and when she wasn't goin' on about Miss Linwood, she's a smart lass. Her ambition is to be a nurse, can ya believe it? She wants somethin' better for 'erself."

"Most of us want something better for ourselves." Phyllis looked off into the distance.

"Yes, yes, Wiggins, that's nice." Mrs. Jeffries struggled to keep the impatience out of her voice. "But what did she say about Miss Linwood? Had she seen anything when she was outside of the club? Had she heard anything?"

He gave a negative shake of his head. "Annabelle told me she didn't say anything like that, so if she saw or 'eard somethin', she didn't share it. But I did find out about the other bits you wanted me to ask her about. Miss Linwood 'as been a paid companion for over twenty years, Annabelle wasn't sure of the exact amount of time, and she's lived all over the world, Scotland, London, Denver, and finally Toronto before comin' back 'ere."

"What about the slingshot?" Mrs. Goodge asked.

Wiggins laughed and looked at Mrs. Jeffries. "You were right about that. Her Indian friend is the one who taught her to use it. But that isn't all—she said that Miss Linwood carries a gun. She got in the habit when she was in Colorado and someone tried to break into the house where she and the lady she worked for were stayin'."

* * *

The moment the inspector stepped through the front door, Mrs. Jeffries could see he was upset. His shoulders slumped, his lips were a flat, thin line, and his spectacles had slipped so far down, they were almost off his nose.

"Goodness, sir, is everything alright?" She took his bowler and hung it up.

He gave her a strained smile. "Oh, I'm fine, Mrs. Jeffries, don't mind me. It's not been a very productive day."

"Then you'll need a glass of sherry, won't you, sir?" She turned and headed for his study. He followed behind her.

Mrs. Jeffries poured them each a drink, handed him his glass, and then took her own seat across from him. "Now, sir. What happened?"

He lifted his sherry, but instead of taking a sip, he held the glass up to eye level and stared at the lamp through the amber liquid for a few moments. Sighing, he took a sip and then put the drink down on the table. "The case isn't progressing very well. I'm afraid that, despite all our best efforts, I've no idea who might have killed Jeremy Marks."

"But it's only been three days, sir," she reminded him. "Give yourself time."

"Time is the one thing I don't have." He picked up the glass again. "For some reason, Chief Superintendent Barrows is under pressure to get this one solved as quickly as possible."

"Pressure? Did he tell you why?"

"No, but he made it clear when Constable Barnes and I were at the Yard today that it was important to get it solved and behind us. My own suspicion is the Home Secretary is worried about the political consequences of this one dragging on for too long."

She took a sip from her glass. "That's understandable. In the newspapers, Jeremy Marks is portrayed as a self-made man, even though he had a terrible reputation. He wasn't a member of the hereditary aristocracy or even the landed gentry. I think the current government might be worried about how it looks to the electorate if his killer isn't brought to justice quickly. After all, sir, most of your other cases involved the upper class in one way or another."

"I'd not thought of it in those terms, but you might be right." He smiled. "That does make me feel better, Mrs. Jeffries. The truth is, I didn't quite know what to say when the chief superintendent was going on and on about it. But that's not the only thing he mentioned. Barrows thinks that Inspector Nivens is interfering in my current case. He told me that since Nivens has come back to the force, he's taken an extraordinary interest in my old case files."

"How does he know that?"

Witherspoon chuckled. "Nivens pressured one of the Yard inspectors into assigning him an assistant. What he doesn't know is that assistant reports directly to the chief superintendent."

As the inspector hadn't mentioned Nivens more than a time or two since the odious little toad had come back on the force, she chose her next words with care. "Are you concerned about him, sir?"

He thought for a moment. "I should be, but honestly, it doesn't worry me. I'm tired of thinking about the man. What does worry me is the way the evidence in this case is crumbling."

"How so, sir?"

"It started with Hannah Lonsdale." He told her about

the interview. "And the truth is, she very much struck me as the type of person to more enjoy making Marks suffer than killing him outright. But of course, I can't prove it either way."

"You believe her, then?"

"I'm afraid so, and things didn't get any better when we went to interview Mrs. McElhaney." He gave her the details of that encounter. When he'd finished, he drained his glass and set it on the table. "She even showed us her cigarettes. She keeps them in a gold jeweled case. I don't understand, Mrs. Jeffries, when did women start smoking?"

"We've a lot of ground to cover this morning," Mrs. Jeffries said. "So unless any of you have something to report, I'll get right to it." She looked at Hatchet. "This is going to sound strange, but is there any way you can get your source, the one who told you the story about Cornelia Howell going into the dressmaker's shop, to the West London Archery Club today? They're having their monthly meeting and luncheon so the place will be quite full."

Hatchet stared at her curiously. "I don't know. The Manleys might not even be in London. Why?"

"I want her to take a look at Miss Linwood and see if she could possibly be Cornelia Howell."

"But that incident happened years ago. People change. She might not be able to recognize her after all this time," he warned.

"I know, but if I'm right, it could solve this case. Your source is the only one who can identify her. They were quite friendly with one another."

"It's worth a try." He started to get up, but Ruth waved him back to his chair.

"Don't go yet. You need to hear what I found out last night at the Shaws' dinner party. It's about Cornelia Howell."

"Isn't she the woman whose family was destroyed by Marks a long time ago?" Phyllis looked confused. "But I thought we were concentrating on the nasty things he'd done recently."

"That's my fault," Mrs. Jeffries said. "I shouldn't have hobbled our investigation with that assumption. But do go on, Ruth, tell us the rest."

Ruth took a deep breath. "Cornelia Howell's mother's maiden name was Linwood."

No one said anything for a moment. Finally, Mrs. Goodge looked at Mrs. Jeffries. "Thank goodness you told Constable Barnes to keep an eye on the woman this morning. He and the inspector are going to the archery club."

"Cor blimey, Mrs. Jeffries," Wiggins said. "Did ya tell him that Miss Linwood carries a ruddy gun?"

"A gun," Luty exclaimed. She looked at Hatchet. "If you're headin' to that club with a woman that carries a gun, I'm comin', too, and I'm bringin' my Peacemaker."

"No, madam, you are not." Hatchet stood up. "Let's not get ahead of ourselves here. We don't even know if this Miss Linwood is Cornelia Howell, and we certainly don't have any evidence she murdered Jeremy Marks. Furthermore"— he looked at Luty—"I've hidden that wretched weapon somewhere you'll never find it."

"You hid my Colt .45!"

He ignored her and turned to Mrs. Jeffries. "I'll see if Myra and Gerald are in town and willing to try and identify this person. But even if she is who we think she might be, what then?"

"I'm not sure," Mrs. Jeffries replied. "But finding out who she really is would be a good start. She was outside at the time of the murder."

"So were lots of other people," Betsy pointed out.

"But the others either had an alibi or gave the inspector a believable reason for why they weren't in the common room. Only Miss Linwood wasn't where she claimed to be."

"For God's sake, Hatchet, this could be dangerous." Luty looked at him, her expression anxious. "Let me go with ya? Please, I'm beggin' ya. Even without my Peacemaker, I'm a good person to have around if things go wrong."

Hatchet could see the worry in her eyes. He gave a slow shake of his head, reached down, and patted her arm. "No, madam, but please don't worry. I promise, I'll keep the Manleys and myself well out of sight of Miss Linwood. So even if she is our killer, she'll not have a reason to whip out her gun and shoot anyone."

The monthly meeting of the West London Archery Club started promptly at eleven o'clock. The members gathered in the common room and Rufus Farley called the meeting to order.

Inspector Witherspoon and Constable Barnes stood on the left-hand side in the back of the room, trying their best to be unobtrusive. Constables Pritchett and Parker were on the right-hand side.

"Constable Barnes," the inspector whispered. "Was there a reason you wanted to bring the other constables with us today? Mr. Farley was quite annoyed. He accused me of turning his club into a spectacle."

"Better a spectacle than a tragedy," Barnes murmured

softly. "I only wanted them to come just in case something else happens, sir. Besides, having one of your members murdered with a bow and arrow is already a spectacle."

Witherspoon stifled a laugh, which exploded out of his nose into an inelegant snort. "Oh dear, sorry, I shouldn't laugh but sometimes one must. By the way, where is Constable Griffiths?"

"I sent him outside to keep a lookout for Inspector Nivens," Barnes admitted. He lowered his voice as a woman turned and glared at them. "Chief Superintendent Barrows was quite adamant that if we see him, we confront him and ask him what he's doing here." The constable glanced at Miss Linwood. She was sitting next to Mrs. Storch, a black leather bag with silver mountings on her lap.

Rufus Farley announced that a member of the club from each category had qualified for the regionals. A polite cheer and clapping followed.

Mrs. Storch leaned over and whispered in Miss Linwood's ear. A moment later, Miss Linwood got up and quietly made her way to the door.

"I'll just go have a word with Constable Griffiths," Barnes murmured.

"I'll come as well," Witherspoon said. "If one isn't interested in archery, this is a tad boring."

They slipped out the door while the crowd settled down. Constable Griffiths was just coming in the front entrance. "I'm glad you're here, sir." He hurried toward Witherspoon. "I just saw Inspector Nivens outside talking to one of the gardeners."

Barnes surveyed the corridor but didn't see Miss Linwood anywhere.

"Good work, Constable. Where is the fellow?" Witherspoon sighed in exasperation. "Honestly, I've no idea why that silly man . . ." He broke off just as Hatchet along with two other people stepped through the front door.

Just then Miss Linwood came out of the cloakroom holding a knitted pink shawl.

"Hatchet, what are . . . oh yes, that's right, you're a member. But the meeting's already started." Witherspoon gestured at the closed doors to the common room.

"We're just a bit late, Inspector." Hatchet forced a smile. "I've brought my friends with me. This is Mr. and Mrs. Gerald Manley."

Witherspoon extended his hand to Mrs. Manley first and then her husband. "How nice to meet you."

"Likewise, Inspector," Gerald Manley replied as they shook hands.

"Lovely to meet you, sir." Myra Manley broke off as Miss Linwood approached the doors of the common room. "Oh my word, Cornelia Howell, my goodness, I can't believe it's you. It's been years."

Miss Linwood's eyes widened in shock, and she froze. But it was obvious from her expression that something was very, very wrong. "I'm sorry, I'm afraid you're mistaken. My name isn't Howell. It's Linwood."

Barnes had been candid with the Manleys so Myra understood what was going on and she also understood the importance of standing her ground. "Really, you mustn't pretend with me, Cornelia. I've heard you've fallen on hard times and you're a lady's companion now, but we were once friends."

"Pardon me." Witherspoon looked from one woman to

the other. The woman who'd called herself "Miss Linwood" now stared at Mrs. Manley with narrowed eyes and what could only be described as real malevolence. "But are you Cornelia Howell?"

"I'm Miss Linwood. Miss Dorothy Linwood, and if you don't mind, I'm taking Mrs. Storch's shawl to her."

"You sound exactly like Cornelia Howell," Myra called as the other woman turned toward the door. "And I know it has been many years, but you look exactly as I thought Cornelia would."

"Miss Linwood, please let's get this sorted out," Witherspoon suggested. "If you are Cornelia Howell, I've some questions for you. Questions about Jeremy Marks."

She turned back and stalked across the carpet to the counter, where everyone was standing. She tossed the shawl down on it and slammed the black leather bag down as well. The clasp sprang open.

"My name is not Cornelia Howell," she shouted. She turned and glared at Myra. "And I'll thank you to mind your own business."

"My apologies." Myra smiled sweetly. "But the resemblance is amazing and the name is quite a coincidence. Cornelia's middle name was Linwood."

She sucked in a long, deep breath and lifted her chin. "What are you implying?"

"Nothing, I'm simply curious as to your motives. I've no idea why you're pretending not to know me," Myra said. "But we were once good friends."

"We were never friends," she snapped. "You just felt sorry for me because you thought I was an old, ugly spinster and you were heading down that path yourself."

"Don't you dare speak to my wife like that." Gerald Manley grabbed his wife's arm and yanked her behind him.

"I'll talk to her and anyone else as I please," she shouted. "Wife? Really, she got you to marry her? Of course, her family was always rich as sin. I just wonder how much of a marriage settlement you received after the vows were said. That's the only reason she could have married someone who looks like you."

"If you were a man, I'd thrash you for that remark." Gerald balled his hands into fists and stepped toward her, but he wasn't fast enough as Witherspoon shoved forward, putting himself between the Manleys and the woman he now knew was Cornelia Howell.

Barnes said nothing; he kept his gaze on the open leather bag.

Witherspoon held his hands up in a placating gesture. "Now, now, let's all calm down. I'm sure this matter can be—"

"What's going on here?" Nigel Nivens suddenly stepped inside. "I say, Witherspoon, what's going on? What's all the shouting about? Really, Witherspoon, even you ought to be able to handle this situation."

Everyone turned to look at him, everyone except Cornelia Howell. She stuck her hand in the open bag and pulled out a gun.

Barnes saw it first and silently cursed himself for getting distracted. "Put that away, ma'am," he ordered. "We don't want anyone to get hurt now, do we."

"Don't patronize me," she hissed. "Now, all of you, move aside and get out of my way."

"Miss, uh, er . . . Howell," Witherspoon began. "Please, let's not be hasty . . ."

"Don't tell me what to do!" she screamed. "I'm sick to death of people telling me what to do." She raised the gun and aimed it at Witherspoon.

The door to the common room opened and Rufus Farley stuck his head out into the corridor. His jaw dropped when he saw the gun.

"Get back inside, man, and don't let anyone out here!" Barnes shouted.

Farley quickly closed the door.

"Oh, for God's sake, Witherspoon," Nivens said contemptuously. "If you can't handle this, I'll take over."

"Inspector Nivens, please be quiet," the inspector ordered, but he didn't look in his direction. All he could see was the revolver aimed at his heart.

"I'll not be quiet," Nivens snorted. "If you can't handle one silly old woman—"

"Silly old woman," she screeched. "I'll show you what this silly old woman can do." She aimed and pulled the trigger.

CHAPTER 11

"Good God, what's that stupid cow done to me?" Nivens sprawled on the floor, his gaze on the blood oozing out of his arm.

"Lie still, Inspector!" Witherspoon shouted. "Don't move." He looked at Cornelia. "Please, let me get the inspector to a doctor. Otherwise he's going to die."

The side of her mouth lifted in a sneer. "That's the whole point, Inspector Witherspoon. I like watching arrogant, idiotic men die. That's why I killed Marks." She lifted the gun barrel and used it to scratch the bottom of her chin. "But that isn't accurate. I murdered Marks because he ruined my life."

Constable Griffiths edged forward, but she spotted the movement. "I wouldn't do that if I were you." She smiled at him. "I've still got my gun and I wouldn't mind putting a bullet in you as well."

"Don't move, Constable," Witherspoon ordered. "We don't want anyone else hurt." He glanced at Nivens. He was deathly pale. The blood was seeping out of the wound on his chest and soaking into the carpet.

"Miss Howell, please, that man is going to die if we don't get him to hospital," the inspector pleaded. "For the love of God, he's never harmed you."

"But he has, Inspector. Everyone's harmed me." She broke off and giggled. "But that doesn't matter now. Now, if you'll all move over there"—she pointed the revolver at the space behind the counter—"I'll leave you to it and be on my way."

"You won't get far," Witherspoon warned. "If you turn yourself in now, you might escape the hangman."

"What, and go to prison for the rest of my life? Hardly, Inspector. If I can't escape, I'd rather hang."

Nivens then made the worst mistake of his life. He laughed and then compounded his error by saying, "Good Lord, I don't think there's a scaffold big enough to hold the likes of her." He pointed at her.

Her expression clouded and an angry flush climbed her cheeks. "You're certainly no gentleman," she said as she raised the gun again, aiming it directly at him.

"Don't be an idiot, Inspector Nivens!" Witherspoon yelled. "Miss Howell is a fine figure of a woman. Please, Miss Howell, he doesn't know what he's saying. You strike me as an intelligent, very reasonable woman. Surely we can—"

"Can what?" she interrupted. "Reason together? Don't be stupid. You do understand that all those times I made cow eyes at you, I was simply ensuring that you didn't take me seriously. It's amazing what you can get away with in life by flattering people. I've done it for years and it always works. But then again, human beings are easily fooled."

"Yes, I'd already come to that conclusion myself."

Nivens snickered. "Ye gods, Witherspoon, you were flattered by this old hag. You must be desperate for attention."

"Do be quiet, Inspector Nivens," Barnes hissed. He suddenly felt a faint draft coming from the far end of the corridor.

"When did you learn archery?" Witherspoon asked.

"When my other two attempts to kill Marks failed." She shrugged. "But live and learn, eh, Inspector? Before I took the position with Mrs. Storch, I accompanied a Canadian woman to Toronto, as a paid companion, of course. I became acquainted with an Iroquois chief. He taught me how to use a bow and arrow. I was actually quite good at it. No, no, I tell a lie, I was excellent at it. For goodness' sakes, Inspector, I put two arrows into the man during a raging storm."

"Exactly how did you manage that?" Witherspoon glanced at Nivens, who thankfully had decided to keep his mouth shut.

"It was easy, Inspector. I took the job with Mrs. Storch because I knew she was a member of this club. Jeremy Marks has hung about this place for years. I was a bit disappointed when he got chucked out for cheating, but I knew he'd be back."

"You knew him before," Constable Griffiths said. "Didn't he recognize you?"

"Not really. When he was in business with my father, I

only met him once or perhaps twice. My father did business with him, but we certainly didn't have any social dealings with the man."

Barnes thought he heard a sound. It was coming from the direction of the staircase. He looked around, hoping to find some way to distract her. But there was nothing. Hatchet and the Manleys were standing like statues, Nivens was on the floor bleeding into the carpet, and Constable Griffiths was frozen to the spot. Barnes had an idea. He moved closer to her, stepping to one side so if she looked at him, she wouldn't be directly facing the corridor. "You said your other two attempts to kill Marks failed. How so?"

"My first companion position was with Mrs. McCray. Her husband was a botanist and he invented McCray's Vermin Solution," she explained. "Actually, she always claimed she was a much better botanist that he was, but because she was a woman, he got the credit for it. Unfortunately, Mc-Cray's Vermin Solution works on dogs far better than it did Marks. It was simple to do. I watched the Marks house for two weeks and I saw that the meat delivery wagon came every Wednesday and Friday. Marks wasn't very nice to delivery people, so the lad left it by the kitchen door. It was easy to steal one of the steaks and smear poison on it. But the mongrel got there first." She sighed. "But that's life. If at first you don't succeed, try again."

"And the second time?" Barnes shifted position again as he heard another faint thump from behind him.

"The second time was ten years later. I'd taken a position with an Englishwoman named Mrs. Lacey. She was obsessed with the American West. But she didn't want to go on her own so she hired me to go with her. America's a huge country as well as being a place where one can easily get their hands on firearms. I became quite a good shot." She gestured at Nivens. His face was now as white as his shirt collar. "Just ask him. But I digress, Constable. I tried shooting Marks as he came out of a funeral. Unfortunately, he bent down to pick something up just as I pulled the trigger. All I shot that day was a window."

Witherspoon saw that Nivens was losing consciousness. "Please, Miss Howell, if you've an ounce of humanity left, let me get Inspector Nivens medical attention."

"Humanity," she repeated. "I don't think I have any of that left, Inspector. Do you know what it's like to lose everything? It wasn't just the loss of my status in society or my home and family; Marks cost me the one thing I thought I'd never have—the love of my life."

Barnes saw Constable Griffiths looking down the corridor. He risked a quick glance in that direction and saw Constable Parker moving slowly up the corridor with his back flush against the wall. He carried a police truncheon. If she happened to look in that direction, she'd spot him. Barnes had to keep her focused on him. "I don't understand, Miss Howell."

She stared at him for a long moment and then smiled bitterly. "Look at me, Constable. I'm six foot tall and as that one"—she leveled the gun at Nivens again—"rightly said, I'm a big person. I always was, but Alex didn't care. His name was Alexander Richards and he loved me. We were going to be married, but when Marks ruined us, Alex's father forced him to give me up, and he broke our engagement. That's when I decided Jeremy Marks had to die. It took me a long time, but I did it."

Nivens started moaning. "Witherspoon"—he barely got the word out—"help me. This harpy is killing me."

"Harpy!" she screamed. "How dare you?" She aimed the gun and pulled the trigger just as Gerald Witherspoon threw himself in front of Nivens.

The shot grazed Witherspoon's hand but hit Nivens in the stomach just as Constable Parker threw his truncheon at Cornelia Howell, bashing her arm. Constables Barnes and Griffiths leapt at her. Barnes knocked the weapon out of her hand and shoved her hard against the counter. Constable Parker raced toward them as Constable Griffiths yanked her arms behind her back. A moment later the two of them got her in handcuffs.

Barnes knelt down next to Inspector Witherspoon. He'd taken his handkerchief out of his pocket and was using it to try and stop the blood pouring out of Nivens' gut. "Hold on, Inspector Nivens," Witherspoon urged. "We'll get you to a doctor."

The inspector's hand was bleeding, but he didn't seem to notice. The constable pulled his handkerchief out as well, hesitated a second before adding it to try to stanch the flow of blood from Nivens' belly.

"Someone get a doctor!" Barnes bellowed. "Quick, we've two wounded men here."

"It's too late for that, Constable." Nivens smiled gratefully at Barnes. "But thank you for trying." He looked at Witherspoon. "You really are one of nature's gentlemen. Ye gods, Witherspoon, you tried to save my life." He broke off and gave a short, sad laugh. "While I've spent years trying to ruin yours. I'm sorry. I'm so very sorry."

* * *

"What's taking so long?" Mrs. Jeffries looked at the clock for the hundredth time. "Smythe and Wiggins should have been back by now."

"And Hatchet, he ought to be here, too," Luty said. "I know I shoulda gone with him to that danged archery club. Hell's fire, he works for me and I shoulda threatened to sack him if he didn't take me with him. That woman has a gun— what if she spots Hatchet and his source? If she gets recognized as Cornelia Howell, she might pull the danged thing out and start shootin' at everybody."

"Let's not get ahead of ourselves, Luty." Mrs. Jeffries tried to stay hopeful. "What's more, you know Hatchet. He'd have let you sack him rather than put you in danger." She had a dreadful feeling in the pit of her stomach, and from the worried expressions on the faces of the other women, she knew they sensed it as well. Something was wrong.

Betsy had taken Amanda home to her neighbor but returned and was sitting next to Luty, holding the elderly woman's hand. Mrs. Goodge was staring off into space like a silent statue, her face a mask of misery and her body tense with fear.

"We don't know that anything bad has happened," Ruth said softly. "I'm certain that Smythe and Wiggins will be back any moment now."

"We shouldn't have let them go to the archery club," the cook muttered. "We should have made them stay here, where it's safe."

"Mrs. Goodge, they've gone out dozens of times when there was a chance our inspector was going to make an arrest," Ruth said softly. "They're grown men who make their own decisions. I don't see how we could have stopped them . . ." She stopped speaking as they heard the back door open and then close.

Fred, who'd sensed the change in atmosphere, barked and leapt up, scrambling to race down the hall.

"It's alright, old fella." They heard Wiggins' voice.

"Oh, thank God, they're both alright." Mrs. Goodge gave a short sob, wiped her eyes, and turned as the two men came rushing into the kitchen.

Wiggins was pale as a ghost, Smythe's mouth was set in a flat, grim line, and for once, he looked every year of his age. Both were disheveled and out of breath.

Betsy stood up. "Are you all right? What's happened? You've been gone so long."

Smythe hurried to his wife and pulled her close. "I'm fine, love, but I'm not so sure about the others. We were outside but we heard shots fired. We don't know what happened inside the club. A constable came rushing out and raced off, blowing his whistle as he ran to summon more police. We tried to get inside, but Constable Griffiths and another policeman were by the door and they know us by sight."

"All we could find out before we 'ad to go was that two people 'ad been shot," Wiggins added.

"Was it Hatchet? Is he alright?" Luty demanded.

"I don't know," Smythe admitted glumly.

"I'm fine," Hatchet said as he came into the kitchen.

Luty jumped up and hurried to him. "Thank goodness you're alright. I've been worried to death. What happened? We've all had a bad feelin' about this. Is the inspector alright?"

Hatchet took both her hands and gave them a light squeeze. "Give me a moment, madam. It's been quite a day." He took a deep breath and then turned to look at Ruth. "Inspector Witherspoon and Inspector Nivens have been taken to hospital. They were both shot by Cornelia Howell. I don't know the extent of their wounds."

Ruth stared at him in disbelief. "Gerald was shot? No, that can't be right. He's a good, good man."

"Dear God, this can't be happening," Mrs. Jeffries murmured.

Betsy moaned softly. Smythe pulled a chair out from the table and gently eased her into it. "Sit down, love. Let's not get het up. We don't know 'ow bad it is."

Wiggins shook his head. "I don't believe it. I just don't believe it—not the inspector."

Mrs. Goodge had tears in her eyes. Phyllis jammed her fist into her mouth to keep from sobbing.

"It turns out that Mrs. Jeffries was right. Miss Linwood is Cornelia Howell and she shot both of them. She's been arrested for the murder of Jeremy Marks. Let's sit down and I'll tell you what happened from the beginning. It'll be a while before we hear anything."

It took a few minutes to get settled and then Hatchet told them the details. "After she fired the second time, Constable Parker hurled his truncheon at her, and Constable Griffiths and Constable Barnes jumped her and managed to wrestle the gun away before she could shoot anyone else. She was screaming like a fishwife, howling to the heavens that she'd had her revenge and Jeremy Marks was now in hell. It was dreadful to witness, absolutely dreadful. It took all three of them to get her bundled into the police wagon and taken to the station. The Manleys and I went as well and Constable Griffiths took our statements. The Manleys went home and I came here. Constable Griffiths promised someone would be here soon with news."

Mrs. Goodge got to her feet. "I'll make tea."

They didn't speak much as they drank their tea and waited for news. After what seemed like hours, they heard the front door open and footsteps upstairs. Mrs. Jeffries leapt up and dashed toward the back stairs. Everyone else got to their feet and started after her.

But before anyone could get upstairs, Inspector Witherspoon came down the staircase. His left hand was wrapped in a bandage.

"Oh my gracious, thank the good Lord you're alright, Gerald," Ruth exclaimed as she raced toward him. "We've all been so worried."

He clasped her in his arms and gave her a quick hug. "I'm fine, my dear, the police surgeon said it's only a graze." He looked at the others. "Oh dear, I suppose Hatchet told you what happened and I can see by your expressions that I've worried all of you. I'm so dreadfully sorry."

Mrs. Goodge wiped her eyes. "I'll get you a cup of tea, sir."

"Do come sit down, Inspector," Mrs. Jeffries urged.

"I've told them what happened at the club," Hatchet explained. "And that the Manleys and I went to the station and made formal statements. But we don't know what happened after that."

Witherspoon and Ruth sat down. The inspector looked at Hatchet. "Before I begin, I wanted to ask you something. Why did you bring Mr. and Mrs. Manley to the club today?"

"As I told Constable Griffiths when he took my statement, they were thinking of joining and they wanted to have a look at the place before they made up their minds."

"Hatchet told us that Miss Linwood is really a woman named Cornelia Howell and that she killed Jeremy Marks," Luty said.

"Indeed she did," Witherspoon said. "She's being charged with murder. She's quite mad. I think it's the type of madness that has been festering and growing for a long, long time." He paused and looked at his bandaged hand. "Dr. Procash was at the hospital when we arrived. They took Inspector Nivens into surgery and he bandaged my hand. I went back to the station. I got there just as Cornelia Howell formally confessed to murdering Jeremy Marks."

"What did she say, sir?" Phyllis asked. "I mean, if I can ask such a thing. It's just you know how much we all love hearing about your cases, sir."

Witherspoon smiled broadly. "Of course you can ask, Phyllis. Truthfully, seeing all of you here touched me deeply. I am very grateful for all of you."

"We're just happy you're safe, sir," Phyllis replied.

"Cornelia Howell had planned to murder Marks for a long time," the inspector explained.

"I told them about her first two attempts to kill him," Hatchet said.

"Oh yes, the poison and the shooting at the church. Both of them failed but she was quite proud of the fact that she succeeded this time around." Witherspoon took a sip of the tea Mrs. Goodge had put in front of him. "She took the position with Mrs. Storch deliberately because she knew Mrs. Storch was a member of the West London Archery

Club and, more importantly, that Marks was a member. She was annoyed when he got chucked out for cheating, but as she said, she knew he'd be back."

"Why was she so sure of that?" Ruth asked. She remembered what Octavia had told her about Marks, that the club was his "hunting grounds."

"She said that the archery club was where Marks met rich women and she was proved right when he got engaged to Hannah Lonsdale. But her plan to kill him went wrong when the storm started and the competition was postponed. She'd taken a bow and arrows and hidden them upstairs in the Ladies' Dressing Room. Her original plan was to wait until the end of the competition when everyone was outside and the scores were unofficially announced. She was going to shoot him from the window, drop the weapon, and then get back outside with Mrs. Storch before anyone noticed she was missing. As she put it, 'No one pays any attention to someone like me.'" Witherspoon shrugged. "In one sense, I suspect she was correct. Society does tend to treat some people as if they were nothing more than pieces of furniture. But I digress. When the storm started, she realized the competition was going to be postponed so she went upstairs and retrieved the bow and the arrows she'd hidden. She put the bow and the arrows by the passageway into the practice room, intending to put them back in their proper places later. By that time, the rain was coming down hard and the members were on their way back inside. She was sure she'd have to postpone her plan."

"What made her change her mind?" Luty asked.

"She spotted a folded tarp behind the door. She said it gave her an idea. But she couldn't execute it until a bit later, when she saw Marks going through the common room at the same time that Mrs. Storch asked her to go down and take the picnic hamper to the Storch carriage." He took another quick sip of his tea. "Miss Linwood, I mean Miss Howell, nipped down to the kitchen, gave the footman a shilling to take the hamper and told him she'd be under the willow tree, supervising. She went outside with him, and when he wasn't looking, she dashed around the side of the building, nipped into the practice room, and grabbed the tarp, the bow, and the arrows. She went to the abandoned property next to the club, used the tarp to keep the rain from dripping off the trees onto her clothes, and waited till she saw Marks outside searching the grounds. Originally, we thought he was stealing arrows, but it turns out he was looking for a very valuable bracelet that he'd given Miss Lonsdale. That's when she shot him. She dropped the bow and arrow, covered it with leaves, and then took the tarp to the abandoned carriage house and put it in an upstairs room."

"Why didn't she just drop the tarp with the bow and arrow?" Betsy asked. "Why go to all the trouble of going to the carriage house?"

"Because she saw two club members standing on the kitchen porch and she was afraid they'd see her. She managed to hide the bow and arrow under the leaves, but she didn't have time to hide the tarp. After she'd hidden it, she came back to the club, tidied herself up a bit, and went back into the common room as if nothing had happened." He smiled sadly. "It's a dreadful story, and unfortunately, it caused a man's death."

"But where did she learn how to shoot a bow and arrow?" Luty demanded. "Did she tell ya that?"

"She did. She said when her other methods failed, she decided to, as she put it, 'face the bastard on his own ground' and take up archery. She paid an Iroquois Indian to teach her how to use a bow and arrow. Apparently he was a very good instructor because she is an expert archer. She'd have to be to have been able to kill Marks during that storm."

Betsy put her hand on her belly and shook her head. "I'll bet when she was born, her mother had no idea how her life would turn out. I'll bet her mother loved her and tried her very best to raise her right. But life wasn't very nice to Cornelia Howell. It's frightening when you think about it. None of us know what is going to happen."

"Don't fret about it, love." Smythe put his hand over hers. "Our little ones will do just fine. We'll make sure of that."

"I think the inspector is right," Phyllis declared. "Cornelia Howell must have been slowly going mad all these years. She dedicated her whole life to killing a person. How can anyone live like that? Imagine, spending your life doing that."

"Yes, it is unimaginable." Mrs. Jeffries thought of someone else who'd spent a great deal of time trying to harm another. "How is Inspector Nivens, sir?"

Witherspoon looked away for a moment and then took a deep breath. "I'm afraid he's dead."

The inspector insisted on walking Ruth across the communal garden to her home. "Don't wait up for me," he instructed Mrs. Jeffries. "It's been a very trying day and I'd like to spend some time with Ruth before coming home."

"I'll leave the back door unlocked, sir," she replied.

As soon as he and Ruth were gone, Mrs. Jeffries hurried back to the table.

"I never liked Inspector Nivens," Luty murmured. "But it's right sad that he ended up dead."

"I know," Phyllis agreed. "No one deserves to die like that."

"Perhaps he'll find a measure of peace now," Mrs. Jeffries said.

"Alright, tell us how ya figured out it was Miss Linwood, or should I say Cornelia Howell, who was the killer?" Luty demanded.

Mrs. Jeffries smiled. "To be truthful, I was at a loss until that one fact we learned from Constable Barnes. The one about Miss Linwood going to Scotland to be a paid companion to Mrs. McCray."

"Of McCray's Vermin Solution," Phyllis reminded them.

Now that the waiting was over, the sense of relief in the kitchen was palpable. Mrs. Goodge put a plate of brown bread and butter on the table. Mrs. Jeffries went to the pine sideboard and pulled out the bottle of whisky she kept for emergencies or celebrations.

Phyllis got the glasses and Betsy made another cup of tea for herself and Hatchet.

When they were all settled in their places, Luty repeated her demand. "Don't keep us waitin'. Tell us how ya did it. I gotta tell ya, I had my doubts we'd solve this one."

"So did I, Luty." Mrs. Jeffries poured a small shot of whisky for each of them.

"So it was the comment about Scotland that set you on the right path?" Phyllis passed around the whisky. She wanted to understand because she had her own plans for the future. The world needed a private inquiry agency run by and for women!

"Yes, but it didn't happen immediately. It was when I reread my notes on the case—"

Phyllis interrupted. "You keep notes? I thought you kept everything in your head."

"I haven't done that in a long time. My memory isn't as good as it used to be." She smiled ruefully. "So after every meeting with all of us, or Constable Barnes or the inspector, I write everything down, especially the details. It's a good thing I did. Otherwise, I'd have missed the fact that Ruth's source told her that Cornelia Howell had to take a position as a paid companion and that it was in Scotland."

"Weren't you afraid it was just a coincidence?" Hatchet asked.

"I was, but that, coupled with several other facts, pointed toward Miss Linwood. She was the only one who wasn't where she claimed to be when she was outside. Mick, the footman, told the inspector he'd gone back to thank her again for the shilling she'd given him. But she wasn't under the willow tree and she couldn't have left after making certain he put the hamper in the Storch carriage, because it only took a moment to put it inside, and when he turned, he never saw her come out from beneath the tree." Mrs. Jeffries took a sip of her drink. "Emmett Merriman wasn't in the common room, but he had an alibi."

"He was in the attic, telling Mrs. Harland their affair was over," Hatchet murmured.

"Yes, and admitting to infidelity is better than being accused of murder," Mrs. Jeffries said. "Mrs. Harland confirmed his whereabouts. Miss Lonsdale was outside as well, but she had no reason to kill Marks."

"But she did. After reading the letter Marks wrote to Alice McElhaney, she knew he was only marrying her for the Lonsdale fortune," Phyllis protested.

"I'm not explaining this very well. I meant to say that instead of deciding to kill him for what he'd done, she'd come up with a far more diabolical plan for Marks. She told our inspector she was going to ruin him financially and she appeared to have the resources to do so."

"But weren't you afraid she was lyin'?" Wiggins helped himself to a slice of bread and reached for the butter pot and the knife.

"I considered that, but Miss Lonsdale had only been engaged to Marks for a short time and he'd never humiliated her publicly. She was the one who ended the engagement. If she'd wanted him dead, why break off the engagement? Why not just kill him and pretend to be a grieving woman who'd lost a fiancé? From the way Inspector Witherspoon described her demeanor when she found out he'd been murdered, she didn't sound as if she was desperately in love with the man."

Phyllis nodded in agreement. "And murder for vengeance usually means someone's so hurt and obsessed, they can't think of any other way to make the pain go away. She sounds like she was just angry at him, but that's different from having your whole world destroyed. But what about Alice McElhaney?" She looked at Mrs. Jeffries. "You said that Marks hadn't humiliated Miss Lonsdale, but he had humiliated Alice McElhaney. She was outside."

"She claimed she was there smoking a cigarette." Mrs. Goodge shook her head, her expression disgusted. "I don't know what this world is coming to when supposedly respectable women sneak about outside to smoke."

"She did show the inspector and Constable Barnes the cigarette packet." Mrs. Jeffries chuckled. "She was also a very good archer."

"That's what I don't understand," Phyllis said. "You didn't know that Miss Linwood was an archer. But he was killed by someone who was an expert. How did you figure that bit out?"

"When we found out that Miss Linwood had an Indian friend in Toronto, an Iroquois chief, a man that she regularly corresponded with," Mrs. Jeffries explained. "That got me to thinking. Then when Wiggins told us about how she killed a rat with a slingshot and that her Iroquois friend was the one who taught her to use it, it didn't seem much of a stretch to wonder if he'd taught her to shoot a bow and arrow."

"Which 'e did," Wiggins said. "But you musta 'ad more to go on."

She took another sip. "I did, but it took some time before I saw the connections. First of all, when you ran into the carriage house to hide from the constables, you saw what you described as big footprints, which I assumed must have been made by a man. But later on, Hatchet commented that Miss Linwood was as tall as he was."

"Which means she could have made those footprints." Phyllis was delighted she was now able to see the same connections as Mrs. Jeffries.

"Right, but I didn't realize it until yesterday. The one aspect of Miss Linwood's behavior that convinced me to look more closely at her was the way she acted toward Inspector Witherspoon."

"How so?" Hatchet helped himself to a slice of bread.

"From what we know, Cornelia Howell has only been back in England for a year; at least that's how long she's worked for Mrs. Storch. Yet she told our inspector that she'd followed his last case in the newspapers and implied that she'd been an admirer of his for a long while. But that isn't possible."

"Our inspector isn't one to blow 'is own 'orn," Wiggins guessed. "Is that what you're sayin'?"

"That's right. He gets his name in the papers occasionally, and on one level, he's quite famous, but he's not a household name and he never gives interviews to the press. He leaves that up to Chief Superintendent Barrows. Yet according to Constable Barnes, every time she came near the inspector, she gushed at him like a schoolgirl. There was something about the way he described the encounters that struck me as being very calculating, almost like a script had been used."

"She admitted that herself," Hatchet added. "Just after she'd shot Inspector Nivens, she said she'd only made 'cow eyes'—her words, not mine—at the inspector to keep him from taking her seriously."

"That was a bit too clever on her part," Mrs. Jeffries said.

"Sounds like she overplayed her hand," Luty snickered. "Just like a lot of bad poker players do."

"Indeed she did. Mrs. Harland told the inspector she saw someone running toward the carriage house holding something over their head. She thought it was to keep the wet out, but I suspected it wasn't just that but also to keep from being identified."

"It worked, too." Betsy glanced at the clock.

"The last thing that pointed me toward Cornelia Howell was when Wiggins found out that she carried a gun."

"Ain't nuthin' wrong with carryin' a weapon," Luty declared. "I used to carry my Peacemaker all the time."

"Nonsense, madam, you only carried that wretched weapon when we were on the hunt," Hatchet argued.

"I stopped carryin' it because you nagged me so much."

"Nonetheless, once we found out the woman was armed, that put a whole different light on the matter."

"So you figured it out usin' just these little bits and pieces." Wiggins grinned broadly. "Cor blimey, Mrs. Jeffries, you didn't 'ave much to go on, but you sussed it out."

"I'm not so sure I didn't just get a bit lucky."

Everyone laughed, and a few minutes later, they were tidying up and getting ready to go their separate ways.

Betsy struggled to gain her feet. Smythe held her upper arms and helped her stand. "Oh no." She clasped her stomach and looked down at the floor. "Smythe, my water just broke. The baby's coming."

"The baby's coming! Blast a Spaniard, my love. Why didn't you say anything!"

"Because it just happened."

"Let's get you home and then I'll get the midwife." He put his arms around her shoulders and started to hustle her to the door.

"I'll go," Wiggins said. "You get Betsy 'ome safe. Where does the midwife live?" As soon as Smythe gave him the address, he took off like he was being chased by the devil.

Smythe bundled Betsy out the back door, promising to send them word as soon as the baby arrived.

"Let's get you home as well, madam." Hatchet put Luty's cloak around her shoulders.

"But the baby's comin'," she protested. "We oughta stay."

"You're exhausted and so is everyone else. Mrs. Jeffries will send word when it happens and we'll come back tomorrow. Now, don't give me an argument about this—even you know that babies take their time coming into this world."

"Do go home, Luty. I promise we'll let you know as soon as we know," Mrs. Jeffries assured her. She could tell by the worried look on the elderly American's face that she was concerned about the birth. Every woman in the room knew how risky childbirth was for a woman.

"Alright, alright, I'm goin' home and I'm goin' to git on my knees and pray that Betsy and the baby are safe. That's all I want now, for the two of 'em to be safe."

"That's what we all want," Mrs. Goodge agreed.

The kitchen was quiet after everyone was gone. Mrs. Jeffries insisted that both Phyllis and Mrs. Goodge go to bed. When Wiggins arrived home, she sent him off to sleep as well.

Mrs. Jeffries sat down at the table and waited for the inspector to arrive home. He was surprised to see her still up. "Mrs. Jeffries, I told you not to wait up. It's late and you must be tired."

"I am sir, but I've news I wanted to share with you. I thought you'd want to know that Betsy has gone into labor. Smythe took her home and Wiggins went for the midwife."

"That's wonderful news." Witherspoon grinned broadly. "What a day this has been. The case was solved, and for every human life that is lost, another one comes into the world."

"You're very philosophical tonight, sir. Are you thinking about Inspector Nivens?"

Witherspoon looked thoughtful. "I am. I know he hated me, Mrs. Jeffries, and for the life of me, I don't know why. But the point is, I didn't hate him and I'm sorry he's dead."

Mrs. Jeffries marveled that Witherspoon could be so honorable, could try to save the life of someone who'd tried to destroy him. "You're a good man, sir."

"And I'm blessed with a wonderful household that I consider family. I do hope things are going well for Betsy and the baby. I don't know what I'd do if I lost any of you."

"Don't think like that, sir." Mrs. Jeffries held up her hand, showing her crossed fingers. "Let's hope all goes well and that both mother and baby are safe."

At half-past seven the next morning, they learned that all had gone very well.

Smythe came into the kitchen. He was grinning from ear to ear. "I'm pleased to announce the safe arrival of Matthew James Smythe. He weighs a healthy seven pounds and five ounces."

ABOUT THE AUTHOR

Emily Brightwell is the *New York Times* bestselling author of the Victorian Mysteries, featuring Inspector Witherspoon and Mrs. Jeffries.

Ready to find
your next great read?

Let us help.

Visit prh.com/nextread